Three Day Nights

Sandi Huddleston-Edwards

Published by Hear My Heart Publishing

ISBN: 978-1-945620-32-4
A product of the United States of America. Written by Sandi Huddleston-Edwards
This book is a work of fiction and documented historical non-fiction.

Dedication

This book is dedicated to two people. First is my husband, Barry R. Edwards, who loves and supports me in every aspect of my life. Throughout our thirty one years of marriage, we've learned the beautiful gifts of acceptance and forgiveness, and we are still learning as our two paths continue this journey of life. I cannot imagine a better partner to have. Thank you for believing in me and supporting me in everything I do.

This book is also dedicated to my best friend, Margaret Parks Westmoreland, who supports me in so many ways, but especially in her Christian advice. In the context of my writing, she reads the early manuscripts of all my books and gives me the honest feedback on which I can rely and for which I appreciate. Her friendship is a God-given blessing for which I treasure and am grateful. Thank you for being more than a friend.

Acknowledgements

With gratitude, I would like to thank the following persons for their gifts of time, assistance, and patience in helping this book to come to fruition.

Anthony Aycock: Thank you, "writing buddy" for our shared passion for writing and for taking me by the author's hand in 2004 and telling me a story neither of us will ever forget. Thank you for the use of your unpublished essay, What Thing in Honor.

Thomas Black: There could never be a better "Hoke" for me. Thank you for all the miles you've driven me in pursuit of the written page.

Cheryl Burwell: It's your sweet and generous gifts of muffins, candies, and ripe tomatoes you silently leave on my doorstep when you know I'm heads-down writing that show you care and support me. Thanks, friend.

Vicki Cleveland: Thanks, friend, for using your "Master's knowledge," and helping me with the genre for this book.

Sheriff Dan Good: Thank you for the love you've shared for a fallen friend and for your encouragement and time you gave to this story and my writing.

Arthur Keith: Thank you for your life-long achieved knowledge and wisdom you are always willing to convey in lay terms I can understand.

Patty McQuillan and Keith Acree, Department of Corrections: Thank you for helping me gain permission to tour specific areas of Raleigh's Central Prison.

Officer Dan Murphy, CPCC: Besides ensuring safety and security at our campus, you've given your expertise and time unselfishly whenever I had a question, and that meant a lot. Thank you.

Beth Wilson: There could never be a better publisher to work with. You follow your heart and then your head, and because of this, your books are inspiring and successful. Thank you for your patience and your love for the written word to glorify God. And thank you for believing in my writing and my stories.

Contents

Introduction

It happened thirty-eight short or long years ago, depending on your involvement and perspective. But people still talk about it. They talk about the vodka, the unlicensed rage, the call to police, the feelings of shock and terror, and the penultimate relief. One man was arrested after triggering a thirteen hour manhunt involving more than two hundred law enforcement officers --the largest manhunt in the history of Rutherford County. The locals ask if you've watched *Damon's Law*, also entitled *The Rutherford County Line,* a melodramatic "B" movie about a contemporary local legend, Rutherford County Sheriff Damon Huskey. The climax of the movie is the pursuit and capture of James Hutchins, who shot and killed the Sheriff's younger brother.

The horrific and heartbreaking events of May 31, 1979, and their aftermath could not be imagined by the strongest of writers. Or those who were impacted and are still haunted by the glaring realization that life is a precious nanosecond by nanosecond journey. It can be terminated all too easily by the maliciousness of a single, reckless act. This was indeed true for on this day in Rutherfordton, North Carolina, history, the courageous lives of three dedicated officers were taken unmercifully, unceremoniously, and unpredictably. Because of their murders, the lives of their loved ones, peers, and countless friends were scarred forever when James Hutchins, a reportedly "good-hearted man until he took a drink," murdered Captain Roy Huskey and Sergeant Owen Messersmith in Hutchins front yard when they had come in response to a domestic dispute report. After fleeing the horrendous carnage he'd created, Hutchins then murdered Trooper Robert "Pete" Peterson in pre-meditated "cold blood" on a back road fifteen minutes later.

When the jury sentenced Hutchins to die, the trial judge editorialized him as "the most dangerous man I have ever seen." And Governor Hunt, who denied him clemency, defended his lack of mercy by stating, "... the murder of a law enforcement officer is not only the cold-blooded killing of a human being, it is an assault on the fundamental rule of law in our society."

The people who were traumatized by this man's actions remember the time and shudder. As I write about it, I do the same.

They say this man, Hutchins, was a loving husband and father, who was quiet and stayed to himself. JoAnn Huskey Keyser, widow of Roy Huskey, who was the first victim of Hutchins's rampant rage, said, "He supposedly was good-hearted except when he'd get to drinking. There was nothing to lead you to think something like this would happen."

"James, I think, had a lot of good in him, as well as the bad," commented one of his neighbors after the murders. The good, it seems, may have been interred with his bones, but the bad he created continues to live on after his death, leaving a story of tragedy and a multitude of questions behind.

Steve Owens, Charlotte Hutchins's (the eldest daughter of James Hutchins) former boyfriend, is quoted as saying, "They had to work for everything they had. It didn't come easy. They weren't like an *Eight is Enough* type family, but they loved one another."

They also call Hutchins a killer who deserved to die. They speak in low voices, carefully selecting their words about his execution, which took place on March 16, 1984. Lieutenant Mike Summers of the Rutherford County Sheriff's Department was an official and invited witness to the execution. His comment was spoken like a resolved poet and is quoted here: "The whole thing took four or five minutes, but it felt like fifteen or twenty. His face went cherry red, then ash gray." Hazel Peterson, mother of the slain highway patrolman, Robert L. "Pete" Peterson, is quoted as saying, "It really didn't bother me either way [electric chair or lethal injection just as long as they put him to death."

When my friend Anthony Aycock and I began researching this project in 2004, our interviews with family, friends, and co-workers couldn't help but stir my emotions my sympathy, empathy. I was angered at the irrational behavior, which caused the deaths of these brave men. I immediately grew to respect and admire the family members, friends, and co-workers who recounted how they had endured their worst nightmares. They worked through their anguish, gathering up the remnants of lost lives and silenced memories in order to survive and move forward. Their accounts became more than my hand scribbled notes on paper for a future essay or book. They became real-life stories I couldn't forget no matter how many times and years I placed them aside. This story of lost hope and lost lives has traveled many miles with me throughout the years. It tugged ever so gently at my soul. My writer's desire to take these scattered thoughts and to create something meaningful became somewhat overwhelming and demanded the submission of a book proposal. After receiving one publisher's rejection and two publisher's acceptance offers within the course of five months, I then realized this book was destined to be written.

As a fictional writer, I wanted to explore the happenings that led up to the fateful day when he detonated and afterward when he was sentenced to death. Did the devil make him do it because he was a bad person, or was he a human being who committed terrible crimes of passion? And more importantly, I wanted to explore the act of ***forgiveness***. Is it possible to excuse someone who committed such shocking acts as these? As a Christian, all sins are equal in the eyes of God. No matter what sins are committed in this lifetime, God's grace and mercy offers unconditional love and forgiveness when it is accepted with remorse and repentance because Jesus's death on the cross already paid the price for our sins. His precious blood covered them for us. But if it is so easy for God to forgive us, why is it so hard for us to forgive others and ourselves? Could I forgive someone who took the life of one of my loved ones? Could I forgive myself if I took the life of another person?

It is important for all of us who have been touched by similar events or who will read this story of irrational acts, to recognize on May 31, 1979, we, too, became victims of a callous disregard for life. It was wielded at the hands of a deranged individual, who turned to his alcoholic addiction for temporary solace and reached for a gun to end his oppressions and perceived oppressors. Once we realize we are fellow journeyers on this road called life, can we stop being the outsiders looking on and pointing critical fingers at the beater and the beaten? Instead, can we seek to understand why those choices are made? Can we work diligently as individuals and a society to ensure different solutions and alternatives are not only possible but accessible? Can we learn to extend our hands to each other, especially those in need – the hungry, the sick, the imprisoned, the destitute, the grief-stricken, the orphan, the widow? Can we recognize we are all created in God's image, loved equally by God, and forgiven for our sins, which are equal, by God?

For the survivors of May 1979, the events may seem like yesterday. For a writer, they are today. And for fellow journeyers, this story is written with the hope and a whispered prayer that these events won't happen tomorrow.

Author's Note

Because the events of May 31, 1979 have become more pervasive today, this is a fictionalized version of real events. I will use the actual name of the town and county where all this took place. I will use the real names of the victims and those quoted in newspaper articles and other document. Otherwise, fictional characters will be used.

I have used a poetic license and have modeled after Truman Copote's literary nonfiction novel genre. My version of the story is – an amalgam of events, rumored stories, composite characters, imagination, and my own assertions regarding this man's life. He was impacted by a myriad of issues: domestic abuse, poverty, depression, lack of education, and alcoholism.

I invite you to read along as my two fictional characters, Alex and Tony, pursue their dreams of writing a true crime novel. Blinded by unscathed innocence and naiveté, they begin their research on what made this murderer tick. But along the way, they discover much more than they bargained for when they encounter the fictional enigma, Charles Lefrere, who leads them on an unexpected journey of self-discovery and atonement.

Prologue:

The End of a Journey

March 16, 1984

"You exist in a half-world suspended between two superstructures, one self-expression and the other self-destruction. You are strong, but there is a flaw in your strength, and unless you learn to control it, the flaw will prove stronger than your strength and defeat you. The flaw? Explosive emotional reaction out of all proportion to the occasion."

Willie Jay, from a letter to Perry Smith, reported in Truman Capote's *In Cold Blood*

Prologue

"Forgiveness is unlocking the door to set someone free and realizing you were the prisoner!"
Max Lucado

JAMES WILLIAM HUTCHINS

The circles on calendars led up to March 16, 1984; the clocks were striking 1:30 a.m., moving each second closer to 2:00 a.m. – the appointed hour of death for one individual. Ambiguously, Hutchins was confronted with the harsh reality of how *few* steps the last leg of his journey would take – only about ten paces. As he stumbled out of the Death Watch Area with its blue concrete floors and white institutional walls for the last time, the single caged light bulb secured over the frosted glass doors seemed to flicker goodbye. He glanced over at the uniformed and armed officer standing silently at guard behind the window. With head nods, they respectfully acknowledged each other. The convicted man immediately read the numbers "111" over the Waiting Chamber's door as he was led the short distance across the hall to the Preparation Room. He was accompanied by four officers, Warden Rice, and the prison chaplain. How ironic he'd take his last breath on the other side of this wall -- only a few feet outside the huge doors that had defined his parameter for the last days of his life. It was half an hour before execution.

"Okay, James," the bald prison guard said. "Please strip down to your shorts and socks. This is all you're allowed to wear."

"I can wear my wedding band, right?" he asked while glancing around the 5' x 10' white-walled chamber and the new, white framed metal gurney he'd be the first to use.

"Yes. That's right. Not everyone gets to, but your request was granted," the officer stated.

Hutchins's thumb instinctively tucked itself underneath his ring finger and protectively twirled the thin gold band like he had done thousands of times before when he was nervous. An unexpected surge of emotions consumed him. Reluctantly but yet obediently, he complied and began to unbutton his shirt. As he slipped the garment off, removed the sneakers, and dropped his trousers, he fought back the overwhelming desire to run – to cry. That's when he focused on the adjacent room, Number 117, the Execution Chamber. He'd chosen lethal injection over the gas chamber. What a choice! He would be the first inmate to be executed in North Carolina after a twenty-three year moratorium and the first person to be lethally injected in the state of North Carolina. *What a mark to make in history!* He thought. Suddenly, Hutchins had an urge to laugh, but the surreal reality jerked him back to his senses.

"What do I do with these?" he asked, while reminding himself of the promise he'd made to keep his faculties in check and remain composed rather than releasing the boyish tears, which suddenly welled up behind his eyes. Even after all these years, he could still feel his father's stinging backhand lingering on his face and mingled with the salty taste of blood running from the corner of his mouth.

His father had yelled and cussed at him countless times throughout his childhood. "You got yourself into this [expletive] mess, and now you'll have to pay. Stand up, you [expletive] and take it like a man instead of the yellow-livered coward your momma raised."

He shuddered at the timeless echoes of the endless disdain his father had showered on him, which had penetrated the walls of self-esteem and torn down his feelings of self-worth. Thankfully, he was relieved from these painful memories when the second heavy-set prison guard offered to help.

"Hand 'em here, James. I'll take 'em for you."

The officer extended his stubby fingers and gently took the garb he'd changed into after his last, twenty minute shower earlier that night. The guard diverted his attention – compassionately(?) – apologetically(?) -- toward the floor, refusing to meet his eyes.

"Now, climb onto the gurney and lie flat on your back," the bald guard commanded. His voice was stern but kind, reminding the convicted man this was "no joke" and certainly "no option." Memories of his knee surgery surfaced, primarily because the orderlies had instructed him to slide from his hospital bed onto the operating room gurney. Unfortunately, there would be no recovery room this time.

"Uh huh, okay, Captain," he obediently replied. "And, uh, uh, be sure there is no autopsy. I asked that there'd be no autopsy."

"No autopsy, James. I'm sure," Warden Rice stated. "The Superior Court Judge issued an order to stop it. You don't need to be worrying about that now."

"Just making sure," he stated matter-of-factly. Ironically, it seemed like they were friends chatting about nothing major, like how short to cut his hair.

Hutchins's motor actions became robotic even though his heart was racing. Suddenly and uncontrollably, he began shivering from head to toe from nerves. He feared his wobbly knees would buckle, and he'd collapse before he could hoist his hips onto the narrow steel bed – his death bed. But somehow he succeeded with his last physical act and lay back on the green sheet, placing his head on the make-shift pillow of several folded sheets. Immediately and perfunctorily, two guards firmly grabbed his shaking wrists and ankles while the other two guards began tightening the leather restraints around them. One of the guards covered him with a top green sheet. Then they fastened the leather belt across his chest and the one across his thighs. Within a matter of seconds, Hutchins was strapped to the gurney – helpless and immobile. All too soon, one guard mumbled "goodbye" and disappeared.

His eyes blurred with moist tears as the walls and ceiling began to spin; time and events were moving much too quickly. He licked his parched lips but realized he had no saliva. His tongue felt as rough as a piece of 36-grit sandpaper. This five year old nightmare was finally happening. It had been an unwelcomed recurring dream, but this time, he wouldn't awaken. De ja vu' was coming true. He was living his last hour and coming face to face with his Maker in a matter of minutes. His eyes focused on the single, black caged light bulb hanging over the bed.

His thoughts were racing; his mind struggled to slow down -- to stop. He couldn't comprehend what meeting his Maker would be like, but he always thought it would be something that occurred unexpectedly, like a heart attack or a stroke or even a gunshot wound. It would happen quickly, without premonition or a state scheduled execution date. Death was on a far-away calendar with no set year, no set month, no set date, and no appointed time. But here he was with death staring him in the face and taking away the life of a healthy 54 year-old (ten days before turning 55). He yearned to live but was being forced through his final moments – and taking his last erratic breaths. There was one word for this: *Agonizing.* How could a man come to terms with the knowledge he was actually going to die in the wee hours of Friday morning? That's why he'd always avoided fortune tellers. He never wanted to know what the future had in store for him because somehow he'd always known the superstitious prophecy would end up haunting him as his past behaviors and dealings with the law had done. Besides, he had no need for fortune tellers. He'd foretold his own demise every time he became drunk and abusive. And on the tragic afternoon in May, he'd set a bunch of tumbling dominoes in unstoppable motion.

Suddenly, a wave of anxiety gripped him, tearing him away from the memories of his last day. Any inner peace he'd felt after talking to Geneva, the kids, the prison chaplain, his own preacher, and his only friend sank like heavy vapors in the thick air. He'd hoped their visits and calls would have provided resolution and courage to make it until his appointed death hour -- 2:00 a.m.

He began to worry. *But what if there isn't life after death for me? What if Jesus hasn't forgiven me for killing those officers, killing the truck driver, shooting Junior and the other guy, or getting drunk and beating my family with fists and slurred drunken words? What about my other sins? Would I awaken in heaven or in hell?*

The convicted man began silently pleading. *I don't want to go to hell, dear Jesus! Please believe me when I say I'm sorry. I'm so sorry for everything bad I've ever done. I was wrong to shoot those men. I was wrong to get drunk. I was wrong not to live my life in a better way, the way you'd wanted me to live it. I hope you've forgiven me and will allow me into heaven. If I could turn back time, I'd change a lot of things. I'm sorry I didn't do a better job during the fifty four years you gave me. I hope you're hearing me now. Please hear me! I don't want to go to hell!*

His silent prayers were interrupted when a male technician, who reminded him of the actor Boris Karloff, peered down at him. "Mr. Hutchins, I'll be inserting intravenous catheters into your arms."

"Okay, I guess. But can you put them in my hands instead?" He stammered uncontrollably. "I don't much like needles."

"I understand," the technician replied in a kindly voice, while he placed EKG monitors on Hutchins's chest. "Actually, it hurts worse going in the hand. We have to insert an IV in both of your arms, but I'm authorized to give you sedative injections first. This should ease the discomfort before I insert the IVs. You'll only feel a couple of bee sting-like pricks," he continued. "Now, please form a fist with your right hand."

Out of the corner of his eye, he watched as "Boris" tied rubber tubing tightly around his upper arm and rubbed the area with a wet cotton ball of alcohol. When the veins in the middle of his arm stood at attention, the sharp needle pricked his flesh and was shoved further, invading his veins. "Boris" worked mechanically. In a matter of a few minutes and mercifully done with little discomfort, both IVs had been inserted, and clear tubes ran from three plastic bottles now hanging from a stand alongside the gurney. These were his impersonal executioners.

He almost laughed aloud from nervous jitters. *I can't believe this is really happening. Oh boy! I guess it's all downhill from here.*

He hoped beyond hope this was a dream, and he'd awaken with sweat popping from his forehead and running down his face as he had so many nights before over the past five years. He closed his eyes and hoped. *When I open my eyes, I'll be lying on my cot inside my cell. I'll mop across my forehead with my sleeve. Then I'll reach for the Bible to read some verses to settle my nerves. Afterward, I'll drift back to sleep. Then I'll have an early morning cup of coffee and a tasty breakfast. Wake up! Wake up!* He opened his eyes and his heart sank. *I am awake. This time, the dream is really happening.*

Afraid, he reminded himself of the case worker's explanation the previous day. *I'll be administered with a combination of three drugs. One will make me uncon-*

scious. I'll drift off to sleep. The last one is a muscle relaxer, which will cause death -- my diaphragm and lungs will be paralyzed, so my heart will stop. He promised I shouldn't feel anything. I'll go to sleep.

"Boris Karloff" raised the head of the bed so Hutchins's upper body was elevated about 30 degrees. Then he pulled the green sheet all the way up to Hutchins's neck, covering his arms and the tubes. He scanned the walls for a clock, but there wasn't one for him to see. "Doc, what t-t-time is it?" he stuttered.

"It's 1:50, son," the man answered.

The prison chaplain stepped forward and said a prayer. Then he recited the "Twenty-Third Psalm." Next, the two prison guards reappeared, and with the help of "Boris Karloff," they wheeled the gurney bearing the frightened man away from the wall of the small Waiting Chamber, Number 111. "Boris" followed along with the metal stand and the three dangling bottles. There was a two inch high threshold at the doorway of the Execution Chamber, Number 117, so they had to lift the gurney over the threshold into the white metal-walled room. Hutchins noticed the evenly spaced rivets and the dull gray floor out of the corner of his wide eyes. This had been the gas chamber in the past; the hungry wooden chair stared back sullenly, jealous of the young gurney. *Sorry, chair,* Hutchins thought. *You didn't get to claim this one.*

The pounding of his heart sounded like horses' hooves to his ears. The three men rolled him beside the wire-meshed window, so the eyewitnesses could get a full side view. *Thank God the curtain is pulled!* Then a contemptuous thought invaded his mind. He suddenly thought of himself as an exhibition at the fair or at the circus. *Ladies and gentlemen! Step right up. The show's about to begin. I know there are some of you who have been waiting for this moment for a long time. Well, your wait is almost over.*

The hair on the back of his neck and arms stood up – literally. He had no desire to see the people on the other side of the window watching him die, so he turned his head slightly to the right and laid there motionless, counting the beats of his drumming heart. Besides, he already could feel their hatred and disgust penetrating through the draped window. *To them, I must be a heartless monster. Even so, how can anyone with an ounce of human compassion want to watch this happen?*

Somehow, he even believed in his mysterious friend's promise to be with him during this time. How? He had no idea, but Lefrere had never let him down in the months and years since they'd met. But Hutchins knew with all the wads of sticky red tape the prison system had, the chances of him being in the Witness Room was slim. Whether he was physically there or not, he was there in spirit, and maybe this is what Lefrere had meant. The friendship he'd shared with Lefrere gave him strength and eroded the negativity that would be projected by other onlookers who were happy to watch him die.

He thought to himself, *Thank you, God, that none of my relatives are here to witness this. I was adamant they shouldn't attend. But honestly, I almost wished I'd allowed Geneva to stay. Knowing she was on the other side of this glass would have been comforting because now, I feel so all alone – so scared. Dear Jesus, I'm afraid. Please let my death somehow repay the families I have wronged. Please give them peace. And please be with me. I can't do this alone.*

He heard the bald guard's footsteps as he crossed the tiny room and stood ready to open the blue curtains drawn across the glass window beside the reclining man. Hutchins noticed the officer was avoiding any eye contact with him. Then there was complete silence except for the beating of his heart and the footsteps of three anonymous volunteered and who had been selected by Warden Rice to administer the drugs. They remained out of view, standing behind a white curtain partition. All Hutchins could see was their silhouettes like in the movie the kids used to watch when it came on television. *What was it called?* The Wizard of Oz? *Yeah, that's right. They must be called the Warden's Wizards. Hey! That was actually good if I must say so myself.*

He tried to swallow twice; these were obviously nervous reactions because he had no saliva whatsoever to swallow. He glanced up at the three plastic bottles, one holding the lethal dosage.

Isn't my whole life supposed to be flashing before my eyes? Isn't that what they say happens when you are dying? The only thing I see flashing is the single light above my head.

He forced himself to think good thoughts – about his family. *I hope Geneva will be okay. She stood beside me the whole way even though I haven't always treated her right. She's been my strongest supporter, urging my attorneys to file appeals and even meeting with the governor to plead for my life. She's been strong for so long; she deserves better than what I ever gave her. Maybe after I'm gone, she'll have a better life. Maybe she'll find someone who can make her happy. I love my kids. I hope they can remember the good times – not just the bad – and live good lives, happy lives.*

Now Warden Rice was asking him once more if he had anything to say. Again, Hutchins shook his head. Before leaving the Execution Chamber, Warden Rice had given a signal for the bald guard to open the curtains. As the officer began drawing back the blue folds, the scenes on both sides of the window were exposed to each other.

The convicted man's acute senses heard Warden Nathan Rice's voice echoing from the Witness Room on the other side of the glass. Drums were pounding in Hutchins's ears. He stared up at the bottles again – his death agents hung silently in a row.

Then Warden Rice reappeared in the execution chamber and gave the signal to begin. Hutchins focused on the light bulb above his head as the translucent liquids began dripping and flowing into his veins.

Okay – make it quick, he thought.

He closed his eyes, preparing to say the "Lord's Prayer." His lips moved as he began reciting the words, which his sweet, Bible-thumping mama had tried to teach him long ago.

Our Father, who art in heaven,

Hallowed be thy name.

He was having difficulty remembering the words, but he wanted to pray it once more before it was too late. That's when he heard the compassionate voice he'd come to know. His eyes flew open wide in search of his friend's face, but Lefrere wasn't within his peripheral vision, and Hutchins refused to turn his head the slightest degree to the left for fear of meeting the eyes of hostile witnesses. His eyelids involuntarily closed for the last time. But all that mattered was his friend had found a way to be with him as promised. Lefrere's comforting voice led the dying man in prayer.

Thy kingdom come, Thy will be done

On earth as it is in Heaven.

Hutchins took several quick breaths in and continued reciting the words. He felt calm and relaxed; his friend's ever-present voice made dying less frightening. The lightbulb's intensive heat was searing into his closed eyelids even though its brightness was beginning to dim.

Give us this day our daily bread,

And forgive us for our trespasses as we forgive those who trespass against us.

And lead us not into t-temp-temptation

But, but d-del-deliver me…. He was becoming extremely drowsy

From e-evil….

Am I floating? He wondered. *I must be!*

For thine is the

Kingdom and the pow –er and the glo—ry….

Then he heard Lefrere's gentle voice saying, "It's okay, James. Now let go and come with me."

And that's what he did -- he – just -- let -- go.

Part One:

Return to the Beginning

May 31, 1979 – September 21, 1979

Chapter One

The Gift of Innocence

"For children are innocent and love justice, while most of us are wicked and naturally prefer mercy."
G.K. Chesterton

TERRI TUNNEY

The long-anticipated cramps woke Terri at dawn with the tightening of her abdomen beginning slowly, stretching the skin taunt with every rise, and then mounting to a visible peak. The discomfort was manageable as she timed the contractions, which were coming consistently every five minutes. After waddling to the bathroom in her pink, fluffy slippers and emptying her uncomfortable bladder, she stood and massaged her rounded belly with gentle fingertips.

"I guess you're wanting to be born, little guy," she cooed. "You want to see the light."

Then she turned and automatically reached for the handle to flush the toilet. But she stopped when she noticed *the* blood-tinged mucus plug floating in the yellow-tinted water. *So this is what it looks like,* she thought. *Oh no! Then these aren't Braxton-Hicks pains. These are real labor pains. This is it! I'm officially in labor!*

Panic seized her; she didn't know if the sudden wave of nausea was a part of the labor process or the realization she had crossed a threshold for which she could not return: Motherhood. It was as if the past nine months had been a wondrous dream and journey. Wearing maternity clothes had been fun and even comfortable. Receiving special attention and care from family and friends and even strangers had been delightful. She had been the "center of attention" as the cliché goes. But now she knew it was no longer a dream. The painful part of the journey was upon her as it had been for her mother and her mother's mother and all the other "mothers" in the world. She silently prayed for strength.

Without hesitation, she headed for the bedside table. She grabbed her Bible and read Genesis 3:16, which she had bookmarked earlier when she found out she was pregnant. "To the woman he said, 'I will make your pains in childbearing very severe; with painful labor you will give birth to children. Your desire will be for your husband, and he will rule over you"' (NIV). Unfortunately, the passage didn't ease her anxiety any more than when she read it the first time, so she prayed. *Dear Father, please give me strength to get through this labor; help me to bear the pain of childbirth. I'm really scared. But most of all, I want my baby to be okay. Please let my baby be born healthy and strong with ten fingers and ten toes. And if it is your will and you don't mind me asking, please let it be a little boy. I pray these things in the holy name of Jesus Christ. Amen.*

She curled onto the mattress beside her sleeping husband and lovingly watched as he made the familiar soft whistling snores she'd grown accustomed to. *Starting now, no longer will it be you and me. We're having a baby – an addition to our family. In a few hours, we will be three. A precious part of you and a precious part of me.*

She raised up on her elbow and bent over to gently kiss his stubbly cheek. "Mark, wake up. It's time. We need to go to the hospital. Wake up and get dressed."

His response time was perfect. He sat up quickly causing tousles of black hair to fall across his wide-opened eyes. A boyish smile parted his lips, showing his white even teeth and deep dimples. "Are you sure?" he asked.

As she watched his endearing reaction, she nodded and half-whispered, "I'm sure. The contractions began around 6:30 and have continued every five minutes. I've timed them for over an hour. And I lost my mucus plug."

"Your what?" He asked while rubbing the sleep out of his dark brown eyes as he climbed out of bed.

"Never mind. It's a pregnancy term. Part of the process. Come on. You need to hurry."

"You get dressed while I shower and shave," he said while already tossing clothes onto the bed and grabbing his tennis shoes.

"Are you kidding? Do we have time for it? I don't want to deliver the baby myself," she giggled feeling a little nervous.

"We have time as long as I don't take my customary twenty minute shower. So you hurry up. I want a doctor to deliver our baby, too -- someone who knows what he's doing. Come here a minute," he said crossing the room to her and grabbing her shoulders. "Honey, are you okay? Are you nervous?"

She melted into her husband's awaiting arms and pressed her face against his bare chest. Unexpected tears began to flow. She felt the insurmountable dread of the unknown. *How long will my labor be? What will delivery be like?* She had been told by the Lamaze instructor that every woman's experience was different. *Did we do the right thing by trying to have the baby naturally? Will Lamaze work? Will I be able to manage the contractions? Would there be complications? Will the baby be okay? Will it be a little boy or little girl?* All these questions flooded her mind. *All I want is for the baby to be born healthy.*

She pulled back and wiped her nose with the back of her hand. "I'm sorry. I'm acting like a child. I want our baby to be healthy. And," she stuttered, "I want you to be proud of me."

He drew her back into his arms and stroked her hair. "Honey, I am already proud of you. Everything is going to be fine, and our baby will be perfect! Wait and see!"

Terri longed to be a little girl again, so she could cry for her daddy. She pictured him walking toward her with open arms as he had done when she burned her hand on the wood stove at the age of four. Or there was the time when she'd cut her finger while trying to peel an apple with an "off-limits" paring knife when she was seven and had to get stitches. He'd even known what comforting words to say when her pre-teen heart had been broken by Ronnie Burwell on the night of the first junior high dance. When Ronnie had broken up with her to go with Nancy Jo Fields, she thought she was going to die. No matter what the hurt or disappointment had been, she could always bury her tear-stained face against her father's strong, unyielding shoulder. His simple presence and tender touch could soothe away the worst pain or diminish the frightfulness of an awful nightmare.

But daddy was gone now; both of her parents were gone -- victims of a terrible automobile accident on New Years' Eve three years ago. Mercifully, they were killed instantly and never suffered, according to what the paramedics and doctors later stated. The accident had been caused by a deranged man who was driving under the influence for the second time and with a revoked license. He had crossed the center line of a two lane road only five miles from her parents' home. She was grateful they had died together, which was how they would have wanted it to be. Her parents' marriage and devotion to each other had been an inspiration to everyone who knew them but especially to Terri and her brother, Tony. Terri remembered how ecstatic her parents had been on her wedding day and how daddy had choked up when he answered the minister's question about giving her away. "Her mother and I do," had been his response. Then he had kissed her, winked, and placed her hand in Mark's.

Her dream of having a happy marriage had been fulfilled for the past four years. And now she was a wife and was becoming a mother. *Grow up,* she told herself. *Mark is my husband. I can turn to him with my fears, and we'll face them together.* Suddenly, she felt ashamed and pulled back from her husband's embrace to wipe her wet cheeks and force a smile.

"Hey sweetie," Mark whispered while he continued running his fingers through her hair. "You are going to be a great mother. The best mother anybody could want. I will be with you the entire time. I won't leave you for a minute. I promise. I love you, Terri."

She smiled at his tenderness. "I love you, too."

"Now go and put on your big girl panties if they still fit," he said with a laugh, "and let's head to the hospital. I want to meet our child."

Chapter Two

The Gift of Grace

"For we do not have a high priest who is unable to empathize with our weaknesses, but we have one who has been tempted in every way, just as we are – yet he did not sin. Let us then approach God's throne of grace with confidence, so that we may receive mercy and find grace to help us in our time of need."

Hebrews 4:15-16 (NIV)

JAMES WILLIAM HUTCHINS

Well, I finally did something right, James Hutchins thought to himself as he drove the white Ford Fairlane toward Chesnee, South Carolina. It was 10:30 on Thursday morning. He was feeling emotional as they drove the twenty three miles from their house in Rutherford County because it was "dry." He lowered the visor to block out the morning sun's glare and glanced sideways at his seventeen year old daughter who was his pride and joy. She always had been, but she tended to be a little feisty at times, and he could do without this part of her.

He was lost in his thoughts. *Tonight is Charlotte's big night. She'll be graduating from R-S Central High School, and we'll finally have a high school graduate and diploma in the family. I wonder what my old man would have said about that. Me, his good for nothin' son, having a daughter who made it all the way through high school. Probably he said nothing good. He never had anything good to say – especially to me.*

He noticed his daughter was smiling, probably because she was getting her way. He'd taken the day off from work to celebrate with his family. Charlotte had convinced Geneva and him to allow her to have a few friends over after the graduation ceremony this evening. *What was wrong with giving in?* He asked himself. *She deserved to have a party. What was wrong with having a few friends over? Besides, I'm proud of the way the house looks now, and I know they are too. It's only natural for them to want people to visit.*

He had always been ashamed and felt bad about his inability to provide adequately for his family. But in 1977, two years earlier, he had landed a good-paying job at Stonecutter Mills. He supervised a crew of four or five men. After taxes, he was able to bring home $101.00 each week. Maybe his luck was on the up and up now. The new job's extra money allowed him to install paneling on the walls and tile on the floors of their white-framed rental house. He had even shown the kids how to keep chickens and plant a vegetable garden out back. Geneva had planted perennial flowers in the yard and around the house. It had begun to take shape, to look like a home. But unfortunately, a leg injury he'd suffered in 1974 flared up again, interfering with his ability to work, so he'd been forced to have the knee operation he'd been putting off for years. His recovery had kept him out of work for almost a year. But he'd been able to return to work the month before; the sky was blue again.

Hutchins remembered the conversation last night when Charlotte had asked her parents if she could serve punch – spiked punch – at the party. He thought, *Of course, I wasn't on board with that initially because I didn't want to be responsible for a bunch of kids getting drunk at my house. Besides, I've finally gotten back to work after being out for a while. With only Geneva's paycheck and insurance to live on, it's been tough. We've had to scrimp to get by; even Charlotte had gotten a job at the drug store to help. Vodka or gin were not necessities and were expensive on a tight budget. There were other things we needed, but as usual, I relented and decided to buy her the vodka even though she was underage. I want my kids to have more than I ever did. And sometimes I wonder if they are appreciative enough of what we give them.*

When they reached the package store to buy a fifth of cheap vodka, Hutchins picked up a twelve-pack of beer for himself. After all, he was celebrating too. As they drove back to Rutherfordton, Charlotte kept count of the empty cans as they piled up in the floorboard, realizing her father had drank ten of the twelve beers in the short duration.

When they arrived home, she hustled into the house with the punch ingredients and the vodka. She found her mother in the kitchen preparing snacks and food to serve at the party. As she gathered the contents and the punch bowl, Steve Owen, her boyfriend dropped by to take her shopping for a few hours and to see if there was anything he could do to help with the party preparations. Everyone was cheerful, and everything seemed under control. Charlotte poured the appropriate quantities of pineapple-orange juice, apple juice, Hawaiian Punch, and a jar of maraschino cherries for the punch. But then, she emptied the entire fifth of vodka into the glass punch bowl and stirred the different liquids with a large wooden spoon. Even though her father was acting a little irritable, she announced she was going shopping with Steve for a few hours. There were things she wanted to purchase for her room and the party. Charlotte was beaming when she left, insisting her father be the first one to taste-test the red-colored concoction while she was gone.

At approximately 5:00 p.m., Steve dropped her back home. After gathering her packages and happily walking inside, she was met by her angry father.

"Good gosh, girl! This punch is too strong. What did you do? Pour the whole fifth in there? Are you trying to get everyone drunk? It's too strong," he yelled. "You can't serve that to a bunch of kids!"

Immediately, she was disappointed at his disapproval and also because she'd used the entire bottle of vodka. So she argued, "No, it's not too strong. It's fine, Daddy. It'll be okay when I add ice to it. I need to add ice."

"No it's not going to be fine. I know what I'm talking about, and this is too strong for a bunch of kids to drink." His voice was getting louder; his face was getting redder.

"It's fine," she replied softly with a pleading smile on her face, hoping he'd calm down. "Besides, it's not your punch. It belongs to my friends who helped me pay for it."

"And I'm telling you it's not." He was getting angrier. "Give me half of it and dilute the rest."

"No!" she cried.

"Give me half of it like I said."

Adamantly, Charlotte grabbed the punch bowl, sloshing liquid across the countertop, and poured out almost all of the punch. Then she replaced the bowl's contents with water. "It's not too strong now. We can drink it and not get into trouble."

After a few expletives, he yelled, "I'm going back to Chesnee to get more vodka. Then I'll make some punch, and it will be all mine."

"Please don't. Don't ruin my graduation, Daddy." She left the room in tears, deciding to tend to her afternoon purchases instead of argue. She'd bought plants and macramé basket holders to hang. When she returned to the kitchen, she was carrying a hammer in her hand. She needed nails to hang the plants.

Enraged, Hutchins left the room and returned moments later, holding the family's graduation tickets. He waved them in front of Charlotte face, while Geneva, Jamie and Lisa were frightened and held their breath. With a quick flick of his thumb, he opened the top of his cigarette lighter, pressed the lever, and torched the five tickets while his family looked on in horror. Geneva began weeping while the two younger kids pled for him to stop. Charlotte defiantly stared him in the eyes.

"What are you doing?" Charlotte screamed. Her eyes were wide with bewilderment.

"Burning these tickets. No one is going to celebrate tonight." He yelled spatting his words.

"You're just a mean and cruel man!" Charlotte shouted. "I'm glad you're not going."

A stinging slap across her face halted the words on her tongue. Defiantly, her stare dared him to smack her again. Instead, she felt his rough hands grab her around the throat and begin to squeeze the air out of her body. His eyes looked distant as his contorted face twitched with rage. Her eyes bulged. She couldn't breathe. She clawed at his vise-like hands, trying desperately to pry them away.

Lisa grabbed at his arms to pull him away from her sister. "Daddy, stop, stop. Don't hurt her!" She wanted things to calm down so the graduation ceremony and party wouldn't be ruined by her father's sudden rage.

But instead of relenting, he smacked Lisa across the face. Her face stung, as well as her heart. This was the first time in her life she'd been struck by her father.

She was no longer a virgin to his tirades and reckless antics.

As Hutchins wrestled to get the hammer out of Charlotte's hands, he raised it above her head. That's when Geneva screamed. Jamie and Lisa joined their mother in tackling the "head of household," and pulling him away. They tearfully begged him to calm down and come to his senses.

Their distraction was enough for him to release Charlotte. She jumped up and bolted out the door, running across the road to their closest neighbor's house, leaving her family behind to deal with the aftermath. When their neighbor answered the door, Charlotte was gasping and out of breath. "Daddy's drunk! He's beating on us! He's beating on my mom.... We need help!"

The neighbor stood aside and allowed the girl to enter. She offered to hide her under the bed, but Charlotte declined. Unfortunately, the girl couldn't have known the family quarrel had already subsided. Geneva and Lisa had returned to the kitchen to finish making the snacks and to prepare dinner, while Jamie and his father sat side by side on the living room sofa with James repeatedly yelling the family wouldn't be able to go to Charlotte's commencement.

She asked to use the telephone, so the woman quietly handed the receiver to her, so she could call the sheriff's department. Unfortunately, the neighbor had heard all of this before; Hutchins's abuse was too familiar. While Charlotte dialed the number to the sheriff's department, the elderly woman consoled the sobbing girl by patting her back and giving her a glass of water. When the dispatcher answered, Charlotte began crying into the phone.

Chapter Three

The Gift of Today

"Therefore do not worry about tomorrow, for tomorrow will worry about itself. Each day has enough trouble of its own."

Matthew 6:34 (NIV)

CAPTAIN ROY HUSKEY / SERGEANT MILLARD OWEN MESSERSMITH

This day in Rutherfordton and surrounding towns in the county had an air of excited anticipation like Christmas as everyone was abuzz with thoughts and plans for Graduation Day in Rutherford County. It was a school holiday. JoAnn Huskey was hurrying to finish all of her daily tasks at the insurance company in Spindale when the phone rang. She pulled a brass chain on the banker's lamp to turn off the intrusive, glaring light shining through the green glass shade.

"Giles Insurance Company, may I help you?" she answered.

"It's me," said Roy. "What are your plans for tonight? Are ya'll eating supper at home?"

"No. Remember? Sherry and I are going to graduation at Chase. We thought we'd eat supper at the Western Steer. Why don't you join us before your shift?"

"No, ya'll go ahead. I'll fix a sandwich."

"Are you sure?" she asked.

"Yeah. I'll be fine. Ya'll go ahead, and have a good time. Tell him [their nephew] congratulations for me. And make sure you tell the Baby [Sherry] what happened on her soap [*The Edge of Night*] today."

"Okay. What happened?" JoAnn asked.

Roy's voice seemed more enthusiastic. "Someone was sitting at a desk and the character was shot."

"Who shot him?"

"Zack shot Steve, and it showed Molly standing behind the door," he replied.

"Did he die?" JoAnn asked, engrossed in the soap opera's storyline.

"Don't know. I think he was shot twice. But you know how these soaps are. They come back in ten years."

She shook her head and laughed as she hung up the telephone receiver. She loved her hard-working, "neat freak" husband who enjoyed soap operas as much as her daughter did. As a boy, Roy had told anyone and everyone, "When I grow up, my house is going to be clean." She chuckled and thought how true this was. There were times when she had been reading a book and would get up to go to the bathroom. When she returned, she'd search for her book only to find it replaced on the bookcase shelf. Their white kitchen sinks were spotless because he used Comet all the time. And his neatness didn't stop at home. One of the deputies laughed as he never tired of recounting the story of when he'd thrown a cigarette butt on the ground and twisted the toe of his shoe over it. He could see Roy was antsy to pick it up.

Roy was an honest man and a teetotaler. Sure he cursed a little, but it had gotten to the point his cursing was not too bad. She loved to hear him sing in the shower in the mornings. *I'm thankful for my husband. If only I could get him to go with me to the Baptist church more often.* JoAnn reminded herself to work on that one. Then her mind wandered again. It seemed like yesterday when she and Roy had met.

Glenn (*I can't remember his last name*) was the boy JoAnn had been dating from Harris. She and her best girlfriend, Shirley Freeman, attended Cool Springs, but they preferred dating boys from Harris. After JoAnn and Glenn decided they wanted to date other people, they broke up but remained good friends. Even so, when he caught the mumps two weeks later, JoAnn went by the following Sunday afternoon to check on him. On Monday night, she was going to date a new guy. He was from Caroleen and had promised to take her to the movies to see *Across the Wide Missouri.* She giggled at the memory. He had been an octopus – all hands. During the movie, he kept putting his arm around her and trying to get fresh. Finally, to JoAnn's relief, a voice from the row behind them said, "I wish you'd sit still, so I can watch the movie." JoAnn glanced around to locate the person with the welcomed admonishment. He was sporting army fatigues. And he happened to be sitting beside a friend of Glenn's.

"I thought you and Glenn were going steady," the friend whispered.

"Not any more. We broke up two weeks ago. But I checked on him yesterday; he has the mumps."

"Oh. That's too bad," the friend paused. "Then can I have your phone number?"

"Sure, I guess so." She gave it to him, and then addressed the guy in the army fatigues with a question. "Are you in the National Guard?"

"No," he answered. "Army. I'm home on a thirty day furlough." She was curious and found out his name – Roy Huskey.

Evidently, Roy had been listening whenever she had given her phone number to Glenn's friend and had memorized it. When he called her and asked her out, she said "Yes," but she had a different answer when he'd asked her to marry him on their first date.

"Ask me the next time you come home," she had told him. One thing she had learned about Roy early on was he was outspoken. You either liked him or you disliked him. And you knew exactly where you stood with him, too.

Because they dated each other every night for thirty days, JoAnn learned a lot about Roy and his family dating back a century. The Huskey family had settled in Cherokee and Spartanburg counties in South Carolina and Cleveland and Rutherford counties in North Carolina. His grandparents, Thomas Clifford Huskey and Millie Ann Rollins Huskey, had four sons, and both of his grandparents lived to be almost fifty eight years-old. They were buried in the Rollins Family Graveyard outside of Gaffney, S.C.

Their son, Richard R. Huskey was born on January 15, 1888. He married Hattie Mae Henson, who was born February 2, 1899. They had seven children: Daniel Billy, Damon Howard, Robert Lee, Thomas Max, Roy, and twins, Betty Jean and Billy Dean. Richard Huskey worked as a sharecropper. After giving birth to her twins, sadly, Hattie Mae had died on June 9, 1935, of pancreatitis. They buried her at the Sulphur Springs Baptist Church Cemetery in Rutherford County. For six months, Richard and his boys struggled to perform their demanding chores and care for the needy babies. Eventually, he had made the difficult decision to place them in the Rosemont Home for Children.

One Sunday when Richard had gone to visit his two children at the Children's Home, he was shocked to learn they were gone. Roy wasn't sure if it was Social Services or the Welfare Department who had taken the children and placed them with a family named Hoffman who lived in New York. But they had adopted the twins and had renamed them entirely. Neither Richard nor any of Roy's brothers ever had contact with them over the years.

JoAnn enjoyed learning about Roy's family, so when he got his next furlough, he returned home and called her. Roy had spent the nights with his high school friend, Terry Robbins at Robbins Lake, where people paid to fish. Roy would walk all the way from Robbins Lake to meet her after school each afternoon. Over the course of six weeks, they dated every night, with him once again asking her to marry him.

"Ask me the next time you come home," she repeated.

That "next time" would come sooner than expected because Roy's father had been hospitalized in July. Roy was able to get an emergency furlough to come home. Being persistent, he once again asked JoAnn to marry him.

He wore me down, she thought to herself. They were married on July 16, 1957; he was twenty and she was sixteen. *Have we really been married twenty-two years?* She wondered. *It seemed like a short time until you heard the number.*

Roy was known to be a character, who enjoyed talking all the time, which was different from his quiet older brother, Sheriff Damon Huskey. Roy loved an argument. He never really got mad – he loved having serious conversations.

Roy was rarely seen without his sunglasses; they were a staple of his normal attire, but few knew he used them to camouflage his lazy eye he'd been born with. He had inherited the eye muscle weakness from his mother and had shared the same condition with his sister, Betty Jean, who was later renamed as Barbara Ann. It was most noticeable whenever his sister was tired; one of her eyes would "wander" off center.

As a child, Roy had endured lots of teasing about his condition. This, along with the early death of his mother, had planted seeds of concern, fear, anxiety, and insecurity in his soul, a child's soul, which was rich for the plantings of self-awareness, self-esteem, and self-discovery. Unfortunately, these seeds had taken root and sprouted feelings of possession and jealousy.

After he joined the Army, surgeons had attempted to correct this condition, and while they did correct the weakened muscle, the overcorrection resulted in an inability to focus with strong light. So thick, tinted glasses became a requirement – not an optional adornment. Because of this, he withstood still more teasing throughout the years because some of the guys he worked with thought he was wearing sunglasses to be cool. Some even nicknamed him "Hollywood," but he never corrected them or explained. Instead, he accepted their ribbing with laughter. Others who didn't know him as well may have viewed him as being cocky. He was a hard person to get to know, but once you did, he was nice to know. Roy was good to almost everyone he knew.

When they had bought their current home on the site of one of the historical mills, the land was overgrown with spreading kudzu and honeysuckle. Roy rented a bulldozer and spent five days clearing away acres of the thick vines, filling in a gulley, and cutting off the edge of a hill. Afterward, he kept the land and their yard well-manicured. JoAnn used to joke and tell others, "He'll stand and wait for a twig to fall, so he can pick it up." She was thankful for the money his skills and hard-work had saved them over the years. They'd started their family and had two children, Rick and Sherry, but now it seemed like they were grown and leaving home before she had turned around once.

JoAnn fondly remembered when they had bought Sherry's horse when she was nine. It was a beautiful horse: Half Arabian and half American Quarter Horse. They had gelded him. JoAnn smiled to herself. *Then there was the squirrel monkey. She always had lots of animals around the place.*

But the well-rooted emotions of jealousy and possessiveness had blossomed like a perennial and threatened his marriage of fifteen years. JoAnn had left him for a year and a half because of his "terrible temper" and because "he was afraid someone was going to take me away from him." Desperate to get his wife and children back, Roy endeavored to change his ways and control his temper. During their separation, he worked an interim job for Duke Power, driving a bulldozer in Sandy Marsh. He deposited his paycheck in the bank every week and came to visit his wife and children on the weekends. Finally, he turned to his minister, asking him to visit JoAnn and convince her to come back to him. And she did. Their last twelve years have been their best years.

Sherry's love for animals was why she was working on her B.S. in biology at UNC-Charlotte and planned to attend NCSU College of Veterinary Medicine to become a veterinarian. "Daddy's Baby" already had earned her A.S. at the community college. She was home for the summer, which made him happy.

They were proud of their son, Rick, who had attended UNC-Charlotte to become a civil engineer. He had married a lovely girl in April, whom they were happy to welcome to the family.

Captain Roy Huskey was back on the job at the sheriff's office, counting down the minutes until he'd officially be on duty at 6:00 p.m. A couple of officers joined him at the gas pumps, chuckling at some of his arrest stories. Roy nudged his ever-present sunglasses back to the bridge of his nose to block out the sun's rays and kept on laughing.

"Hey Roy," the new dispatcher called as she walked outside. "There's a caller who is asking for you."

"Who is it?" Roy asked.

"I don't know, but she wants to talk with you."

Roy followed her inside and picked up the waiting receiver. On the other end was Charlotte Hutchins. She was sobbing. "He's beating on my mom. He's got some guns. I don't know what he's going to do next."

Roy tried to calm her. "Well, hold on. We'll get somebody up there."

He returned to the waiting officers and said, "Another domestic disturbance call. Hutchins is showing his ass again. I guess I'll have to go handle it once more. His daughter says he's beating his wife and has guns. She's scared."

Getting calls from the Hutchins's place was nothing new, and because Roy lived less than a mile and only a few roads from Hutchins, he normally was the one asked to respond. Most of the time, the calls amounted to nothing. But one time when Huskey had answered a call at the house, he had found Geneva and the three kids in an overgrown field where they'd taken refuge. They'd spent the night there from fear of Hutchins and his .30-06. Another time, which had happened more recently, Huskey had been called out again to the house where he found Hutchins in the yard with a shotgun in his hand and screaming at the sky. He wasn't sure if this call might be like either of those two, especially since Charlotte had said, "He has guns; I don't know what he'll do next."

"Want me to tag along as back-up?" his friend Sergeant Owen Messersmith offered. They were good friends, both on the job and off. The balding and popular Messersmith was 58 years old and preparing to retire in a few months. He'd been on the job for four and a half years and was assigned to the Lake Lure and Chimney Rock areas where he was active in the Lions Club and Rotary Club and was known to enjoy talking about his two sons, Emory and Raymond Rude.

"I thought you were off duty," Roy said.

"I am. I pulled first shift, but I don't mind. It'll be my last call for the day."

"Okay, if you're sure"

Messersmith nodded. "I'm sure."

"Then follow me out there," Roy agreed, happy to accept his assistance. "You remember it's about a mile from my house. I'll turn into the driveway. You hang back on the road. It shouldn't take too long."

Chapter Four

The Gift of Victory

"Where, O death, is your victory? Where, O death is your sting?"

1 Corinthians 15:55 (NIV)

CAPTAIN ROY HUSKEY / SERGEANT MILLARD OWEN MESSERSMITH

Roy's life had taught him to be sensitive to those who were treated unfairly. He believed officers were not above the law; they were there to enforce the law and bring about fairness to all people. He wanted to ensure everyone was treated equitably by him and others. He endeavored to do what was right and found flaws in laws that didn't protect the victims, especially when they seemed to protect the perpetrators. So in 1963, he had joined the Sheriff's Department and dedicated his life to making a difference.

His life had been a series of events and stories suitable for a television soap opera. Dan Huskey, his brother, was a gospel singer with the Blackwood Brothers and had appeared on the *Arthur Godfrey Show*. After their mother had died giving birth to his younger brother and sister, the twins, his father had placed them in a children's home. Later, they had been adopted by a family from New York, so his family had lost touch with them. Over the years, Dan had tried to find them. Every time he visited New York, he'd search for their last name in phone books. But Dan had been unsuccessful, and the family had not been reconciled. That is, not until Marge, his sister-in-law, challenged her husband, Sheriff Damon Huskey, to use his connections to locate them. His older brother was up for the challenge – meeting it in 1978.

By knowing their new names, Damon was able to locate a woman named Barbara Ann Hoffman living in Detroit. When Damon and Marge traveled there to meet her, they were disappointed to discover it wasn't her, but the woman did inform them there had been another Barbara Ann Hoffman in her high school class. She now lived in Kansas. So Damon called the Sheriff's Department in Kansas, and surprisingly, the dispatcher knew of Barbara Hoffman who had come into the office to inform them her phone was being disconnected the next day in case anyone wanted to get in touch with her. She was moving closer to her brother, Peter Hoffman, who worked at the EPA in Washington, D.C. Afterward, Damon and Marge were excited to telephone her and explain who they were. They had been separated for forty years, but now the siblings were reunited. Roy had known his younger sister and younger brother for one year.

After driving north from Rutherfordton for four miles to Mountain Creek Road, Roy steered his cruiser into Hutchins's dirt driveway and coasted the fifty yards up to the white-framed house. He adjusted his sunglasses to block out the brilliancy of the setting sun. It was a few minutes past 6:00 when he parked his car and got out. He noticed Hutchins was standing on the screened porch. He couldn't have known Hutchins "was feeling he'd reached the lowest point of his life." They exchanged a series of menacing shouts.

"I told you never to come back to my house, or I'd kill you!" Hutchins yelled.

That's when Roy noticed what Hutchins had been holding.

"You get out of this yard," the enraged man yelled. "This is my business. You get out of here. I have a gun." Hutchins aimed toward the grille of the cruiser, shattering the headlight with an undeniable warning he meant business this time. Then he stormed inside the house and returned momentarily with another gun – a .30-06.

After the shot, Roy instinctively drew his revolver before getting back into the car. This action was not lost on Hutchins. Roy shoved the gearshift into reverse and began to back out of the driveway. But it was too late; he didn't get far. When Hutchins fired again, the bullet shattered the wind shield, striking Roy's right shoulder. His revolver was knocked to the backseat of his cruiser. When Hutchins shot the third time, the bullet smashed into Roy's forehead, shooting him between the eyes.

That's when Hutchins noticed the second cruiser entering the driveway. And he was ready. Owen Messersmith had been parked halfway on the road and halfway in the driveway as Roy had instructed when he heard the shots. Immediately, he responded, stopping behind Roy's cruiser – a fatal mistake. As he quickly exited the car without drawing his weapon, a .30-06 bullet entered the right side of his body and exited the left side. Falling to the ground beside his car, the officer died instantly. Mercifully, he felt nothing. His death was the result of a bullet and unbridled rage.

Hutchins grabbed his two guns and the box of cartridges and left in his white Ford Fairlane.

After finishing the call to the sheriff's department and relieved they were on the way, Charlotte had telephoned her boyfriend, Steve Owens, who immediately traveled to the neighbor's home. As he was reaching the neighbor's driveway, he passed Hutchins, who was speeding out of his driveway. Upon arriving and finding Charlotte bruised face, he applied ice, and while doing so, Charlotte mentioned she'd heard four shots and saw her father leaving hastily. Steve hurriedly ran to his car and drove across the road. When he pulled into the driveway, he parked behind the last cruiser where Sergeant Messersmith lay sprawled out on the ground.

"I thought at first he was hiding out. And then I remembered Mr. Hutchins had left. Then I went up to the officer. He was lying down.... I looked up closer to the blood....I started asking if there was anything I could do to help....his eyes were still open ...he wouldn't say anything. Blood was pooling under his punctured right eye."

He didn't go to the first cruiser for fear of what he'd find. So he grabbed Messersmith's radio microphone and started yelling. He was terrified over what he'd seen and was scared to death Hutchins may return.

"If anybody can hear me, I'm not kidding; a policeman's shot!" he screamed hoping someone would hear him.

Geneva, Jamie, and Lisa hurried out of the house. Relieved they were not harmed, Steve gathered them in his car, went and got Charlotte, and drove them to the Rutherford County Jail for their safety.

Lieutenant Lloyd "Junior" Boone, a deputy sheriff, who was retiring that same day, heard Steve's dispatch loud and clear. "Stay with me and tell me where you are." Owens did, so Boone rushed to the tragic scene at the Hutchins's residence.

Boone recalled later, "I pulled in just back of Messersmith's car. I immediately went up to him. I checked him for a pulse. I used his radio to say I had found one officer and he was down, to send an ambulance."

He continued by relating the horrible scene. "I could see the door of Captain Huskey's car was open." He had initially thought he saw Huskey moving and that he was okay. "His left toe was holding the door open, but I later realized a dog had jumped into the car with him." Boone walked to the driver's door and looked inside. "His whole face was blowed away. The blood was oozing. Just by looking at him, I knew he was dead." He radioed for backup.

State Trooper Sorrels heard the broadcast for officers to watch for Hutchins's white Ford. A little later, Peterson responded. When Spears heard Peterson's response, he fell in behind.

When Deputy Philbeck got home that afternoon, he heard transmissions on his scanner radio. "Someone was screaming 'Officer killed! Get some help. Policeman's been shot!'"

While JoAnn and Sherry were eating their supper at Western Steer, JoAnn noticed several people staring at them, which was puzzling. Realizing they didn't have a bow for their graduation gift, they decided to stop at Sky City on the way to the graduation ceremony at Chase. Sherry braked behind a car at the stop-light. As the light turned green and they were turning left onto Church Street, they heard sirens and watched several troopers' cars whizzing past them. The cars had almost run over them.

Shaken, they pulled into Sky City's parking lot. A lady who had been in the car ahead of them got out of her car and scurried toward them. "They almost hit me!" she exclaimed.

"Do you know what's going on?" Sherry asked.

"Yes. On the radio they are saying two highway patrolmen are dead."

Apocalyptically, Sherry said, "Mother. It's Daddy!"

"No," JoAnn replied, shaking her head. "Don't worry. Your dad is probably home eating a sandwich." Even though she tried to reassure her daughter, her stomach felt like it was twisting itself into knots.

"Yes, it's daddy! Let's call and find out," Sherry cried.

When they located a nearby pay phone, Sherry called the sheriff's office. When the female dispatcher answered, Sherry identified herself. The dispatcher didn't say a word.

That's when the phone was passed, and Deputy Junior Boone's voice came on the line.

"Junior," Sherry said, "Was my daddy one of the officers who was shot?"

He hesitated. "Are you sure you want to know?"

"Yes. I want the truth," Sherry responded. She was shaking.

"Are you sure?" he asked.

"Yes."

Junior said sadly, "I think they are taking them to the hospital."

"Is he dead?" she asked.

"I think so. I'm sorry."

Sherry and JoAnn ran to the car and headed for the hospital. Sherry drove as fast as possible without killing them. They stood outside the Emergency Room doors, waiting for the ambulance to arrive. It seemed they had been waiting for a long time when a newscaster who JoAnn knew walked outside and laid his hand on JoAnn's shoulder.

"JoAnn, I'm so sorry," he said sadly.

They had been given no information and didn't know where Roy was.

They noticed three or four surgeons walking together from a room

"Daddy's dead." Sherry whispered.

"No, no, darling. Don't think the worse," JoAnn chided her.

"No. I know how things work. Surgeons wouldn't be walking out together." For one of her college summer jobs, Sherry had worked at Isothermal in admissions. Her job had been to help admit patients and complete their insurance information.

A few moments later, their nightmare was confirmed as the doctors relayed the tragic news. The grieving process began with shock. In shock, they telephoned Rick to give him the bad news about his father. Shortly afterward, heart-broken Sheriff Damon Huskey and his wife, Marge, arrived at the hospital and accompanied Sherry and JoAnn home.

In the blink of an eye, these two dedicated officers were gone without an opportunity to say goodbye to their loved ones. They were not treated fairly by Hutchins or by fate. Their wives, children, relatives, and friends would be forced to bring about their own closures and pick up the pieces of their lives without them. How is this possible?

Only six days earlier on May 25, Sherry Huskey had baked her father a cake. Unknowingly, the family had celebrated his last birthday. His journey of forty-two years [May 25, 1937 – May 31, 1979] had instantly ended from a massive head wound caused by a high-powered rifle.

Deputy Owen Messersmith had traveled his journey for fifty-eight years [June 20, 1920 – May 31, 1979], leaving behind his wife and two sons and being known as a "nice guy" who smiled all the time.

Their watches ended on May 31, 1979.

Chapter Five

The Act of Duty

"Let us have faith that right makes might, and in that faith let us to the end dare to do our duty as we understand it."

Abraham Lincoln

PATROLMAN ROBERT L. "PETE" PETERSON

It is possible random travelers entrenched in their daily routines passed by N.C. State Highway Patrolman Robert L. "Pete" Peterson on May 31, 1979, as he was parked at the county line on U.S. Highway 221 alongside a fellow trooper to talk "shop" about their neighboring counties; Peterson was assigned to Rutherford County, and the other trooper was assigned to McDowell County.

"Hey, some of the fellows were talking about you the other day. They said you were known as 'super trooper' because you were the toughest trainer in the history of the N.C. Highway Patrol. They say you were like a 'machine,'" the young trooper stated with unconcealed admiration. "Does being a former Marine have anything to do with this?"

"Is this what they say?" Peterson asked, downplaying the attention. He adjusted his mirrored Aviator sunglasses, so they wouldn't rub so hard behind his ears and squinted at the sun's blinding rays. "Naw, well, I don't know. In the Marines they teach you discipline; that's for sure."

"Did you serve in Nam?"

"Yeah. One tour."

When Peterson obviously didn't care to elaborate and the conversation ebbed, the younger trooper searched for something else to say. "Yes, sir. They say you're like a mythical figure. So, how long have you been in this area? You didn't train me when I was a cadet."

"I transferred here a little over two years ago. After handling ten trooper cadet classes, I was ready to do something different. I've been in the Patrol for nine years total."

"So is it true you made the cadets run fifteen miles in the morning?"

"Fifteen miles?" Peterson laughed. "That's hyperbole! I only made them run fourteen."

The younger trooper chuckled good-naturedly and then stopped. He looked puzzled. "You're kidding, right, Pete?"

"Yeah, I'm kidding." His eyes peered through the steering wheel at the visible gauges. "Naw, all kidding aside. We ran three to five miles each morning, five days a week. Not bragging, but most of the time, I'd take off afterward and run another mile to the public golf course, play eighteen holes, and make it back to the Center in time to conduct the daily training sessions. Sometimes they asked me to work in the evenings to help cadets with remedial training needs. I did because I had the time."

"Philbeck told me he ran with you sometimes. He said, 'You know what the rascal did while we were jogging? He'd turn around and start running backward, yelling at me the whole time to get into shape because he was in top shape."'

Peterson laughed.

"Wow. No wonder they call you 'super trooper.' I'm glad I didn't have you as my trainer."

"I'm probably glad you didn't either," Peterson joked. They laughed together. Suddenly, their chuckles were interrupted by loud, undistinguishable words and static.

"Wait a minute." Peterson signaled to the other trooper to hush with the palm of his hand. The distorted radio traffic on his scanner continued. It was being transmitted from the Rutherford County Sheriff's frequency. Like many other troopers, Peterson had taken it upon himself to purchase a scanner for his patrol car, which allowed him to monitor local law enforcement frequencies. They were transmitted on high-band frequencies, unlike the State Highway Patrol's transmissions, which were on low-bands.

"I can't make it out. Can you?" he asked the other trooper.

"No," he replied, leaning farther outside of his window to try.

"Okay. Then maybe I'd better check it out. See ya later."

Hastily, he pulled his car onto the asphalt and headed toward Rutherfordton. He picked up his radio to contact the State Highway Patrol Communications Center in Asheville. After identifying himself, he asked, "Can you contact the Rutherford County Sheriff's Department to see if anything's wrong? There's a garbled dispatch, but I can't make it out. Make sure everything is 10-4."

"Standby," the dispatcher called. A few minutes later, the dispatcher returned. "We're unable to get anyone on the telephone. We've tried several times, but the lines are busy. We've tried getting a computer reply, too, but haven't been successful."

As Peterson crossed into the city limits, a speeding car ripped past him. Spontaneously, Peterson turned his vehicle around and chased the vehicle. He instinctively turned on his blue light and siren and lifted his radio to contact the Communications Center again. "In pursuit of a speeding car on U.S. 221 heading north. It's a white Ford Fairlane. Will radio license number when I get closer."

Unfortunately, Peterson didn't realize the driver he was chasing had killed two law enforcement officers. He throttled the accelerator and applied his astutely trained driving skills, but somehow, momentarily, the fleeing car left him behind, distancing itself from the trooper's. After rounding several curves and straight-away lanes, Peterson finally saw the car ahead of him slow down and turn onto the road behind the massive Gilkey Lumber Company.

His car slid as he braked to make the turn onto SR1533. He slammed the car into reverse and turned onto the road. This provided a few extra seconds for Hutchins to collect his thoughts and plan his next move.

"I just seen a white Ford going behind Gilkey Lumber Company. I see him now. I don't think he knows I'm behind him."

Trooper Spears radioed, "I'm sitting right behind you, Pete."

As Peterson radioed the dispatcher with an update "He's slowing down," he noticed the woods were thick on both sides, resembling a tunnel.

Alarmingly, the officer saw the white car had come to a complete stop in a ninety-degree curve and was blocking the road. The driver's door was open. He watched as the anonymous driver rounded the front of the Fairlane and assumed he was heading toward a close-by clump of trees. Peterson also noticed he was carrying a rifle looking like a .30-06.

Peterson radioed the dispatcher one last time. "He's got his door open; he's fixing to hit the woods."

Peterson slammed his foot on the brake pedal and locked it down. He wrestled with the rigid steering wheel, forcing it right to correct the skid. The tires smoked and screeched as the rear end of the patrol car slipped and slid. Unfortunately, Peterson had miscalculated. The man wasn't running; instead, he was hunched down on the other side of his car, pointing the barrel of the gun in the trooper's direction. There was no place for Peterson to go. Hutchins had been waiting to ambush him. Three calculated, rhythmic shots hit the fender of his car. As he'd trained others and had been trained himself, his last thoughts were to quickly open his door and dive for cover behind the vehicle engine's block. Simultaneously, he grabbed his .357 revolver from his belt holster, knowing the cylinder was full. He always kept it full.

He rose slightly to take aim at the defiant man who stood between him and eternity. Everything was happening in slow motion. It was if the trooper could see through the length of the lowered rifle barrel to the bullet that would end his life.

Instantaneously, as he squeezed the trigger of his revolver in the direction of the man, his head reeled backward in reaction to the bullet ripping through the windshield and into his brain, rupturing his skull with its forceful impact. Peterson never heard the fatal blast or the fifth bullet from Hutchins's gun.

Peterson's assailant ran to the ford and drove north another mile or so before realizing his front tire was flat. He shouted a litany of superfluous words. He had no other option but to grab his guns and box of ammunition and disappear into the dense thicket.

Trooper Robert Kaiser arrived shortly afterward in response to the radio calls he'd heard Peterson make. As he rounded the curve, he parked his car closely behind Peterson's bumper. The Fairlane was gone.

"Peterson? Peterson? Are you okay?" he called, hoping to hear a reply.

But there was no answer. Kaiser hurried toward the other patrol car and took in the entire scene. Peterson was unmistakably deceased, having been shot in the head. Like a shaken rag doll, the brave and fallen officer's body was slumped in the front seat of his car, under the steering wheel. His left foot was on the ground. A large pool of blood stained the asphalt under his head, which was leaning outside the door. Residual shards of the windshield's glass continued to fall from the fresh bullet holes. His revolver was on the floor-board.

Multiple voices on Kaiser's and Peterson's radios were high-pitched and squawking. Peterson's car was still running, and the transmission was in drive. The Fairlane had been found abandoned down the road.

Patrolman Dan Good, Peterson's best friend, had been working the late shift that day on the southern end of the county. When he arrived moments later, he was met by the two other patrolmen who already had reached the horrific scene. As he knelt beside his best friend, he knew Pete was dead. The bullet had hit him in the center of his forehead. Through tears, he watched his fallen friend's dead body jerking with muscle spasms. The other patrolman stood over the two officers and looked on in shock and horror.

Many years later, when asked about the events of May 31, 1979, Good would state, "I was in Vietnam. I killed people. I saw people killed. I earned the Purple Heart. But the two worst things in my life are the death of my daughter and my friend Peter Peterson being shot."

Within three miles of the two slain officers' bodies on Mountain Creek Road and some ten minutes later, life had ended for N.C. State Highway Patrolman Robert L. "Pete" Peterson, a courageous and dedicated young man who had displayed a strong sense of discipline and duty to his peers and subordinates. Five spent cartridges gleamed against the grey asphalt to mark the spot where his assailant had waited to ambush him. Lake Lure's Medical Examiner Dr. William Burch later stated,

"He never knew what hit him. The bullet tore off the top of his head." Peterson's spent cartridge was never found. He left behind a heart-broken family including his parents, his daughter, Melanie Paige Peterson, and two sisters.

Robert L. "Pete" Peterson's journey had lasted only thirty seven short years, but in those years, he had lived an exemplary life. This included becoming a U.S. Marine, who gallantly served his country in the Vietnamese war; developing into a rigorous and respected N.C. Highway Patrol trainer who became a legend; and being an endearing and beloved father, son, brother, and friend who had made his family and others proud.

With the sun dropping behind the horizon, Peterson's watch had ended.

Chapter Six

The Gift of Generosity

"Generosity is the most natural outward expression of an inner attitude of compassion and loving-kindness."
Dalai Lama XIV

ALEXANDRA (ALEX) WELLS

"But Daddy! You and Mama don't need to give me anything else! Giving me a surprise party is more than enough!" cried Alex. She was being led outside their sprawling ranch house by her doting parents. A small group of family members – aunts, uncles, cousins, and intimate friends followed closely behind the trio, afraid they wouldn't discover the surprise before Alex's blind-fold was removed. But when the gift came into view, there were collective gasps, refrained giggles, and a cacophony of superlative words.

Rob Wells released his daughter's hand and turned around to address the onlookers. He was an attractive middle-aged man with more pepper than salt in his hair. His olive complexion belied popular accusations that he conducted a perpetual affair with a tanning bed. Now his handsome face was beaming amidst a broad smile and twinkling dark eyes. And according to this proud father, his popular and gorgeous daughter had inherited his good looks and reputed outgoing personality. Whenever he was asked about his wife's contribution to their daughter, Rob's pat answer was "brains and a love for reading."

He held up his palms in a motion to silence the onlookers. "Betsy and I want to thank ya'll for coming today to help us celebrate our daughter's recent graduation from college. We're very proud of her and relieved not to have to pay tuition and room and board any longer," he joked.

"Oh, Rob," Betsy groaned. "Be serious."

Everyone laughed.

"Okay. So I have to be more serious." He turned to hug his daughter close. "Alex, I hope you know how much your mother and I love you. We've always been proud of you and grateful you are our daughter. And to show you how proud and grateful we are, we wanted to give you a special graduation gift you won't forget and one that hopefully should last you a long time." He held up crossed fingers in an exaggerated display. Everyone laughed at the implied message hidden beneath his words.

As her father removed a tie-dye scarf left over from the '60s, her mother excitedly grasped her right hand more tightly. Alex opened her eyelids and struggled to adjust her vision to the late afternoon sunlight, which seemed to be blinding her. She couldn't believe her eyes when she was able to focus and comprehend what was parked in the circular driveway of the house. Underneath a HUGE red bow was a dark blue metallic 1979 Corvette with sunroof T-Tops. She covered her gaping mouth to squelch the scream that was quickly traveling upward from her diaphragm.

"Oh, my gosh! It's beautiful!" she exclaimed. "It's absolutely beautiful! Mama! Daddy!" Then she released the pent up tears that exploded onto her pink cheeks. "I can't believe this is real." She hugged her mother's shoulders before pulling back and wiping her own face. "Is my mascara running?" Their combined tears and girlish glee were mingled together in blatant warmth and affection. As she turned toward her father, she found him patiently waiting with open arms.

Rob embraced his daughter and lifted her off her feet, as if she were still his little girl. He kissed the wet cheek now rubbing against his own sand-paper version. "Are you happy, Baby? Do you like it? Did we make you happy?"

"Oh Daddy!" she smothered his face with kisses. "I love you and Mama so much. Thank you! This is beyond real! It is perfect!" After he lowered her sandaled feet to the sidewalk, she led her father and mother toward the sports car.

Her dad opened the driver's door and inhaled deeply. "Smell the interior, Baby. Doesn't that leather smell great?" he asked.

"Wow! It smells wonderful, Daddy," she answered, breathing in the scent.

"And I love the color, inside and out," her mother said while rubbing her hand across the dark blue seat. "Do you like the color, Alex? Your dad let me pick it out."

"Of course! The color is perfect, Mama. You know blue is my favorite color. It's perfect. Ya'll are perfect!

Today is perfect! Everything is perfect!" she exclaimed. "Thank you both!"

"What's under the hood, Rob?" Alex's Uncle Tom called to him.

"An L82, 350," her dad replied. "And it's a manual 4 speed. Come look."

"Manual? Why'd you get a manual transmission?" Uncle Tom asked. "She won't be able to drive it for a while."

"Of course, she will, Tom. I taught my daughter how to drive a manual transmission before she learned how to drive an automatic. She can shift gears with the best of them."

He turned toward his daughter and flashed his broad, boyish grin. She had always admired his white, even teeth. Alex was sure he was one of the most handsome men in the world – at least in her world. And with raised eyebrows and a mischievous smirk, he held up his hand and dangled a set of shiny keys in front of her face. She grasped them tightly, and giggled. "Everybody, come and see my present!"

The cheerful party attendees gathered around the car to smother Alex with congratulatory hugs and to share their own accolades and goodwill wishes. Alex was elated. The astonishment had worn off, but immense gratitude was taking its place. She felt it oozing from her pores and escaping with every word. She could hardly contain herself as she tried to remember ever being this happy. Then she realized there had never been a moment when she hadn't been happy. And it was primarily due to her parents.

Mama and Daddy are the most generous parents in the world, and I'm so glad they're mine," she thought. *I love them so much, not because they gave me a car, but because they are who they are. I know I used to wish for a brother or sister, but I don't know if I could ever share Mama and Daddy with anyone else. And to-day makes me glad I don't have to.*

"Okay, Baby," her dad called. "Your mom and I flipped a coin, and guess who won? Me. I get the first ride with my daughter in her new car."

Betsy was frowning, nodding her head submissive-ly, and shrugging her shoulders. Then she burst out laughing. "I lost, but what's new? I'm sure he used the special penny of his, which has heads on both sides. You didn't think I knew about your penny, did you?" she teased while pointing her index finger in her husband's face.

"Would I cheat?" he asked while chuckling.

"Yes you would!" Alex and her mom yelled in unison.

Everyone cheered in response. "It's about time you got caught, Rob. You were a cheater our whole child-hood," Uncle Tom said accusatorily. Several other men, primarily his golf buddies, agreed.

"This is not fair!" Rob cried. "I'm being ganged up on!"

"It's about time," Betsy agreed. "But ya'll go ahead and take your ride you won fair and square. The rest of us will go inside and have dessert. Those hamburgers and hot dogs we ate earlier are long gone. Follow me, everybody. We have homemade vanilla ice cream and a buttercream pound cake for dessert. Cindy, can you help me?"

As the small crowd disseminated from the car, Alex watched as her mother disappeared into the house, with a line of people following in single file. Alex eagerly climbed into the driver's seat and wrapped the seat belt around her hips. She watched her dad fasten his seat belt before turning the ignition key. She listened as the motor instantly turned over and purred its expected low roar. Alex placed her left foot on the clutch and throttled the engine; she engaged the clutch and moved the gear shift from reverse to first. As they rounded the driveway in first gear and arrived at the junction of the road's pavement, her daddy chuckled. "Let her rip, Baby."

And she did.

Chapter Seven

The Gift of Safety

"Blessed is the one who perseveres under trial because, having stood the test, that person will receive the crown of life that the Lord has promised to those who love him."

James 1:12 (NIV)

JAMES WILLIAM HUTCHINS

After aiming the sights of his gun, Hutchins had pulled the trigger and, as expected, saw the patrolman's head jerk backwards by the force of the bullet hole drilled into the middle of his forehead. Satisfied he'd outfoxed the officer and defended himself from capture, Hutchins knew the man felt nothing. Mercifully, death had come instantly with the bullet. Hearing high-pitched sirens in the distance, he rushed to his car to escape and drove another mile. But the retreaded front tire had gone flat. He began cursing every four letter word he could remember and angrily kicked the rubber hard with the toe of his boot. Quickly, he grabbed the two guns and a box of ammunition from the front seat before disappearing into the overgrown thicket.

Adeptly, he scampered through the dense woods, dodging low limbs and clumps of trees and leaping over rocks, babbling creeks, stumps, and low bushes. He successfully stayed clear of tangling vines and leaf-hidden holes that could trip him or turn his weakened ankle. After about twenty minutes, he stopped to catch his breath and wipe perspiration from his eyes with both shirt-sleeves, never releasing the guns or box of bullets from his iron-clad grasp. After his panting slowed and his heartbeat stabilized, he held his breath and listened with acute hearing: sirens in the distance at the murder scene and surely where he'd abandoned his car in the road. He ascertained their distance to be about three quarters of a mile away. More distance was needed, so he picked himself up and darted into the darker woods, not stopping for another twenty minutes.

In a matter of minutes, the area was transformed by a deluge of law enforcers and patrol cars. Officers and patrolmen from several neighboring cities and counties, SBI agents, FBI agents, and deputized volunteers were arriving by the minute, and more were on their way. Most had either heard the radio transmissions or had been told about them and listened in disbelief and dread, hoping beyond hope this was a huge and horrible mistake. Maybe someone was playing a terrible joke, like the 1938 broadcast Orson Welles did on "The War of the Worlds." There was hope because never in the history of North Carolina had three officers died on the same day in the same county by a single killer. Officers didn't get shot in Rutherford County – no one had been killed in the line of duty since 1895. This was 1979. Peterson was known as "Super Trooper." How could this have happened?

While their trained expressions were cool and composed, they hid feelings of anger and sorrow. They spoke in low-pitched voices, conveying the incredulousness of the cold-blooded repercussions that brought them to this less populated site. As humans, they were devastated by the callous and calculated disregard for life this deranged individual had displayed, not once but three times within a span of fifteen minutes or less. As officers and members of a brotherhood, they were as much a victim of these atrocities as their three dead comrades. The reality of these collective events accosted their senses; they took offense to having their brotherhood reduced by three. Badges were proudly worn to distinguish them as helpers of the oppressed and enforcers of the law. In this killer's haste, he had disregarded their symbol of solidarity and not only convicted their brethren as the oppressors, but had executed them as such. But unlike he who had acted out of anger, distrust, and revenge, they were here to ensure this person's rights would be protected; justice should prevail for even him. Only then could they and this community heal.

A command post was established immediately at Gilkey Lumber Company on U.S. 221, across the road from the school. By 7:00 p.m., hundreds of officers and volunteers were tracking on foot, holding back bloodhounds, or crowding the bright-lit sky in helicopters and airplanes. This included the Charlotte Police Department's helicopter dubbed as "Snoopy." They established a perimeter around a three hundred acre tract of land in the Gilkey Community. The country backroads and railroad tracks were ablaze with spot lights, flood lights, flashlights, and vehicle lights. It was brighter than daylight.

Officer Ray Dixon was pragmatic and had sent someone to retrieve a picture of Hutchins and then make copies of it, so they could distribute them for accurate identification. When Sheriff Damon Huskey called Dixon to say he planned to stake out an area of the railroad tracks near the edge of the woods, Officer Dixon sent two other officers to join him. After all, his brother had been killed, and Dixon knew diplomacy wasn't one of the Sheriff's strong points – and possibly wouldn't be right now.

Police Officer Tom McDevitt from Forest City was placed in command. His job was to bring about a successful end to this manhunt by deploying officers and volunteers where needed and coordinating all communications. They began plotting the area and planning a strategy for capture. Knowing Hutchins was armed and dangerous, McDevitt stressed for the officers to be extremely cautious. Then he deployed the men to handle their different assignments.

Undaunted by the danger of their mission and propelled by their dedication to law and order, they were determined to see justice done for their fallen friends. They had a job to do, which involved placing their lives on the line as they always did. Without hesitation, five officers volunteered to go into the woods and apprehend the suspect.

Patrolman Good, flanked by Patrolman Davis and Patrolman Hines, entered the woods shortly after 7:00 p.m. The three men were accompanied by two McDowell county officers, Ken Hollifield, and dog handler, James Boyce, and his bloodhound named Rosey.

"This man is a seasoned hunter, and he was in the service," Good said, reminding the other four men. "He's trained to move quietly and know where his opponent or prey is at all times. Any light we give off or any noise we make – even a twig breaking – can give us away. He'll anticipate our moves, so we have to be careful. Remember, he's already killed three officers; he won't think twice about killing a few more."

These brave officers had no idea if they'd ever return from the woods alive. Based on the catastrophic nightmare this suspect had left behind for them to deal with, they knew he was capable of killing anyone and everyone who crossed his path.

Their earlier watch had not ended. It was being extended. It had just begun.

Chapter Eight

The Act of Birth

"Before I formed you in the womb I knew you, before you were born I set you apart; I appointed you as a prophet to the nations."

Jeremiah 1:5 (NIV)

Mark peered into the open doorway of the maternity ward's waiting room. Among the other visitors, he immediately spied his brother-in-law, Tony, doing what Tony normally did -- reading a book. A good-looking blonde of about twenty-five sat across from Tony, who was slumped in the chair with his long, lanky legs outstretched in front of him. His wire-framed glasses were nudged down on the brim of his nose the same way an older man would wear his. After the blonde returned Mark's lingering smile, he began crossing the room and was beside Tony in three long strides. Tony was startled to find Mark sitting beside him in the plastic chair and extending a cigar with his hand.

"Congratulations! You have a nephew, Uncle Tony! Seven pounds, fourteen ounces and 20 ½ inches long. Here! Have a cigar!" Mark almost shouted it.

Everyone in the waiting room began clapping and chattering "Congratulations" to the two men. Tony shuddered silently with relief and gladness the waiting was over for his sister and for him. He'd spent a miserable day in the crowded and cluttered waiting room, hoping and praying Terri and the baby would be all right.

"Is Terri okay? Is the baby okay?" Tony perked up and couldn't refrain from stuttering because of his excitement and raw nerves.

"Yes. Your twin sister was a trooper. You'd have been proud of her, Tony. She had a hard time, but she is doing well, and the baby is great – 7 pounds, 14 ounces and 20 ½ inches long."

"Is that good?" Tony asked. "That sounds little."

"Of course it's good! Wait until you see him. He has lots of black hair and strong fists. And he's got a strong set of lungs, too."

"Great, Mark. That's great. I'm really happy for ya'll. Congratulations -- Dad," Tony jeered. "Wow! You're a dad and my sister is a mom. It's all starting to sink in."

Delighted, they shook hands and embraced quickly, clapping each other on the back as men do when they feel awkward and uncomfortable. But the young woman caught Mark's eye again.

"Miss, would you like a cigar?" he offered.

She perked up, sitting straighter and crossing her shapely legs. "No, thank you. I don't smoke. But congratulations on your son!" she said smiling.

"Thanks," Mark grinned. "Are you waiting for someone yourself?"

"Yes. My best friend is having her baby – I guess, I mean, I hope soon. I've been waiting all afternoon," she pouted.

"Well, I know what you mean," Mark said. "Well, I hope everything goes well for your friend."

"Me, too," she said with a smile.

"When can I see Terri and my new nephew?" Tony asked, annoyed at their lingering gazes.

"Well it may take a while longer for you to see Terri. She ended up having to have a Cesarean section. She pushed for three solid hours before they decided to go ahead and take him. His heartbeat had started dropping, and she couldn't push him out. By then, she was too swollen and too exhausted. But it was the best thing for her and the baby."

Tony suddenly felt sick; his knees felt weak, so he sank to the chair. As siblings, he and Terri were close, but as twins, they had an even tighter bond than other siblings – being able to complete each other's sentences or interpret each other's covert actions or decipher each other's thoughts easily. The only person Terri had seemed closer to was Dad. He'd always been her special hero.

Quickly noticing Tony's pale face and sinking reaction, Mark guessed his brother-in-law needed reassurance. "But she's okay, Tony. She's fine. They are sewing her back up. It takes a while. Terri sent me out to tell you about the baby and to make sure you were okay. You'll be able to see her tonight in a few minutes. She wants to see you. Come on. We can go ahead and see the baby in the meantime. They're keeping him in the nursery until Terri is moved to her room. Come on. Let's go meet your nephew." Mark grabbed Tony's limp arm.

"Goodbye," he called over his shoulder to the blonde. "And good luck!"

"Goodbye," she cooed with a flip of her long hair and smiled.

Relieved to be moving, Tony followed Mark down a long corridor to stand before three nursery windows. Tony was amazed at the rows and rows of babies. The population was booming all in one night! Amused, he noticed how some babies were crying loudly and some were sleeping.

How can they be sleeping with all the noise? He wondered. *Thank heaven the windows are sound proof so we don't have to hear all the racket.* He and Mark stretched their necks to read over all the last names. Finally, they found the Tunney Baby Boy about the same time. He was one of the calm, sleeping babies. Amazed at the tiny body who somehow now belonged to him, too, Tony pressed his hands against the cool glass and allowed himself to smile at his nephew. *He's so little. So you are what was in my sister's stomach for nine months. Nice to meet you, little fellow. I'm your Uncle Tony. And to think something as small and innocent as you are can change people's lives forever. Wow! I know you'll change theirs and probably mine, too. I hate to tell you, kid, but you aren't all that cute right now. You look a little wrinkled and beat up like you've been in a bad fight where your opponent got the best of you. Your hair is sticking straight up. I hope it will lie down eventually or....*He didn't want to think he might be an ugly kid, sort of like Tony thought he, himself, had been.

Everyone had talked about what a cute baby Terri had been, but no one ever said anything about him, even though they were twins. But honestly, they hadn't looked alike. But he was the oldest by three minutes. So he had this to hold over his sister's head.

I'm sure you'll grow up to be a handsome guy. After all, I think your mom is alright, even if she is my sister. And your dad thinks he's good looking, so maybe he is.

"See how big he is?" Mark asked. He was beaming, a typical proud parent. "He looks like me. And look at all his hair. No wonder your sister had heartburn the entire time. I bet he plays football in high school and college like his old man did."

"The thing about heartburn is an old wives' tale, Mark. An educated man as yourself should know. Heartburn isn't an indication the baby will have hair. It means she was eating too many spicy foods and overloading her stomach with donuts, and the baby was pressing on her stomach. And let's hope he doesn't play football." Tony replied with a joking smile. "Maybe he'll play soccer and baseball instead and become a writer like his uncle."

"Well, he'll probably do all of the above," Mark offered as a compromise. He was too elated to argue with his nerdy brother-in-law. "My kid will be able to play football, basketball, soccer, and baseball. And he'll probably grow up to be a doctor and find a cure for cancer. So, I had forgotten. You played soccer and baseball, didn't you?"

"Yes," Tony replied. "My parents made me. It's not easy having a sister who is athletically gifted and you're a guy. But I wasn't totally inept at athletics; I still enjoy all sports, but not as a participant, generally."

Mark had lost interest in the conversation and turned back to the window. "He's got my dark hair and my brown eyes. And look at those fists. He has big fists."

Tony laughed. "You can't tell a baby's eye color for a while, Mark."

Tony thought, *Boy, he's really gotten infected quickly with the proud father syndrome. It didn't take him long at all – not even an hour after seeing the kid. He's forgetting Terri has dark hair and brown eyes, too. Oh well.* He chuckled aloud. *My brother-in-law deserves this happy moment, and with all he's gone through today becoming a father, I'm sure he's entitled.*

The day had been long and the waiting agony, but his sister was okay. There was a new baby in the world, in his family, and the baby seemed healthy. Tony gazed at the baby's kicking legs and waving arms. *Life's not easy, little one, but it's an adventure, a wonderful journey you've been given. Thank you, Father God. Thank you my sister and nephew are okay.* Tony blinked back sudden tears.

"What's wrong, Uncle Tony?" Mark asked.

"It must be the bright lights."

Chapter Nine

The Gift of Family

"All the glory of his family will hang on him: its off-spring and offshoots – all its lesser vessels, from the bowls to all the jars."

Isaiah 22:24 (NIV)

TONY ADAMS

Terri wasn't returned to her hospital room until 11:45 p.m. As physically and emotionally exhausted as she was, she felt wide awake as she lay listlessly on the crisp white sheets. Fortunately, she wasn't feeling any pain yet even though the doctors had warned the anes-thesia soon would be wearing off. The nurses had given her pain medication and promised to give her a sedative to sleep tonight. As tired as she was, she couldn't imag-ine why she'd need a sedative, but the nurse had warned adrenaline and the other meds may counter-act her ability to sleep. Terri was relieved they didn't expect her to nurse the baby yet. She was still undecided about whether she truly wanted to nurse or not. Mark was all for it, but the young mother didn't feel confident. Her eyelids felt heavy, but they quickly opened when she heard quick, heavy footsteps entering the hospital room.

Mark was leading the way with Tony following behind him. Her brother eagerly craned his neck to see her, and she was glad. These past few hours had been something they could not share, but now the birth was over, they could experience the glories of adding a new member to their family. When the twins' eyes met, they both smiled. Tony hurried to his sister's side, almost pushing Mark out of the way. She struggled to lift her limp arms, but when she did, she folded them tightly around his neck. Sister and brother embraced for a long time.

"I'm glad you're okay, sis. I've been worried. So are you okay?"

She laughed. "I'm fine, Tony. I'm fine. You're happy I'm okay, and then you ask me if I'm okay. Be glad you weren't the one born a girl, or you'd be the one lying here after giving birth."

"We've had this conversation before in the past. Remember?" he asked. "Besides, does that mean I'd be married to Mark? Yuk!"

Mark frowned and the two siblings laughed again.

"No seriously, congratulations, Terri." Tony said.

"Thanks, brother. Did you see our son, your nephew, yet?"

"Oh yeah. Your husband came bounding into the waiting room and announced the birth of his son to any and everybody, and then before I could catch my breath, he dragged me down the hall to the nursery to see him."

"And?" she pried. "What do you think?"

"Well, he's little, huh?"

"Not from my perspective," she said with a giggle.

"Well, he seemed little. He was sleeping when we saw him, so I couldn't see his eyes. But I did notice he's got a lot of hair, a lot of hair."

She was beaming with a questioning look in her eyes, so he continued.

"Yep. Well, I think he's a handsome little fellow," Tony lied.

Through her exhaustion, she forced a smile. "Good. I'm glad you like him." She closed her eyes, and mumbled. "All of a sudden, I'm really tired."

Tony stepped back, so Mark could get closer to Terri. He took her cool hand in his.

"Honey, after all you've been through today, you deserve some sleep. I'm so proud of you," Mark said. "Try to get some sleep. I love you."

A white uniformed nurse entered the room with a tray holding a plastic cup of water. "Visiting hours were over long ago, and you gentlemen need to be saying your good-bye's so this tired young mother can get some sleep. She's had a hard day; she needs her rest." She plumped up the pillows and straightened the sheet and blanket covering Terri. "Becoming a mother isn't easy -- especially the first time. You two should try it sometime."

Tony and Mark exchanged puzzled looks. Tony returned to his sister's side and softly kissed her forehead. He whispered into her ear, "Mom and Dad would have been proud of you. I wish they could have been here today. I wish they could see their grandson."

Two lonely tears escaped the corners of Terri's closed eyes and traced their way down her cheeks. Tony gently wiped them away as Terri opened her eyes to peer into his. Mercifully, when he blocked out the room's overhead light, there seemed to be a halo forming around his head.

"Me, too, Tony. I thought of them so many times today and wished the same thing," she whispered. "But you were here for me, and I'm so glad you were. I'm glad we can share this moment. Thank you, big brother. I love you."

"Love you, too," he stammered, a little embarrassed. "Get some rest. I'll be here tomorrow afternoon to see you and the little fellow."

She laughed. "Little fellow. That's so lame. Hopefully, his father and I will have decided upon a name for the little fellow by then." She watched a smile cross her husband's face. "His daddy has to decide on some contenders his mother has suggested several times."

"I still like junior, but I promise to give it more thought, honey – tomorrow. It's now my top priority to name our son."

"Oh, Mark. Have you telephoned your parents yet?" she reminded him.

"Not yet, but I will as soon as I get home. Mom will want all the details, I'm sure. Dad will be rushing us off the phone, so he can book a flight as soon as possible. He will be excited to have a grandson. I don't know what he'd have done with a grand-daughter."

"You'd be surprised," Terri said slyly. "Little girls have a way of wrapping a daddy and a grand-daddy around their fingers."

"I can attest to that," Tony groaned.

Terri giggled. "Ya'll go on and get out of here. You both look tired. Better get some sleep yourselves."

Mark kissed her lips, lingering for a moment. "I love you; thank you for our son. I'm so proud of you, Terri." As he bent to kiss his wife once more, Tony cleared his throat loudly.

"Can ya'll wait when I'm not here?" he asked with a chuckle. "And I'm sure this nurse is getting tired of waiting for us to leave."

"Okay, Okay. Uncle Tony," Mark groaned. "I'm coming. Sweetheart, I'll be here first thing in the morning – right after I stop by the office."

"The office? Do you really need to go by?" Terri sounded dejected.

"Well, if I don't, I'm sure Kelly Elaine will call me. You know what a dutiful secretary she is. Besides, I need to pass out cigars."

Dutiful? Terri thought to herself. *I guess you can call her dutiful along with being gorgeous, sexy, and unattached.* With a shiver, she shook off her momentary jealousy.

"Call me if you need anything from home, sweetie. The doctor said you and the baby may be here for a week."

"A week?" she asked and looked toward the nurse who was nodding her head.

"Yes," Mark replied. "Remember from Lamaze class? That's normal procedures after Caesarean sections. You need some time to get your strength back. So try to enjoy this extra time."

"Okay. Okay," she replied, processing this forgotten information. "I will. Love you both. Goodnight."

After both men mumbled a "thanks" to the stern nurse who stood with her arms folded and tapping her foot, Terri could hear their steady footsteps disappearing down the hall. The kindly nurse handed her a pill, following it with a cup of water. "Here, honey. Take a sip of this."

Terri obeyed and thanked the nurse before closing her eyes.

"Do you need anything else?" the nurse asked.

"Yes ma'am. There's a verse in the Bible I recall about childbirth and being able to forget the pain. Do you know the verse I'm talking about?"

"Yes, I do," the nurse answered.

"Will you read it to me, please?" Terri's eyes were shut, and she was beginning to slur her words. "It's crazy, but as bad as the labor pains were at the time, I can't really remember them."

"I surely will read it to you," the nurse agreed, impressed with the request. She opened the bedside table's top drawer and removed a *Gideon Bible*. She thumbed through the pages. "Ah, here it is. I've read it to many women over the years because it is so true regarding labor and delivery. And I know firsthand it's true because I had four children of my own. Thankfully, they're all grown now. This comes from the book of John, sixteenth chapter, twenty-first verse."

"'A woman giving birth to a child has pain because her time has come, but when her baby is born she forgets the anguish because of her job that a child is born into the world.' And here's another one I like to read to new mothers. It's from Psalm 127, verses three and four. 'Children are a heritage from the Lord, offspring a reward from him. Like arrows in the hands of a warrior are children born in one's youth.'"

She softly closed the book and replaced it in the drawer. Looking down, she smiled at the young slumbering mother.

"Welcome to Motherhood, young lady," she whispered. "You've begun a beautiful journey that will last the rest of your life. And it's one you'll never finish. But it's the most rewarding, the most fulfilling one you'll ever have. And besides, it's one only a woman can do. God bless you and your child forever."

The nurse turned off the flickering fluorescent light above the bed and tiptoed out, closing the heavy door behind her.

Chapter Ten

The Act of Giving

"Each of you should give what you have decided in your heart to give, not reluctantly or under compulsion, for God loves a cheerful giver."

2 Corinthians 9:7 (NIV)

ALEX WELLS

"Mama, you and Daddy shouldn't have bought me a car." Alex teased as she spread blackberry jam over a slice of buttered toast. "But I'm glad you did."

Betsy smiled. "What? Are you eating again? Didn't I see you eating a hot dog and a hamburger and a big bowl of homemade ice cream earlier tonight?"

"Yes, but I'm famished. The party and the new car took a lot out of me."

"Okay, young lady. Finish your midnight snack. I'm trying to get the kitchen cleaned up. But you did have a big day, didn't you?"

"Yes," she said. Then she began whispering, "And of course you realize Daddy has an ulterior motive for buying me a car, don't you?"

"He does?"

"Of course, Mama. I thought you knew him. He's always wanted a Corvette, so now he's says he's going to borrow it once in a while, but you know as well as I do he's going to want to borrow it all the time, so he can take you cruising -- something about reliving his younger days."

"Is this what he told you?"

"Uh huh. He's already asked to borrow it next Saturday. I guess I can still drive my old Impala. At least my good ol' standby still runs. You know, the one I've been driving since I was sixteen."

Her mother giggled. "You poor thing! You're such an old lady! Driving around in a six year old car. You poor thing. Well, you do know how to say 'no' to your father, don't you?"

"No, not really. It's hard to tell Daddy no. Besides, it would break his heart if I did." Alex tore the crust around the toast away and shoved it into her mouth.

"Well, your father's a big boy. He's been disappointed before in his life. He's somehow survived a number of broken dreams. It's your car. We bought it for you. But you do whatever you want to do with it."

Her mother finished rinsing the party dishes and placing them in the dishwasher. "Finally! Finished!" Then she sauntered over to the coffee maker and poured herself a fresh cup of coffee and slid back onto the stool at the end of the bar in their kitchen.

"Why don't you buy him a Corvette for his next birthday, Mama? Or better yet. Buy it for your anniversary. That would be the perfect gift. After all, your anniversary is next month."

"Did your daddy put you up to asking me this?"

"No," she lied and started laughing. "Well, maybe. He did mention how much he'd always wanted one and how much he'd love to have a red one like mine. He hinted his birthday is coming soon and your anniversary is next month."

"I thought so. Just hinted, huh? Your daddy knows exactly what he is doing by telling you. You're his biggest advocate. Rob can go out and buy himself a new car any time he wants one. I'm not stopping him. I never have. We've been blessed enough to build this house on the lake, and we've been able to put you through college, thank the Lord. If he wants a new car, and he thinks we can afford two new cars – yours and one for him -- then he should go ahead and buy one. You can relay my message back to him," she said with a smirk.

"How many years is it? I can never remember if I was born two or three years after your marriage," Alex asked. She'd finished her toast and was rinsing her plate.

"You were born three years after we were married. We didn't want to wait long to have a family. Honey, turn on the dishwasher for me since you're finished."

"Okay."

"So, let's talk about you. What are your plans now that you're a college graduate?" her mother asked.

"Well, I'm hoping to teach high school English in the public schools, of course, but I also want to earn my Master's degree in English and eventually earn my Ph.D., so you know, I've already submitted an application to enter the fall term at UNC-Charlotte. And I've already taken the GMAT. Hopefully, I'll be accepted and can get started on my Master's degree. I can't wait to hear if I get accepted. In the meantime, I can teach, earn a paycheck, and get a graduate degree – all at the same time. That will position me to teach English in colleges and universities. And I still can do some writing."

"That's wonderful dear! I'm so happy you've decided to pursue graduate degrees."

"Well, you know my goal is to become a tenured professor. And of course, I still want to write and be a published author of a zillion books."

"You have wonderful goals. And by the way, I can tell you didn't major in math. A zillion? Really? Well, it sounds like you have a detailed blueprint for life laid out before you. I wish I'd gone to college when I was young."

"Why didn't you go, Mama?" Alex asked.

"We didn't have extra money for college. When my mother died, it was all my father could do to work in construction and bring home enough money to pay the bills and buy groceries for all of us. Being the eldest girl meant I had to help out with the household chores, like cooking our meals and caring for the younger kids. Basically, I took on my mother's role," she said with an involuntary shudder. "Besides, even though I was a good student, it was all I could do to finish high school. I couldn't imagine trying to maintain the household and go to college."

"That's sad, Mama. We've never really talked about this before."

"I don't want you to feel sad for me. I did what I needed to do for my brothers and sisters and made the decisions, which were necessary at the time."

"You gave up a lot for Aunt Brenda and Aunt Shirley and Uncle Ken and Uncle John. Do they realize that?"

"Sure they do. We've always been close, and they have always told me how much they appreciated all I did when they were younger and after Mom died."

"What kind of cancer did grandmother have?"

"It showed up initially as breast cancer, but by the time she was fully diagnosed, she had it in other parts of her body. She died a month later."

When she noticed Alex had hung her head in sorrow, Betsy rushed to change the topic to a more positive one.

"But good things happen for those who wait, Alex. Always remember this. When I was eighteen, I went to the soda shop on a Saturday night with some girlfriends. It was one of the first times I'd been able to join them because I didn't have a lot of extra money for frivolous things, like milkshakes and sodas. And something wonderful happened that night while I was drinking a chocolate shake. That's when I met a handsome young junior who was pursuing his electrical engineering degree at N.C. State in Raleigh. After we'd dated long distance for a few months, we knew we were in love. We continued dating with him coming to Charlotte on the weekends whenever he could. We'd either hang out at the soda shop or to the movies on Saturday nights, and then he'd drive back to Raleigh. We did this for a year and a half. After he graduated from college, we got married. We didn't have a big wedding. Neither of us wanted one, so we invited a few friends and relatives and were married in my home church. I wore my mother's simple wedding gown and her short veil. Your dad wore a dark suit."

"Oh, Mama. I love it when you tell me your story. It's so romantic. And I have always loved your wedding picture. Ya'll look so sweet. Now I love it more because I know you were wearing grandmother's gown."

Betsy petted her daughter's hand. "I had two miscarriages – it seemed like I'd never be able to carry a baby to full term, but three years after we were married, we had you. We were so blessed to have a perfect baby girl. Your dad was beside himself with happiness. He said he'd always wanted a little girl – a daddy's girl – and I think he got his wish."

Alex was smiling. "But I'm a mama's girl, too. Daddy and I have different interests that we enjoy, but he's no fun to go shopping with or to get my nails done or to go to the bookstore and buy the latest novel."

"When I got pregnant with you, I quit my job as a cashier in the grocery store, and I never went back. I wanted to ensure my pregnancy went well. And by then, your dad was making a good living, and I didn't have to go back to work. I've been blessed to be a homemaker and mother. Hey! Come to think about it, I've been blessed to be a homemaker and mother figure the majority of my life."

"And a great one at that," Alex replied, smiling. "You're the best there is. Keeping house and raising a child is a hard job. And keeping up with Daddy is too!"

Her mother reached over and squeezed her hand. "Thank you, honey. All I ever wanted was for you to think of me as a good mother and your father think of me as a good wife. That is what makes me happy. Hopefully, I'm both. College would have been nice, but in the end, it wasn't for me. My life took a different turn."

"You're all of the above, Mom. I don't tell you enough how special you are. But you are."

Her mother had the "touched" look like she was getting ready to cry.

"Now, let's stop all this before you start crying. And besides, you need to quit fishing for compliments," Alex warned.

"Who me? Would I fish for compliments?" her mother teased.

They put their foreheads together as they often did and giggled like schoolgirls.

With their gleeful bantering continuing, they had missed seeing Rob enter the brick-walled kitchen. He poured himself a black cup of coffee.

"What are ya'll up to?" he asked. "Girl talk?"

"Nothing could top what you're up to, I'm sure," Betsy replied. "Honey, that's your fourth cup of coffee, and it's after midnight. You're not going to be able to sleep with all that caffeine. What are you watching on television?"

"An old movie. Something with Bing Crosby and Bob Hope. I've seen it several times. It's about to go off."

"Well, you're not going to sleep well tonight, what's left of it, and you won't want to get up in the morning and get to church on time. We have Communion tomorrow."

Avoiding her mother's eyes, Alex said in a low voice, "Mama, I hadn't planned on going to church tomorrow morning. I'd planned on staying here and creating my resume and filling out some job applications.

You know, stuff like that. And I have a new book tonight I'm dying to read. Aunt Shirley gave it to me."

Her mother's voice had a note of disappointed resignation when she responded. "I wish you would reconsider, Alex. I was hoping now you're home, we could go to church as a family again."

"I have been thinking about it, Mama, but please don't insist I go tomorrow."

"Well whether you attend church or not is up to you, Alex," Betsy stated. "You're old enough to make those decisions for yourself. We've raised you in church and have hoped you'd continue attending church as an adult. But like I said, you're old enough to make your own decisions. If you feel the need to take the day off, then do what you think is best. As for me, I've got to roll my hair, so I won't look like a scarecrow. So, I'm going to call it a day. I'm a little tired. Goodnight! I love you both!" She kissed Alex on the forehead and pecked Rob on the lips before heading out of the kitchen.

"Good night, Mama. Love you, too. And thanks again for the party and the beautiful car," Alex called.

"'Nite, honey. I'll head that way after the movie is over," Rob promised.

Alex watched as her mother disappeared into the hallway. "Do you think I hurt her feelings or made her mad, Daddy?"

"I don't think so, Baby. She'll be fine. Now that you're back home after living away at college for four years, it will take her some time to get used to you being grown. We all need to get comfortable living under the same roof again and respecting each other's feelings. You've developed your own habits and have your own ideas. You're no longer our little girl. You're a mature young woman. Don't worry about your Mama. She's resilient. But I do hope you haven't decided church isn't for you."

"No, of course not, Daddy. I believe in God and all the teachings of the Bible, which have been instilled in me as a child, but I no longer find it necessary to attend church services every Sunday. I don't mind attending some Sundays, but I don't plan to attend every Sunday. I hope ya'll can respect my thoughts."

"Hmmmm. Well. That's entirely up to you, as your mother said. You certainly have grown up, huh? I think we can try to respect your decision, but it is disappointing to her. You probably do need some time – a break. But you'll come back, I know."

She watched as he gulped the remaining coffee and washed out the cup with water. He kissed her on the forehead and asked, "Do you want to watch the rest of the movie with me?"

"No, I don't think so. I'm tired, too, Daddy. I think I'll head for bed. Oh and thank you so much for the wonderful party and the most beautiful car in the world! It's the best present ever."

"You're welcome, Baby. We did surprise you, didn't we?

She nodded.

"Glad you were surprised and glad you like your car. And don't forget about next Saturday, okay?"

"What about next Saturday?" she teased.

He looked annoyed. "You've forgotten already? I asked you if I could borrow...."

She giggled, "Of course I won't forget. It means I'll be driving the Impala on Saturday."

He laughed and gave her a "thumbs up" signal. Then he left the kitchen.

Alex sighed miserably. *They have a wonderful way of making me feel guilty without even saying a word. Parents are good at making you feel like an ungrateful, spoiled brat!*

"Neely! Neely! Come!" she called. "Let's go to bed."

Her fawn-colored Yorkshire terrier came running to the bar stool and waited to be picked up and rubbed. Alex reached down and lifted the seven pounds of love she'd had for the past nine years. Her precious dog snuggled her wet nose beneath Alex's chin and buried her head in Alex's neck. Alex treasured the affection they had for each other. She'd missed Neely while she was away at school and came home on weekends whenever there were no sorority parties, big dates, or major papers to write. She scratched the tiny dog behind her pointed ears where she liked it.

"Neely, I need to tell you something," she confided with an exaggerated whisper. "I didn't go to church much while I was in college, but I did go every time I came home – only because they expected it and because I wanted to make them happy. But I hope when my children are grown, I will never make them feel like they've robbed a bank because they choose not to go to church every Sunday."

Chapter Eleven

The Act of Resistance

"You men who are stiff-necked and uncircumcised in heart and ears are always resisting the Holy Spirit; you are doing just as your fathers did."

Acts 7:51 (NIV)

JAMES WILLIAM HUTCHINS

Rosey strained against the leather collar, but Boyce held the bloodhound's leash firmly. Aware of Hutchins's scent from the abandoned car, she was on the trail and leading the men into deeper darkness. It had been almost five hours since they'd entered the woods across from the command post.

Acutely aware even the sound of a breaking twig could become their last, the five men spread out with twelve to fifteen feet dividing them. Not only had the officers been trained for this type of situation, but Trooper Good had served in Vietnam. He knew what guerrilla combat was all about. And many officers in this area enjoyed hunting and knew how to creep about in the woods in search of their prey without being detected. The men were careful to step slowly, heel first with the weight gradually applied until the ball of the foot was lowered. They continued this slow and methodical maneuver through the thick underbrush and overhanging vines. Occasionally, someone would almost stumble over a hidden tree root or a sharp rock. But surprisingly, their surging adrenaline, their relentless determination, and their heighted awareness of danger steadied their footing and propelled them forward. They strained their ears to hear every noise – even to the point of holding their breath until their expanded lungs became too uncomfortable. They strained their eyes and peripheral vision to capture any movement. They were trained to be disciplined, alert, and reactive.

They were all too aware this man, Hutchins, operated by instinct. As a trained hunter, he knew how to anticipate what prey would do, like a deer. He knew a deer would follow an established trail because it was the path of least resistance. Even though humans were more creative, they still followed the law of nature – the path of least resistance. He was anticipating and planning the officers' moves – probably even watching them now. Intent on getting his way, he wasn't going to give up easily. Besides, he was irrational. But they felt confident there was no way he could escape the number of officers surrounding these woods. But he would try, and they were the only thing between him and freedom.

Hutchins's shoulder was slightly sore from the recoil; his ears were ringing from the multiple rounds he'd shot that afternoon even though when he'd pulled the trigger, he hadn't heard the guns' explosions or felt the powerful recoil, which pushed his shoulder back two-three inches. A seasoned hunter never did hear the shot or feel the recoil because the ability to concentrate on the target blocked out everything; you entered into a temporary zone of nothingness except for you and your target.

Hutchins was lying on his stomach at the crest of a hill where he'd been for at least three hours. From his perch, he could see them before they got too close. Two tree trunks had joined, forming a "V-shaped" opening. The trees' malformation shielded him from them. At the base of the incline, there was a wide gulley that formed a dry moat. Behind him, the dense stand of trees and thicket were impenetrable. But he knew they were coming for him. It was a matter of time. He'd be ready, and they'd be sorry, like those two deputies and patrolman. If they'd minded their own business and hadn't trespassed on his land, none of this would've happened. For reassurance, he squeezed the rifle and tucked it closer. Beside it was the double-barrel shotgun. The night was quiet; not even owls were hooting. Beams of the various search lights bounced off the night sky, shining in the distance. *That's where they are*, he thought. Occasionally, the nuisance sounds of a helicopter would fly over, but the woods were so thick here, only the sun and the moon knew how to penetrate the darkness. But tonight, the waxing crescent moon offered little illumination in the dark woods. His mind wandered to his family.

Wish I knew what Geneva and the kids are doing and where they are, he thought. *Probably hauled off somewhere, so I'll never see 'em again. I wonder if Charlotte's sorry now. If she hadn't poured in a whole bottle of vodka, none of this would've happened. And then she went and poured it out because I didn't want a bunch of drunk kids at my house. So I hit her – it's not like I haven't hit her before. Then she goes and calls the law on me again after all I've done for her. They didn't need to come. Those SOBs were trespassing on my property. I have the right to defend my property and family. Besides, I told Huskey to leave. I warned him I had a gun.*

He rubbed his itchy eyes with grimy hands. His stomach growled and his mouth was dry. A twig snapped, jolting Hutchins from his thoughts. Vigilant, he held his breath and slowly scanned the darkness from left to right, right to left. Something snapped again – this time from the left. Finally, he saw the culprit: a wandering opossum with eerie green eyes about thirty feet away and unaware of his presence. James relaxed his tense muscles and breathed freely.

"James!"

Startled, his head jerked. "Whose there?"

Whoever it was had approached without detection. Hardly breathing, his eyes swept the area for several minutes. His ears strained with readiness. Finally, after being convinced there was no one, he exhaled. *Must have been my imagination! Must be my nerves.* Hutchins shifted his weight, rolling to his left side and shaking the numbness out of his right leg.

"James!"

There it is again, he thought. *This time I heard it for real.* He peered around little by little. *Someone's out there. Probably a cop.* But once again, after a few frozen minutes, there was no movement, no further sound. Even the opossum had scurried away. Once again, he eased his tight grip on the gun.

"James!"

Lefrere! That sounds like Lefrere! But how can that be? How did Photo Man find me? They must have sent Photo Man in here to talk me out. In return, he probably can take pictures for the newspaper. Well, Lefrere made a big mistake this time because I'm not giving up. I'm not giving up for nobody. Besides, I thought he was my friend.

After two or three minutes of lying still and hardly breathing, Hutchins relaxed again. This tenseness and his crazy imagination were wearing him out.

Must be my imagination running wild, he told himself. *Lefrere – Photo Man.* He remembered their several meetings in the woods.

One autumn morning, around dawn, he'd been restless, so he'd left Geneva and the kids sleeping while he drove to the woods behind Gilkey Lumber Company to try out his new shotgun. He knew he'd better do it before the hunters took over. The woods were his preferred home, especially in the morning when the sun's rays penetrated the trees' branches and stroked the forest's floor with finger-like dewy fog. He felt peaceful and alone in this quiet and eerie world.

After firing a few rounds with his .44 Magnum, he adjusted the sights on his new shotgun. That's when he was startled as he glimpsed a man approaching him from the left. The stranger was calling, "Hello! Hello!"

Cautiously, Hutchins slid behind a wide-girthed poplar and spied through scruffy bushes as the man got closer. What was this guy up to this early in the morning? And why in the world would he approach a strange man who had been target practicing? A camera swung freely from the man's neck; he carried a worn, brown leather backpack.

The man didn't seem startled when Hutchins suddenly stepped out behind him. Rather, he spun around, smiled, and extended his hand in a friendly gesture.

Suspicious, Hutchins had hesitated.

"I'm Lefrere, Charles Lefrere," the man had announced while introducing himself.

Hutchins recalled his thoughts. *I remember staring at him like he was crazy. Why did I care who he was? Hey guy, you need to leave me alone. I'm not bothering you; don't you bother me.*

"Hutchins."

"I'm sorry if I disturbed you," he had apologized with a smile.

"Yeah," Hutchins had replied. Apprehension had massaged his spine.

"It's a pleasant morning, isn't it? I couldn't sleep, so I thought I'd take some shots." He held up his camera with one hand and the leather bag with the other. "These kinds of shots."

Hutchins had tensed a little before asking, "What'cha carrying in the bag?"

"Oh, only some photographic equipment. Well, let's see." He had unzipped the bag. "I have a 35 *mm Yashica I've had for several years. It's my favorite. This is a Canon 35 mm," he said while pointing to the strap around his neck. "A few lenses – zoom, wide angle – some filters. Ah and here's a tabletop tripod."*

Hutchins had relaxed.

"How about you?" Lefrere had asked. "Looks like we both came out to get some shots." Was that meant to be clever, Hutchins wondered.

"Yeah, me, too."

After a while, their silence had become awkward.

Hutchins broke the awkwardness by announcing, "My son wants a camera for Christmas, but money's really tight this year. I've got to have a knee operation that'll keep me out of work for a while. Got any recommendations for a camera?"

"There are lots of good options; it depends on the amount you want to spend."

He had noticed Hutchins's immediate frown. "But I tell you what. I have some old cameras I'd be willing to sell for a reasonable price. They're in good condition and the right thing for a beginner."

"That might work. I might be interested. My first name's James. James Hutchins. I live about four miles from here on Mountain Creek Road. Do you live in these parts?"

"Not too far from here," he'd answered.

When he didn't offer more information about where he lived, Hutchins had asked, "Come here often?"

"Yeah. I'm always around," he had said. "Probably be back again tomorrow. I like to experiment with lighting. The trees act like natural filters for the morning's sunrays. You can never realize the amount of silent drama that can be captured in a random place as beautiful as this."

When Hutchins returned a blank stare, Lefrere had stood to leave and extended his hand again.

"Well, it's been nice meeting you, James. I've enjoyed our conversation. Hope to see you again soon."

They shook hands.

"Don't forget about the camera," Hutchins had reminded the photographer.

"Don't worry. I won't," Lefrere had called as he strolled away.

Hutchins allowed his thoughts to ramble in the dark of the woods while he waited for the officers who were surely advancing.

Photo Man had been true to his word. I found him the following morning, kneeling behind a tripod and focusing the camera's lens on a clump of moss. It was weird.

Fascinated, I watched as he moved the camera in different angles and even laid on his stomach to capture the right picture. I'd always thought you pointed and clicked, at least that's what I did with my old Brownie.

"Know anything about guns," I asked him.

"No. I have to admit, I know nothing."

"Well, this is a .44 Magnum, my choice of hand guns. Ever shot one?"

"No, I haven't. I've never handled any type of gun," Lefrere had assured him. "The only thing I've ever shot was with a camera."

Hutchins remembered thinking, *I can't imagine not ever shooting a gun. This guy's lived a sheltered life. But he does look...uh, ah, well, what would the other guys call him? Refined?*

"It's a close range weapon", I'd told him. *"But they make a heck of an impact and have one heck of a recoil. When the bullet goes in, it's probably, uh, the size*

of my thumb. But when it comes out, it's about the size of two of my fists. I carry two of these."

"Two? Why on earth do you need two?" Lefrere had asked.

"In case I miss after emptying the first gun."

Photo Man had returned my stare.

I squatted, and Lefrere had followed my lead and squatted too. I remember thinking I was beginning to like this fellow.

"This here's a rifle – a semi-automatic .30-06. It holds five bullets. Going in, the bullet hole is about the size of a pencil; coming out, it's about the size of my fist."

Lefrere had nodded.

"This is a shot gun. You don't use bullets in a shot-gun. You use a shell. Inside the shell is a bunch of met-al shots that spread out – splatter. Here, it's not loaded. Want to hold it?"

Lefrere had accepted my offer.

"Sure, if you don't mind showing me how it's done."

I demonstrated propping the shotgun up against my right shoulder and holding it firmly with both hands. I closed my left eye, squinted down the barrel, and aligned my sights. Then I handed the weapon to Lefrere, who was a good student. He'd listened and learned fast.

Afterward, he held the rifle and then the .44.

"Wow! This is heavy. How can you hit anything with this?" he seemed amazed.

"Like this. Watch," I'd said. Then I took a ten-penny nail from my overalls and strode several paces toward a

tree. After pushing the nail into the bark, I returned and advised him to plug his ears.

After jamming his index fingers as far as they'd go, he had nodded, not understanding what he was about to see.

In one motion, I extended my arm and lowered the gun to eye level. Then I pulled the trigger. The recoil jerked my arm upward. Photo Man ran to the tree and to his amazement, he'd found the nail had been driven into the bark.

Lefrere called it an "amazing feat." Heck, it wasn't a big deal. I've been doing it since I was a boy. But the guy seemed impressed with my accuracy. I had told him, "Accuracy's not hard if you've been trained and practice a lot. Afterward, shooting becomes automatic, a reaction based on instinct. Good eyesight helps, too, but practice makes accuracy second nature."

Photo Man became someone I enjoyed running into. He was always hiking or taking pictures, and I was always hunting or target practicing when we'd cross paths. He was easy to talk to and nonjudgmental, even when I told him about my scrapes with the law, even about the truck driver I'd killed. I'd never had a friend who I confided in until Lefrere. I'd been close to my brother, Billy, and my cousin, Glenn, but we didn't discuss things the way Lefrere and I did.

Our last meeting had happened a week ago when Lefrere had suddenly appeared in the woods. Honestly, I think the guy was a tracking genius even though he never claimed to be. Somehow, he always located me in the woods no matter where I was.

"James!" he'd called in a friendly greeting. "Top of the morning to ya!"

"You sound like a lost leprechaun," I yelled. "I thought Lefrere was French.

"It is French, but I have a little slice of Irish in me, too," he laughed, extending his hand as he always did.

We'd talked about menial things for a while – the weather, how the family was doing. Then he'd cleared his throat and stared into my eyes and suddenly asked me a question: "James, do you believe in God?"

I felt my skin prickle. Okay. Here it comes, I remember thinking. I should have known he was one of those Bible thumpers or what they called Christian zealots, following me around all this time, only to preach to me! I should have known. But it was like Lefrere had read my feelings.

"Don't be angry, friend. I'm only asking." He'd taken a closer step toward me.

"Naw, I mean, I don't know. When I was little, my momma took me to church and taught me a couple of prayers, but it didn't take. None of it made a lot of sense to me. Why? Do you?"

"Yes, I do. I like for all my friends to. And I'd like for you to believe, too, James. I care about you, and I'd hate to think of you spending eternity in hell."

"Well, Photo Man, with all my brushes with the law and my dislike for officers, how am I supposed to make it to heaven?"

"Oh, you've heard of heaven, then," he had chuckled, breaking my icy defense.

"Yeah, I've heard of heaven," I had sneered. "Don't much believe in the hereafter. I believe more in the here

and now. No one from up there's ever cared too much about me, evidently. I've had to scratch and scrimp for everything I've ever had. And no one's cut me any slack. Ever. Not from up there and not from down here. And I've never asked for anything or expected anything from anybody because I've learned people don't care. You have to take care of yourself – nobody's going to do it for you."

Defiant, I had returned his long stare. It was like he was trying to read me from the inside out. Finally, he had clapped me on the shoulder, and nodded his head.

"You've had a rough time of it, James. I don't discount it. But there is always hope for tomorrow – hope things will get better. And with God on your side, it's always better. There is no one anywhere who loves you as much as God does. One of my favorite verses in the Bible says, '...neither height nor depth, nor anything else in all creation, will be able to separate us from the love of God that is in Christ Jesus our Lord.' This means there is nothing we can do to make God stop loving us, James. He loves you as he loves me. And I'm no saint. I've many regrets, but he gave his precious son, Jesus Christ, to die on the cross for me – and you. His blood was shed for you and for me."

"That's hard to believe, Photo Man."

"What?" he had asked.

"That anyone could love me after all the bad stuff I've done. Shooting a man, maybe two, maybe three, getting drunk, beating up my family, cussing, all those things."

"But I promise. It's true. God loves you, James. And all sins are equal in God's eyes. If I tell a lie, it's the

same as when you shot the man. Now, in man's eyes, it's not equal. But in God's eyes, it is."

"What do I have to do? What do you want me to do? Put on a choir robe, read a Bible, and promise to be good from now on?"

"No. It's simpler than that. All you have to do is believe Jesus Christ is your Lord and Savior. Confess the sins you've committed and ask for forgiveness. It's simple, as long as you mean it. But when you do it and mean it, it will change your life forever."

"I'll think about it, Photo Man. That's a lot to digest."

He had clapped me on the back again. "I hope so, James. I hope so."

"Do you have a stick of gum handy?"

"Sure I do. Here."

I didn't see him again and hadn't thought much more about what he'd said. But now, all this has happened.

For the first time in his life, Hutchins felt alone and scared. Suddenly, it was as if Lefrere was standing beside him saying, "James, Come out. Surrender. There is no need for more bloodshed. Too many people have died already. 'Come to me, all you who are weary and burdened, and I will give you rest.'"

The weight of his actions came crashing down, overwhelming him in a sea of confusion and dread. It was the first time he'd cried in thirty-eight years.

Chapter Twelve

The Gift of Surrender

"Come to me, all you who are weary and burdened, and I will give you rest."

Matthew 11:28 (NIV)

For five hours, they slowly and steadily made their way through the woods, walking up and down hills and small mountains until around midnight. They knew the command post and other officers were at least a mile away. They didn't know if others had been deployed into the woods. If so, no one knew where the other was, and no one knew where Hutchins was. That's when a shout startled them, breaking the night's eerie silence and the heavy tension. It had to be Hutchins.

"Who is it down there?" he shouted. From the sound of his voice, he was probably twenty yards or less away.

"We're a bunch of old coon hunters," one of the officers lied.

They weren't fooling anyone, especially Hutchins. He knew who they were and yelled back, "How's that g---ed trooper I shot?"

Admittedly, one officer answered, "We don't know

his condition, but we think he's alright."

Hutchins's response was blood chilling: "I know better than that. I blowed his g—ed head off. I shot Roy and Messersmith because I'm tired of you SOBs coming to my house."

Trooper Good shouted back, "Give up, Hutchins. You're surrounded and can't escape. We have officers all over this area."

His response was, "I'm going to kill every one of you."

Over the following hours, Hutchins, showing his prowess, kept them guessing by alternating his tactics. Sometimes he conversed with the officers; sometimes he shot at the officers, and they shot back. The heavily armed suspect was dangerous and kept them pinned down and motionless, literally eating dirt on the incline where they laid. This kept up for hours; they were extremely cautious with this mad man because if not, death was less than fifty feet away. At dawn, around 6:00 a.m., it was still. Even the helicopter and planes seemed to be at a far distance. Welcoming sunrays penetrated the trees' branches and exposed the crest of a nearby hill. No one was talking; no one was shooting. No one was moving.

Mistakenly reading the silence as something he could take advantage of, Officer Hines looked at Good and Davis and stated, "Boys, I've taken all I can. I've got to have a cigarette." He pulled out a pack of Lucky Strikes from his pocket and struck a match to light the cigarette. As he flicked his wrist to wave out the flame, Hutchins emptied both barrels of a 12 gauge shotgun in their direction, missing them by two feet. Patrolman

Hines returned fire; no one had been hit. But the men flattened themselves even deeper into their shallow bunkers.

Alarmingly, they noticed Hutchins's shots had come from the right this time and not from the hill in front of them where he'd been all night. Unmistakably, Hutchins had meant to kill them. Without detection, the fugitive had stealthily worked his way closer to them sometime during the fleeting darkness.

"He was really slick," Trooper Good said later. "We never heard him." The stark supposition was this man was making his way down the hill and to their right without discovery, so he could take them out if he'd wanted to.

Fortunately, one of the officers had grabbed a walk-talkie before entering the woods earlier. He called for the bell dogs to be sent in. Bell dogs are bloodhounds with bells affixed to their collars.

The standoff was entering its thirteenth hour; nerves were on edge. As shots were fired and dogs were loosed, tensions mounted, causing Chief McDevitt to issue the orders: "Bring him out one way or another. I don't want any more officers hurt. Do not make any concessions – don't listen to anything he says. Put him in custody one way or another."

At 6:57 a.m., the bell dogs were loosed. Within fifteen minutes, the barking and howling dogs had closed in and encircled the suspect. Fearful of their trained vigorous apprehension techniques, Hutchins stepped out of hiding and surrendered.

"Get those dogs away from me," he called.

Within a matter of seconds, Lieutenant John L. Wilkins, also in the woods by this time, messaged, "The suspect is two hundred yards ahead and walking toward us."

"Throw out your guns, Hutchins," demanded Patrolman Good.

He complied by throwing his two guns into a ditch and lying down. Good jumped into the ditch and cuffed him without resistance. At 7:14 a.m. a second message was sent, "The suspect is in custody."

The Rutherford County Jail was filled with officers, staff, and members of the Hutchins family. When the message was heard, they clapped and cheered. Hutchins family members appeared relieved and quietly left the jail. Sheriff Damon Huskey, who had kept an all-night vigil at the railroad track, travelled back to the command post to personally thank all the officers and volunteers for their participation in Hutchins's apprehension. Next, he returned to the county jail to thank the hundreds of officers who took part in the operation.

It was early morning June 1. Hutchins had eluded more than two hundred local police, state troopers, sheriff's deputies, SBI agents, FBI agents, and deputized volunteers and officers. They come from at least six surrounding counties in western North Carolina and upstate South Carolina. They manned and searched the three hundred acre tract of land in the Gilkey Community. At the end of the thirteen-hour manhunt, the largest manhunt in the history of North Carolina, Hutchins had surrendered and been captured in a dense thicket in Rutherford County. Airplanes and helicopters had filled the skies and dedicated men had filled the woods. But it was his fear of the SC State Law Enforcement Division (SLED) bloodhounds had made the capture possible.

Patrolman Good was satisfied the man who had murdered his best friend, Pete Peterson, had been apprehended. Part of his satisfaction included escorting the slender, 5'11" tall suspect out of the woods. Troopers Larry Davis and Bill Hines and Officers Ken Hollifield and James Boyce, and bloodhound, Rosey, accompanied him.

Hutchins had said nothing as they'd walked the mile and a half out of the woods to the parked cars. Good led him over to a sheriff's deputy, transferring custody. The sheriff's deputy arrested him. Good would never again speak to Hutchins.

As surrounding officers audibly discussed the community's tension and where to take him for safekeeping, Hutchins lifted his eyes and quickly scanned the crowd of uniforms and badges: strangers. Then, almost immediately, his eyes landed on a familiar and friendly face. He focused his eyes in disbelief: Charles Lefrere! When their eyes locked, his heavy heart lifted momentarily. Lefrere was a friendly face in the midst of this hateful, sneering crowd who dissected him with their cold, sharp eyes.

Hutchins lowered his eyes, feeling ashamed and small, like each stare removed a cell from his body. But seeing Lefrere embarrassed him. He had the sudden desire to dive into a marsh of quicksand and disappear. Lefrere had tried to find some good in him, and like everyone else in his life, he'd disappointed him, by allowing his anger to get the best of him. There was no good in him. There was no saving him. This time he'd done himself in.

Lefrere wandered over to him. Hutchins anticipated an officer to appear any moment and chastise him about approaching but no one seemed to notice. Besides, he was handcuffed and harmless.

"James, we must talk fast. Remember our last conversation in the woods?"

He nodded, "Yeah."

"Well, it's still true. God loves you and always will, no matter what you've done. The blood of Jesus is more than enough to cover your sins, my sins, their sins," he said, pointing to the crowd, who was getting tighter and closer, so they could see the murderer like he was an exhibit. You are forgiven, James. All you have to do is believe and confess your sins to Christ. Accept him into your heart as your Lord and Savior. He's waiting, James. He will never leave you – no matter what. His unending love can be a comfort to you now, especially in the days ahead."

"Nothing can comfort me now, Lefrere. They have me where they've always wanted me. I got caught and caught good this time," his voice broke.

"You're wrong, James. Christ can open a door to a freedom you've never known. He can set you free – maybe not from a jail cell this time. But he can set you free from the hurts and disappointments you've come to expect in your lifetime. He can fill your heart with joy – even now. He wants to do this for you, friend. Ask him."

One of the officers came over and grabbed Hutchins by the arm and pulled him away toward an unmarked car. He placed Hutchins in the backseat.

Lefrere came over to the car and placed his palm on the back door's window. Hutchins could hear his voice through the glass. "I won't leave you, James. I'm your friend. Think about what I've said."

Three officers climbed in, one beside Hutchins in the backseat. He kept his head low, marveling about Lefrere being there. It had been him in the woods calling his name. But how? Then he began thinking about what Lefrere had said. If ever he needed a friend, he needed one now.

When the driver gunned the accelerator, the car lurched forward, leaving Lefrere and a crowd of two hundred angry but relieved officers behind in a cloud of rising dust.

Chapter Thirteen

The Gift of Comfort for the Grieving

"He will wipe away every tear from their eyes, and death shall be no more, neither shall there be mourning, nor crying, nor pain anymore, for the former things have passed away."

Revelation 21:4 (NIV)

On the following Sunday, June 3, 1979, three victims of a brutal murder were laid to rest under the light of an afternoon sun. Law enforcement officers from across the two states and one highway patrolman from Oklahoma, came together to pay their final respects to the three slain officers from Rutherford County.

First was Captain Roy Huskey. The casket of Captain Roy Huskey of the Rutherford County Sheriff's Department was carried by fellow deputies who served as pallbearers for the slain officer. They were Ronald Jenkins, Ray Dixon, James Sparks, G. W. Roper, Lloyd Boone, and Keith Mitchem. Rutherford County sheriff's deputies Michael Summers and Randy Jolley served as honor guards, standing at attention and flanking Huskey's casket. A local newspaper described them as "stone-faced." Crowe's Mortuary Chapel was packed.

Reverend Wade Huntley said the huge crowd was there "to pay respect to the men who gave their lives so we might go home tonight, to sleep in peace. None of us appreciate our law enforcement officers as we should. I personally appreciate them. I appreciate the score of officers who took part in this endeavor the other day. I appreciate each day they spend on the road, each hour they lose sleep. Pray with me today for the men and the women who enforce our laws today."

Reverend Kenneth Roach also eulogized Huskey and talked of him as a friend and neighbor. He went on to explain he had once lived in the area and on Thursday afternoon had visited the area again. He regretted not stopping by and visiting his friend. "...not realizing my friend's life would soon be taken, I failed to stop and visit with him." He talked about Huskey's CB handle being Big Star, and stated, "...in my book, he was always Big Star. I never saw him lose his temper...but if there was trouble in the community, he always stepped forth with authority."

The Reverend talked about moving into the community twenty years before and living next-door to the Huskeys. "I learned to love Roy then, and through the many years, we have never been other than friends." He went on to say, "[Huskey and the other officers] gave their lives that we might live. They protect you 24 hours a day – not because of the money involved, but because they feel there is a job that needs to be done."

Over thirty patrol cruisers with their blue lights flashing led the funeral cortege from the Chapel to Sunset Memorial Park in the Oakland Community where Huskey was interred.

Next, was Sergeant Millard Owen Messersmith. Law enforcement officers from across the two states formed double lines on both sides of the entrance to the Church of the Transfiguration in Bat Cave in honor of their fallen comrade. Sergeant Messersmith's casket was carried by fellow deputies who served as pallbearers: Ronald Jenkins, Ray Dixon, James Sparks, G. W. Roper, Lloyd Boone, and Keith Mitchem. Rutherford County sheriff's deputies Michael Summers and Randy Jolley served as honor guards, standing at attention and flanking Messersmith's casket. Because the small church couldn't hold the crowd of people, many had to stand in the church yard where they stood quietly while Father John Palmer said last rites.

After the ceremony, lasting twenty minutes, an officer from the Asheville Police Department presented Messersmith's widow, Alice Messersmith, with a Bible in memory of the fallen officer. Final rites for Highway Patrolman R. L. "Pete" Peterson were held in Black Mountain with a large crowd of uniformed Patrolmen paying their last respects as his parents, daughter, sisters, and innumerable grievers mourned his death. He was buried in the Hopewell Baptist Church Cemetery.

Final rites for Highway Patrolman R. L. "Pete" Peterson were held in Black

Mountain with hundreds of people and hundreds of uniformed law enforcement officers paying their last respects at the gravesite service as his parents, daughter, sisters, and innumerable grievers mourned his death. He was buried in the Hopewell Baptist Church Cemetery in Swananoa, N.C. where he was born and raised. Highway Patrolman Dan Good, his best friend, served as one of the pall bearers.

A newspaper, *The Enterprise*, reported on June 6, 1979, that "what started as a family argument and a routine domestic call for Sheriff's Deputies, ended with the brutal shooting deaths of three law enforcement officers in a spree that lasted less than fifteen minutes. They had been three well-liked and respected lawmen."

Chapter Fourteen

The Act of Justice

"Do not pervert justice; do not show partiality to the poor or favoritism to the great, but judge your neighbor fairly."

Leviticus 19:15 (NIV)

The dark night had been grueling. The community and over two hundred officers and volunteers were still tense with emotions running high even after the surrender. So officials decided the most appropriate decision would be to take Hutchins to the Cleveland County Jail in an unmarked SBI vehicle where he'd be held for a short time.

He was secretly transported back to Rutherford County for a closed hearing at the Forest City Police Department. Hutchins was brought before District Court Judge Hollis M. Owens and never spoke. He kept his head low the majority of time while he was arraigned on three charges of first degree murder. The Judge ordered him to be held without bond and set a hearing date for June 12, 1979. After filing a financial statement, Hutchins was found indigent and the judge appointed David Fox, a Hendersonville attorney, to represent him. Ronald Blanchard was appointed to serve as co-

counsel. After he had been granted thirty minutes to speak with his two attorneys, officers returned him to the Cleveland County Jail.

On June 5, Hutchins was transported by the SBI to a probable cause hearing, which was held at the Rutherford County Court House for the purpose of allowing the state to present evidence to determine if the case would be bound over for trial in Superior Court. Sheriff Damon Huskey stated "Hutchins would not be held at any time in the Rutherford County Jail" and "security precautions would include limited access to the court room and searches of all persons entering the Court House."

On June 12, 1979, at the probable cause hearing in Rutherford County, Charlotte Hutchins took the stand and testified. She told them her father had beaten her and other members of the family because they had been disagreeing over the amount of vodka she'd poured into some punch that was to be served at a graduation party that night. When she saw a hammer come up above her head, she had broken free and ran across the road to a neighbor's house to call the sheriff's office. She also stated, "He's bad about grabbing his gun when he gets mad." She also testified that when she heard shots, she thought her father had killed her mother, brother, and sister.

Hutchins was subsequently indicted by the grand jury for murder, and the case was transferred from Rutherford County to McDowell County. Hutchins turned to look at his cousin Glenn and mouthed the words, "I'm gone. I didn't have a chance" to which Glenn returned, "I know it. You're gone."

For whatever reason, Hutchins became convinced that Fox who was a former District Attorney was working in collusion with the state. On August 16, he requested his lawyer be discharged. As a result, Fox filed a motion stating that "no meaningful communication" was possible and requesting he be discharged, but the motion was denied. Hutchins was examined by Dr. George W. Doss on August 28. His attorneys received a preliminary report from Doss on September 6, which stated he [Doss] didn't have enough information to be sure but felt Hutchins was suffering from a "paranoid delusional system."

On the same day, he was transferred 210 miles away to Dorothea Dix Hospital in Raleigh, North Carolina, for evaluation. Their psychology report stated that "at the time in question, Mr. Hutchins was aware of the nature and quality of his actions and the difference in right and wrong." He was returned on September 14 and subsequently refused to cooperate with Dr. Doss on September 17, when the doctor attempted another examination.

Judge Donald Smith presided over the closed hearing, which began on September 17. Hutchins pleaded not guilty after the district attorney demanded he receive the death penalty. Dr. Doss testified Hutchins was suffering from paranoid psychosis and an emotional disturbance at the time the murders were committed. He had committed the murders for the purpose of avoiding arrest, had committed the murders against law enforcement officers, and had committed the murders because they were a part of his course of conduct, including violence against other persons.

It seemed Hutchins's only possible defense was insanity, but his counsel didn't present evidence to support it. Based on the psychology report and Dr. Doss's testimony, he did not possess the level of *mens rea* (a Latin term meaning the intention or knowledge of wrong doing that constitutes part of a crime as opposed to the action or conduct of the accused) to allow a constitutionally permissible imposition of the death penalty. Hutchins was not allowed to testify by his attorneys. In addition, the defense failed to interview witnesses, even though records show counsel spent hundreds of hours preparing for trial. According to Fox, he didn't allow Hutchins to testify because he was afraid the state would bring up Hutchins's prior voluntary manslaughter conviction and his two convictions of assault with a gun.

On September 21, 1979, after four hours of deliberation, the jury found Hutchins was suffering from an emotional disturbance at the time of the murders and returned verdicts of guilty of first degree murders for Messersmith and Peterson and a verdict of guilty of second degree murder for Huskey. Hutchins showed no visible emotions. When the judge asked each juror to stand and declare his/her agreement with the death penalty, he kept his head lowered while holding Geneva's hand. She wept silently.

The sentencing phase lasted one and a half days. After two hours and fifty minutes, the same jury recommended Hutchins be punished by death for each of the first degree murders and life imprisonment for the second degree murder. First degree murder is defined as the "willful, deliberate and premeditated killing or killing while committing another felony."

Judge Smith referred to Hutchins as "the most dangerous man I've ever seen" and set October 12, 1979, as the execution date. The appeals process kicked in and brought an automatic delay. Then Superior Court Judge Lacy Thornburg set October 15, 1981, as the execution date. More appeals pushed the execution date to January 22, 1982. After the State Supreme Court granted a stay for further appeals, a new execution date was set for October 15, 1982. Again, the appeals process delayed the date. But the clock was ticking, the days were passing, and the years were moving ahead.

Part Two:

Fast Forward to the Enduring

Summer 1983 – March 15, 1984

"To actually forgive, we have to expose the rawness of our wounds to the salts of disappointment, the stinging fears of vulnerability, and the infectious frustration, hurt, and anger that poisons and threatens our spirits. Therefore, forgiveness is a strong act of human courage and resolve, fueled by Christian theology, a profound display of love, and the desire for ultimate healing of the soul."

Sandi Huddleston-Edwards

Chapter Fifteen

The Gift of Innocent Anticipation

"It is human nature to want to go back and fix things or change things that we regret."

John Gray

ALEX WELLS

"Hello!" Alex panted. She bent to kiss the soft face of the attractive brunette who sat patiently beside a cheerful window waiting for her. "Mama, I'm sorry. I just dropped Abbie at the Vet's to be spayed. Have you been waiting long?" Her eyes skimmed the table-top to find two glasses of sweet iced tea with lemon, which she expected.

"Hi, Sweetie. Not long, maybe ten minutes. I went ahead and ordered you an iced tea," her mother said with a smile. "But I had no idea what you wanted for lunch. This menu is extensive! Everything sounds good."

Alex hung her shoulder-strapped pink purse over the back of the wooden chair; when she sat, it creaked loudly. She smiled into Betsy's sage-green eyes. "Thanks!" she said before taking a large gulp of the refreshment. She laughed as it dribbled down her chin.

"Sorry. I was thirsty! Besides Mom, you know I'm a creature of habit. I always order the turkey panini." "Well, I thought you might be adventurous and try something different like me. Today I'm going to have the Asian chicken salad."

"That sounds delicious, too, but thank you, no. I'll stick to my good old stand-by."

After Lissa, the waitress, took their order, the mother and daughter sat quietly, scanning the knotty-pine paneled walls of their favorite local restaurant. It was quaint and inviting. They always enjoyed seeing the new consignment pieces painted by local artists. Once a home, Café 100 had been converted into one of the most popular restaurants in Huntersville, and it was among Alex's preferred places to eat a tasty lunch or bring her friends for a cool drink, soothing music, and delicious food on Saturday nights.

Unable to control her excitement any longer, Alex reached for her mother's hands across the maroon vinyl tablecloth. "Mom, I have something thrilling to tell you!"

"What?" Betsy giggled. "Tell me!"

"Tony and I are planning to collaborate on a writing project. It may end up being an extended essay, or it could possibly become a book. We really want to write a book. You know how I've always wanted to become an author."

"But you are! You've been published, sweetie."

"No, Mom. I mean an *author* -- not someone published in a newspaper or who has a short story published in a forgotten magazine no one ever heard of."

"Okay. Then tell me more about this project. What's it about?"

"Well, Tony's family once lived in Rutherfordton. It's a beautiful town he says. Anyway, that's where he grew up until he went to college. You remember his father was a minister, right?"

"Yes, I do remember. But weren't his parents killed several years ago?" "Yeah, in a terrible automobile accident four or five years ago. But they'd moved to Charlotte by then. Well, anyway, in 1979 this deranged alcoholic killed three law officers – two from the sheriff's department and a highway patrolman. Tony knows a lot about the area and feels close to this story."

"What happened to the man who shot them?" her mother asked.

"He's in Central Prison awaiting execution. Tony is totally absorbed by this story. Because he knows I love to write, he asked me if I'd like to collaborate on this project. Possibly, we'll explore the major issues involved, such as alcoholism, domestic abuse, the death penalty – social topics like those and others."

"Oh, Alex. Murder seems like such a dark subject for you to write about. Why not find a happier topic? Can't ya'll begin by writing a children's book? There are plenty of happily-ever- after stories you could create. You have a wonderful imagination."

"I'm not interested in writing a children's book and neither is Tony. Unfortunately, Mama, some endings aren't always happy. Some people experience hard times and live sad lives. Everything isn't perfect like your life is."

She missed her mother's momentary frown as she continued. "Tony and I want to try and make some sense out of these irrational murders and find an underlying message we can give to our readers – something to inspire them and interest them."

"But maybe there is no *sense* to make out of three *senseless* murders."

"Tony and I realize that, but all of this will be fodder for our writing. We're not sure where this will lead us, but we want to try. We'll begin by interviewing the victims' families and friends. We even want to interview the murderer if we're allowed to, along with his family and friends. They must be so ashamed of him. He must be ashamed of himself. I wonder how awful it is to know you've taken three innocent men's lives and have left families devastated and in unspeakable pain. I can't imagine how much hatred I'd feel if someone hurt you or Daddy."

"Alex, do you really want to interview the man who is responsible for all this devastation? Would you be safe?"

"Yes, we do. I know I'll be nervous in the beginning, but if we can get the Warden's approval, Tony says we would be safe. There are a lot of guards, and after all, it is a maximum security prison. But chances are, we won't get to interview him. And maybe we won't have to. Maybe we can find out all we need to know by interviewing people who knew him." The young woman tried to sound convincing to her mother and to herself.

"When did these awful murders happen?" Betsy asked while sipping her tea. Betsy watched as her daughter's eyes blazed and a familiar excitement spread across her face.

"Four years ago in May of '79."

Betsy hoped the excitement was due in part to Tony *and* collaborating on the project. She and Rob really liked Tony, whom they'd invited over for several friends and family cookouts after meeting him two years before at Alex's graduation. They'd both received Masters' degrees in English. His was in literature, and Alex's was in rhetoric and writing.

"That's awful. How tragic for the families. Well, I certainly admire your courage and desire to write about such deep and sad subjects as those."

"Tony hopes to interview Hutchins or at least people who know him. Tony's other idea is to write a true crime book about Hutchins, but I kind of like the idea of writing a novel about it and fictionalizing some of the details and characters. So Tony said the final product will depend on our research and where it leads us. What do you think?"

"Alex! This sounds great, honey! I'm happy for you. Are you and Tony planning to write it over summer vacation? You don't have to teach this summer, do you?"

"No. We have almost two months off. I doubt we'll be able to write anything for a while, Mom, but we do plan to use our time to research and conduct interviews. Writing a book will probably take several years. When you're writing a short story and possibly a book, it's like going to the movies in your mind. You see the events as they unfold. You become all the characters by getting inside their brains and their hearts. You have no dialogue until you create it as you go. Then you scramble to write all the words and the clever phrases coming to you before they evaporate and disappear into oblivion."

"That certainly doesn't sound like anything I could ever do. I'm so proud of you!" Betsy squeezed her hands. "My daughter is going to be an author!" Her mother's pride and enthusiasm was contagious.

Alex blushed; then she began laughing.

Betsy squeezed the lemon into her tea and hesitated before asking, "So is there more to yours and Tony's relationship I should know about?"

"Mom!" Alex groaned. "Of course not, and please don't get started. We are friends – more like a brother and sister. Stop thinking there is anything else between us. We were study partners when we worked on our Masters degrees. We are English instructors. We teach at the same college. We're both planning to get our doctorates. And we both enjoy writing. We have a lot in common and more than anything, we are ***just*** friends – good friends. He calls me *Harper*, and I call him *Truman."*

"Well, I can hope, can't I?" she teased. When her daughter's disappointment didn't disappear, she changed the subject. "Oh those are clever nicknames, Alex. Harper Lee and Truman Capote. I absolutely love *To Kill a Mockingbird,* and I haven't been able to forget *In Cold Blood* since I read it. I guess this is one reason I'd hate for you to have to experience something as dark as what that book was about."

They paused as Lissa returned with heaping plates. "Is there anything else you need besides refills of tea?"

"No, thanks," Alex replied. "I'm good. Mom?"

"No thank you. This Asian chicken salad looks delicious!"

"It is, ma'am. Please enjoy," Lissa replied. "I'll get you refills of tea."

Betsy reached across the table and grasped her daughter's right hand. She whispered loudly, "I love you, Alex, and I'm proud of you. I can't wait to hear updates about your project."

Alex's trepidation had passed. She nodded and said, "Thanks, Mom."

Betsy lowered her head and waited for Alex to follow her lead, which she did. After Betsy asked the blessing, they bit into their delicious entrees.

"This turkey panini hits the spot," Alex giggled. "It's what I was waiting for."

"And this chicken salad is to die for. You should have tried it." Her mother took another bite and said, "By the way, how are the repairs going?"

"Okay, I guess. They're replacing all the plumbing today and tomorrow. It's still ironic that you and Daddy finance this 1940 craft home for me, and Daddy remodels it completely. We buy new appliances, a new water heater, a new furnace, and new furniture. Then I have a stupid water pipe to burst in the ceiling and flood everything." She took a bite of the fresh fruit salad.

"I know. I know. But thank God you had insurance, Alex."

"I know. You're right. The contractors should begin repairing the dry wall next week. Afterward, they'll sand and refinish the hardwood floors. Then they'll move to the kitchen to install the new floor and new cabinets."

"How about your counter tops?"

"I'll have to replace them too since they were damaged. I want butcher block like Dad initially put in. There wasn't much damage, but they can't match it so it has to be changed. So I get new countertops. And I will have to replace the kitchen appliances. By the way, shouldn't I get the same appliances we chose the first time?"

"I think so. They were top of the line. It's a shame they were damaged. Are you still enjoying staying at the motel? You know you can always come back home and stay with Daddy and me. We miss you, sweetie. Your room is always there waiting for you."

"Yes, I'm sure. I'm able to spread out – you know. Have my own space. But thanks, Mama. Everyone at the motel is nice and friendly. They have this wonderful lady, Minnie, who fixes breakfast for all the residents. It's free – part of the rental rate. And on Mondays, Tuesdays, and Wednesdays, they have a social hour for all the guests where they serve free wine, beer, and soft drinks and some savory snacks. You can't beat it! The staff members have gotten used to Maddie's and Abbie's barking. They think my little Yorkies are cute. And, Mom, haven't you ever heard the old cliché you can never go home again? I did once after college. Remember? So I'm fine. Don't worry. Besides, I like being on my own."

"Well, it seems like the two years you worked on your master's degree flew by. But I know you're fine. We miss you. That's really nice for the motel to offer so many conveniences. I bet you're taking advantage of the pool as well, aren't you?"

"Of course. I have had some friends over, and we've enjoyed it a few times." Dad and you should come over and relax with me. We can have a glass of wine together."

"We might. I think your dad needs to relax more. He's been really stressed over this project he's leading at work. He hasn't been himself lately."

"What do you mean?" Alex asked.

"Well, he's irritable, not sleeping, and losing weight. He's already lost a pants' size. Has he mentioned anything that is bothering him to you?"

"No. He's been upset about my house flooding after he did all the work, but he's happy with the contractor and sub-contractors who are making the repairs. Do you think Daddy is sick?"

"No. Don't you worry. He's been a little distant – not wanting to discuss anything with me. He doesn't seem interested in talking about the cruise we had planned to take later this fall."

"Well, you know how Mr. Perfectionist is, Mom. Give our engineer some space. Daddy will be his old self again before you know it."

They stared into each other's eyes before bursting into laughter.

"You're right. I better take advantage of this time when he's quiet," Betsy said. "Hey, I know you're right, sweetie. If anything was wrong, he would have talked to one of us about it. It's probably what I said. He wants to do a really good job on this project. You know how folks get a little worried when they think they are over the hill and can be replaced easily by younger people?"

"Yeah. Maybe it is part of it. But Daddy doesn't have to worry. He's worked for the firm for twenty six years. They wouldn't let Daddy go."

"I don't think so either. He's always done a great job. Your father is actually working from home today.

He's been doing that a lot lately, so he doesn't have to fight the crazy traffic driving to the office uptown. He says he gets a lot more done when he can be alone and concentrate. He only goes into the office on the days when he has meetings scheduled or field visits to make."

"That's good. Fighting traffic is stressful enough."

"When he's home working, though, I'm afraid I will disturb him, so I go shopping or to lunch with friends, or to get my hair done. Being with you today is perfect! Not only do I get to spend time with my favorite daughter...."

"Your only daughter...." Alex corrected her.

"My only daughter. But I get to eat a delicious lunch before my women's club meeting. Then I get to meet you afterward for a relaxing facial. You get lunch and a facial, I get lunch and a facial, and your father gets some quiet time, so he can concentrate. We all win!"

She spooned the last bite of chicken into her mouth and looked at her watch. "And speaking of my club meeting, I need to hurry. It begins in thirty minutes. I'll meet you at 3:30 sharp. Don't be late. They hate it when anyone is late. Here, take this and pay for our lunches." Betsy stood, smoothed her black skirt, and handed Alex a fifty dollar bill.

"May I keep the change?" Alex asked in her teasing voice.

"No ma'am, and I expect the correct change back when you see me at 3:30." She walked a few steps before stopping. "Oh, Alex. Do you think you should take Daddy some lunch? I haven't bought groceries this week, so he may not have anything to make a sandwich. Do you have time to take him something?"

"Sure. What do you think Daddy would want?"

Betsy grabbed a nearby menu off the counter. "Order him the Cali Chicken BLT. He'd like that." Then she returned to their table and swooped down to kiss her daughter's cheek. "Don't stay too long and don't bother him. He'll be happy to see you, but let him get some work done, so he won't be so grouchy with me tonight. I love you."

"I won't stay long. I need to run by Gabby's house and feed her cat while she's at the beach. See you at 3:30 with your dwindling change. Love you, too."

Her mom dashed out the door into the mid-day sun.

"Lissa?" Alex called. "I need an order to go, please. The Cali Chicken BLT. And I think it's a shame to waste time, so I guess I'll have a Chocolate Pot de Crème while I wait."

The waitress returned Alex's conniving smile. "Coming right up," the girl called over her shoulder. They giggled.

Hmmmm, Alex thought. *Life can't get better than this – a nice lunch, dessert, and a facial all in the same afternoon. And someone else is paying for it.* She was excited about working with Tony on this writing project. The summer would be fun.

Then her favorite daydream inched its way into her mind while she waited, and everything else was forgotten. She could picture herself at a book signing where hundreds of patient readers were waiting in line for her signature. She smiled at each person as she signed her signature with a black pen and wrote some clever message as well. Behind her would be a poster – a page from the *New York Times*, where her name would be listed first.

Yes, she told herself. *Becoming a* New York Times *best-selling author was hard work, but someone had to do it.*

Chapter Sixteen

The Act of Disrupting Dreams

"Hold fast to dreams, for if dreams die, life is a broken-winged bird that cannot fly."
Langston Hughes

TONY ADAMS

It was late afternoon when Tony twisted the brass door knob of his apartment and gave it a slight nudge, but nothing happened, so he unlocked the door lock and the deadbolt; then it opened. *Terri must have gone out for both locks to be on.*

As he traveled through the dimly-lit kitchen into the cluttered family room, he noticed food-stained dishes stacked in the sink. He stopped long enough to thumb through the unopened mail scattered on the kitchen table beside an opened envelope bearing a return address from California. A folded check laid beside the envelope. Tony instantly knew it was the monthly child-support payment from Mark. Due to the blue ink being smudged and the writing now illegible, the bank wouldn't be able to cash it. He suspected Terri had been crying when she opened the envelope, and her tears had dripped on the check. An opened box of thawed out chicken nuggets was left on the stove. Tony quickly tossed those into the trash, and walked into the room where he was surprised to find Terri asleep on the couch.

"Unky Tony! Unky Tony!" Johnny came running and shouting in his squeaky voice Tony had grown to love and expect. He ran and jumped into Tony's waiting arms and hugged him tightly around the neck. "I'm so glad you're home, Unky Tony!" he cried. "Did you miss me?"

"Hey buddy. Hey little man! Of course I missed you," he whispered while returning his embrace and patting his little back. He clicked on a nearby lamp. "I'm glad to be here, too." He lowered his nephew to the floor. "What have you been doing? Is Mommy sick?"

"I've been playing. She's tired," the tiny voice replied.

He scanned the room more carefully, while Terri continued snoring softly in her deep sleep. Not even his opening the door or Johnny's excitement had awakened her. The television was turned to a cartoon channel, and the volume was louder than normal. Obviously, Johnny had been pressing some buttons on the remote. Building blocks were scattered across the brown plush carpet. A half-eaten chicken nugget and an empty glass of chocolate milk sat on the floor beside Johnny's favorite stuffed animal, Big Bird.

"Has Mommy been sleeping a long time?" he asked.

"No." He busied himself stacking blue-colored blocks. "Mommy said she needed a short nap."

"Is that all you had for lunch?" Tony asked while pointing toward the empty glass and piece of chicken.

"Nope."

"What else did you eat?"

"I had three chickens and some cookies and chocolate milk."

"So you had cookies, chicken nuggets, and chocolate milk, right?"

"Yep!"

"What did you have for breakfast?"

"Tony Tiger." Tony interpreted these two words to be *Frosted Flakes.*

Tony noticed a wine glass with traces of a pink liquid sitting on the coffee table in front of the sofa. He knew instantly this was her favorite zinfandel she'd purchased a few days ago. Before he opened the refrigerator door to confirm his hunch, he noticed the empty bottle sitting on the kitchen counter. She must have drank the entire bottle today. He hastily returned to the family room and noticed a bottle of valium sitting on the coffee table. The lid was screwed off. This frightened him; suddenly, he became extremely angry.

He managed to have a calm voice when he asked, "Johnny, have you touched Mommy's bottle of pills?"

"Nope."

"Did you touch her glass?"

"Nope." Johnny didn't hesitate with his answers. Usually, when he was fibbing, he wasn't as forthcoming.

"Are you telling the truth?"

"Yep."

He watched the little boy's face when he answered. It never changed. He kept concentrating on his toys.

"Are you sure? I promise you won't get in trouble if you tell me."

"No, Unky Tony. I didn't touch the medicine or the glass." While the little boy sounded exasperated at the number of questions, Tony felt relieved. He believed his nephew.

"Okay. You know you're not supposed to ever touch medicine bottles or drink from anyone's glass by yourself, right?" Tony asked.

"Yes."

"You're a good boy. Come give me a big hug. I need another big hug."

The four year-old dropped his blocks and ran to the gangly man. He jumped into his arms and gave him an exaggerated hug. "Unky Tony, will you ride me on your back?"

"I sure will. Here, slide around." As he helped position his nephew safely, he noticed Terri's snoring had ceased. He watched her chest to ensure it was rising and falling. When he was reassured she was breathing, he made an unpopular suggestion to Johnny. "What do you say we head to the bathroom and get you a bath? Then I'll fix some dinner, okay?"

"No for bath and okay for dinner."

"Nope, smarty pants. It doesn't work that way. Bath first; food next. And the sooner we do those, the sooner I'll get to read you a bedtime story. How does this sound?"

"Great!" he yelled. "Gitty up horsey. Gitty up."

"Hey, pardner. Don't kick the horsey so hard. His ribs might break. Let's go get you some clean PJs and a towel and washcloth."

"I can wear these PJs I have on. They're my favorite ones."

“Nope. Those have honey mustard and chocolate milk all over them. It looks like you were eating in a hurry. Actually, it looks like you’ve already had a bath in chocolate milk. But all little cowboys need clean PJs to wear to bed.”

The little boy nodded his head in agreement. “Gitty up! Gitty up!” he shrieked.

Chapter Seventeen

The Act of Disappointment

"The only conquests that are permanent and leave no regrets are our conquests over ourselves."
Napoleon Bonaparte

ALEX WELLS

On the way to her parent's comfortable home on Lake Norman, Alex rolled down the windows of her corvette and let her long dark hair fly in the wind. The hot sun beat down on her nose, and its strong rays stung her eyes. She could feel the freckles popping out all over her face, but she didn't care. She turned up the volume of her new *Fleetwood Mac* collection. She was excited Tony was coming over tonight, so they could discuss their research and map out the interview schedules. She might even order a pizza.

Wow! She thought to herself. *Wouldn't it be something if we were able to write a best-seller? We'd get to travel all over the place, signing books, giving television interviews, becoming rich and famous.* Her mind drifted to the killer who had taken three innocent lives. *All because of someone who got drunk and shot three people. What a jerk – worse than a jerk. What a monster!*

They should have strung him up in the woods and saved taxpayers the cost of a trial and execution.

As she turned into the long, circular asphalt driveway, Alex's stomach flipped over. *Dad will be excited when he hears my news. He'll be supportive like he always is. After all, he has pushed me to write, ever since I won a poetry contest in junior high school and had a short story published in a no-name magazine during my freshman year of college. Mama is being cautious. She always has been especially where I am concerned. Being an only child has its perks of being spoiled and being the center of two people's worlds, but it also has its drawbacks, like when they are overprotective and overbearing. But, it's because they love me so much, I guess.*

Excitedly, she slammed parking break on, whisked out the "to-go" bag with the sandwich, and ran under the covered porch to the ornate door. Before she turned the front-door knob, she heard a woman's screechy laughter. *Daddy must be watching television. And Mom is concerned I would be taking up too much of his time. He's being a naughty boy! But I will surprise him and catch him red-handed. He'll owe me one.*

She turned the brass knob quietly and tiptoed toward the family room where Daddy would be sitting in his recliner watching television. She'd surprise him with a bear hug from behind. After peering through the doorway, she noticed his chair was empty, and the television wasn't on. There was another high-pitched squeal along with the murmuring of Dad's low baritone voice. *He must be watching television in the breakfast nook.* She continued tiptoeing down the hall until she reached the kitchen's entrance. As she entered the room, she stopped. The sight greeting her made her nauseous. Her heart began pounding, and she longed to scream, only no sound would come. Instead, hot tears poured down her red cheeks, and her knees gave way. She sank to the floor in a heap.

The two occupants of the room were so absorbed in each other, they were unaware of her presence. Her Daddy was standing in front of the new neighbor, Mrs. Walters, whom her mother had called "the widow," who was penned against the refrigerator. His hands caressed her curvy hips, as she giggled seductively and stared into his eyes. Her long, tanned arms were looped around his neck. Alex was overcome by a myriad of emotions: shock, disgust, anger, hatred, hurt, betrayal, pity, and disbelief among the majority. She yearned to turn and run before they noticed her, but her limp, spaghetti legs wouldn't hold her body up, much less move. It was as if her bottom was glued to her mother's clean linoleum floor.

Without realizing what she was doing, she shrieked loudly! "Daddy! What are you doing?" Then she began sobbing uncontrollably, covering her shocked face.

Immediately, her father's arms were around her, lifting her up to unsteady feet, and repeatedly saying, "Alex, I'm sorry. I'm sorry!"

"Is she all right?" asked the blonde woman.

"I'm fine!" Alex screamed. "You get out of my mother's kitchen!"

Frightened by the sudden change of tone and the defiant behavior, the woman stumbled backward.

"I'm sorry, Rob. I'm...I'll see you...."

"No you won't!" Alex cried. "Get out of here, and don't you ever come back!"

"You'd better go, please," he replied without turning to look at her. All of his attention was on his defiant and sobbing daughter.

"How could you? How could you?" she cried over and over again, searching his eyes. "You're my Daddy. How could you do this?" Then she stared into his brown eyes. "Daddy, how could you do this to Mama?"

Her words caused him to gasp loudly.

"Alexandra! I'm sorry. I'm so sorry," he stuttered. The miserable look on his beloved face shouted dejection and rejection and sadness and remorse. "What are you doing here?"

"What am I doing here?" she asked incredulously. "What am I doing here? What are you doing here?" She spat her hurt and anger toward him before shifting her gaze away. "It is absurd for you to ask me! This has always been my home, too. I came to see you, Daddy. I came to bring you lunch because Mama was worried about you not having something to eat. You do remember Mama, don't you, Daddy? How could you hurt her like this? How could you hurt me? You're my father. I've always worshipped you. What were you thinking?"

Grape sized tears ran from his eyes. All he could do was hold his palms up and shake his head. He looked like the proverbial little boy who got caught with his hand in the cookie jar. He didn't respond. He couldn't respond. He had no words.

She hurled the brown bag toward her astonished father. "So here's your lunch, Daddy. Take it. Eat it. Enjoy it. I never want to see you again."

Tears rolled in waves down her burning cheeks. She ran toward the front door and didn't stop until she was sitting in the driver's seat of her car. As she slammed the Corvette's door, she turned the ignition and rammed the gear shank into neutral. Her father was standing at the door with a heart-breaking stare, now pleading in a broken voice for her to come back. "Let me explain. Please, Alex. I love you. Let me explain."

Alex wanted no explanation. There was no explanation. She'd never hated anyone as much as she did Mrs. Walters – and her father. She shoved the car into first gear and flew down the driveway and skidded out onto the open road before safely ensuring there was no oncoming car. Thankfully, there hadn't been.

She pressed the accelerator to the floor, and the car responded. She whipped around curves at an outrageous and dangerous speed, oblivious to laws and other cars and drivers. The sun was blinding, but she didn't care.

What do I have to lose? She asked herself. *I'd rather be dead than have to live through my mother's anguish. I never want to see him again. He's a jerk like all men. My daddy, the man I've loved all my life. How could he be so callous? How could he be so selfish? How could he be so unkind? How could he be like every other man?*

Chapter Eighteen

The Gift of Caring

"It may help us, in those times of trouble, to remember that love is not only about relationship, it is also an affair of the soul."

Thomas Moore

TONY ADAMS / TERRI TUNNEY

The next morning, Tony awoke with dread in the pit of his stomach. He needed to have a conversation with his sister. Terri needed to understand the recklessness of taking pills with wine and falling asleep with a four year-old running around with no supervision. He sat on the edge of the bed and thought about Alex. He wished he'd called her last night to get his mind off his sister. With bare feet, he shuffled into the dimly lit kitchen only to find Terri standing at the sink and holding a cup of steaming coffee in her hand; she was staring out of the window.

"Good morning," he said when she didn't turn to acknowledge his presence.

Terri didn't answer.

"What are you looking at?" Tony asked, while trying to chip away at the icy atmosphere in the room. "Is there some more coffee?"

When she still didn't answer, he reached around her to grab a mug out of the cabinet. After pouring himself a cup of coffee, he sat at the table and sadly stared at his sister's back. He stood and flicked on the overhead light, but when she groaned, he turned it off.

"Terri, why are you upset with me? Come sit with me; let's talk."

He waited. Before extending the invitation again, she plopped into the empty chair across from him. But she sipped the coffee while avoiding his eyes.

"What have I done to upset you, Terri?"

She shrugged her shoulders. "You haven't done anything. It's me."

"Why are you shutting me out, Sis? Talk to me. Let me help you," he pleaded.

"Leave me alone, Tony. There's nothing you can do. There's nothing anyone can do."

"Well, I see differently than you do. Terri, you're not yourself. You haven't been yourself for a while. You're shutting me out; you're shutting your son out. He needs you. He needs his Mommy."

"Tony, don't you think I know that? After all, I am his mother."

"Okay. Well then, let's talk about it. Do you know what I found when I came home last night? He was sitting in the middle of the floor in dirty PJs. Your unscrewed medicine bottle was on the coffee table where he could reach it. Thank God he didn't get into those. And either you had drained your wine glass, or he could have gotten to it with it sitting on the coffee table, too."

"You talk like I'm a bad mother. Is this what you think?"

"No I don't, but I think you were careless last night."

"I drank my wine. Is that a problem? Am I not allowed to drink a glass of wine?"

"Of course you are, Terri, but you drank a whole bottle of wine by yourself. Don't you think it was a little too much?"

She leaned forward and stared into his eyes. "Tony, you are not my father."

"I know better than you I'm not your father. But I am your brother, and I'm worried about you; and I'm worried about your four-year old son. He's not able to care for himself, Terri, and he can't be left unsupervised. Too much could happen."

"You don't need to worry. And don't tell me how to care for my son, Tony. I'm a good mother. I love Johnny. He's my life – what's left of it."

"I know you love Johnny, Terri. But you can't take valium and drink wine during the day. You have to stay awake. He's a curious little boy. I don't want him to get hurt."

When he noticed the rims of her eyes reddening and glistening in the morning sun, he softened his voice. "We can always place him in a daycare."

"Until I can get a job, I don't have enough money for a daycare. His father doesn't send enough money for everything he needs and daycare."

"Well, let me help you," her brother offered.

"I don't want to live off of you, Tony. I already owe you more money than I'll ever be able to repay."

"That's not important. What's important is you feeling better about yourself, and Johnny being cared for while you get on your feet."

"I plan to get a job," she snapped. "I'm working on my resume."

"That's not what I'm saying. I want you to get better – to be my sister again. I want you to get better and be the person you used to be. You can, can't you?"

"Of course, I can! I need a little time. You've never had your whole world turned upside down, Tony. You've had an easy life."

"Oh really, Sis. Really?" He wanted to shout at her but maintained his composure. "I don't think losing my parents, our parents, before turning twenty-five was an easy road. That devastated me like it did you. But you had Mark to turn to for comfort; I had no one except you. But somehow I got through the grief and moved forward. Does it still hurt? Do I miss them? You bet I do, but I haven't found solace with a bottle of valium and a bottle of wine. I keep moving on."

"What do you mean by 'somehow I got through the grief and moved forward'?"

"I moved forward, Terri. I don't believe you have. You're still back there with Mom and Dad. You have to bury them Terri. Accept the fact they are not coming back."

"Oh, leave me alone." She turned her face away. "You don't understand."

"Help me to understand, Sis. Tell me."

She cried softly into the bend of her arm. The fluffy bathrobe muffled her sobs.

"Tony, not only did I lose my parents, I lost my husband, my marriage, my home. I lost everything I ever believed in. Do you know how hard it is when the person you love and trust with all your heart confesses to an affair and tells you he no longer loves you or wants to live with you? He left me for another woman. Can you imagine how it feels – to be replaced?"

"Of course not, Terri. I can't imagine your pain. It hurts me for you and Johnny to go through this."

"Johnny. My poor little Johnny. His father agreed to child support, but because his girlfriend doesn't like kids, he doesn't want visitation. How do you turn on and off your feelings like that? He seemed so happy when Johnny was born – the perfect daddy. But now a woman is more important than his own son! I couldn't conceive Mark could ever hurt us this way. I thought we were in love. I thought he loved our son."

"Nor did I, Sis. Nor did I."

"And I'm sorry, but I hate the drunkard who killed our parents. I know Daddy used to preach against hatred, but I hate him. They didn't deserve to die. He should have been buried under the prison instead of only getting a few years for vehicular manslaughter. What a joke!" Her agitation was growing. "And you, my own brother told him you forgave him, which is absurd! I've always secretly disliked you for that, Mark – I mean, Tony."

"Well, if you'd gone to the trial, you might have understood a little more."

"I didn't want to see that piece of scum. Because he decided to ring in the New Year by getting drunk, we no longer have our parents. Johnny doesn't have his grandparents."

"I've never seen you this angry, Terri."

She calmed down a little, "Well, maybe you should have. Maybe I've been pushed to the edge. Maybe I'm all mixed up!"

"That's why I'm here to help you." He took her hand. She resisted and tried to jerk it away, but he held it tightly. "Sis, you and Johnny are all I have. I love you both. And I want you to understand some things. I disliked the man, too. I actually thought I hated him. When I went to the courthouse, I was disgusted to discover this wasn't his first offense. He'd been caught driving drunk several times, but he'd never caused an accident before. He'd lost his license, stuff like that. I couldn't wait for the judge to pass sentence, and when he did and was told he'd be spending years in prison, I felt elated. That is, until he turned to me, with handcuffs on, and extended his hand. Tears were streaming down his face when he told me he was sorry. I stared into the man's eyes and knew he meant it. So I shook his hand and thanked him for his apology. But when he asked me to forgive him, I was shocked. His question hit me between the eyes. It was like he'd taken a sledge hammer and hit me. I didn't think I could, but I found myself saying 'Yes' before I'd even processed the question fully. And honestly, Terri, it felt good for me. But that's when he almost fell. They shoved a chair under him, and he sat there and cried. I truly believe he was sorry."

"Or maybe he was sorry he was going to prison, Tony."

"Maybe it was. Maybe it was both. But you didn't see his pleading eyes that day. You didn't hear his voice when he apologized. I truly believe he was sincere."

"Well, I'm happy for you, brother. But I'm not that forgiving. He took away something beautiful that night because he was selfish. Mark took away something beautiful from me because he is selfish. Everybody is selfish, only thinking of number one."

Tony had a sudden impulse to shove a mirror in front of her and scream the words, "Like leaving a child unsupervised and drinking a bottle of wine and taking valium with it?" But of course, he couldn't and wouldn't. He loved her too much to hurt her.

The wall phone rang. For half a second, Tony wished it was Alex calling with another interviewee scheduled. He enjoyed working on the book, but more so, he enjoyed being with Alex. When Terri didn't move, Tony stood and grabbed the receiver.

"Hello?" he said. "Oh hello, Mrs. Granville."

He turned to stare at Terri. Mrs. Granville had lived beside their parents for years. Terri appeared somewhat alarmed and shook her head back and forth, mouthing the words, "I'm not here."

"I'm sorry, Mrs. Granville. She's busy at the moment," Tony reluctantly lied. "Can I take a message or help you with something?"

Terri returned his blank stare.

"Yes. She wasn't feeling well. When I got home yesterday afternoon, she was already asleep." He paused to listen. "Sleeping pills? I don't know about them. I'm sure she forgot to drop them by after she went to the pharmacy for you. When we hang up, I'll remind her." He paused again. "Yes, Mrs. Granville. Thank you. Yes ma'am. You too. Yes ma'am. I won't forget."

He replaced the receiver. Terri watched as he wrinkled his forehead. Tony paused before he spoke.

"Terri, do you know anything about a bottle of sleeping pills Mrs. Granville's doctor prescribed for her? She said she called you day before yesterday and asked you to run to the pharmacy for several medications. She found all of them but the sleeping pills."

"Yes, she did call me. She had knee replacement surgery, so she needed someone to go by the drug store and to get some groceries. Her private nurse had the day off, but she needed some of the refills before her nurse returned the following day. Johnny and I picked up her prescriptions and went to the drug store for her. Then we went by the grocery store and bought the things on her list. When we took the pills and groceries by and put them away, she seemed satisfied. I didn't count the prescriptions or the bottles of medicine I got for her. We left, and I took Johnny to McDonald's for lunch."

"Well, she's missing a bottle of sleeping pills," he said.

"She must have misplaced them, or maybe her nurse did."

"She said they'd looked but couldn't find them anywhere. And the pharmacist has records of filling all of them."

"Then I can look in my car," Terri griped. "Maybe they rolled out of the bag. Tony, why don't you go look? You're acting like I took them or something."

He lowered his eyes to the floor. "No. I don't think you swiped them, Sis." Secretly, he prayed she hadn't.

He cleared his throat and drank the remains of his coffee. "I've got to get to Rutherfordton."

"Why in heaven's name are you going back there?"

"Alex and I have decided to collaborate on a writing project this summer. It's about the Hutchins's murders in 1979. Do you remember when a man shot the two sheriffs and the highway patrolman?"

"Yeah. I do. It was a horrible time."

"Well, I'm interviewing one of Hutchins's cousins today. Will you be okay? Do you need any help with Johnny?"

"I'm fine. Quit making a mountain out of a molehill, Tony. Johnny is fine. I'm his mother and quite capable of caring for him and myself. Go on. You're making me irritable."

Tony bent over and kissed his sister's wrinkled forehead. "Love you, Sis. See you later."

When he left Terri sitting at the kitchen table and staring into her empty cup, he shook off an uneasy feeling. He tiptoed down the hall to his nephew's room. He found the tyke curled up on his side with Big Bird tucked tightly to his chest. What a little angel he was. His long, dark lashes rested on his cheekbones. His breathing was deep and long, lost in innocent dreams. Tony longed to scoop his nephew into his arms and tell him everything was going to be okay, to promise him life would be good, and to assure him he'd always be there for him. He longed to believe these things for himself. But he had learned cruelly and painfully life wasn't a friend to promises and honored no guarantees.

Life plays two character roles: a friend and a foe.

Chapter Nineteen

The Gift of History

"Finally, brothers and sisters, whatever is true, whatever is noble, whatever is right, whatever is pure, whatever is lovely, whatever is admirable—if anything is excellent or praiseworthy—think about such things."
Philippians 4:8 (NIV)

TONY ADAMS / CHARLES LEFRERE

At 9:15 a.m., Tony was leafing through a stack of old newspaper articles at the Rutherfordton Town Library. That's when he glanced up and noticed a white-haired gentleman perusing the shelf of photography books. When their eyes occasionally met, each man politely nodded to the other. After this had happened a few times, the gentleman chuckled, shuffling toward Tony and extending his hand in a friendly gesture. The morning sun shone through the window behind him and seemed to dance off his broad shoulders, creating a halo-like effect.

As they shook hands, he said, "Hello. How are you?"

"Fine," Tony answered. "And you?"

"Fine. I'm Charles Lefrere. Have we met before?"

"No, sir. I don't think so. However, I did live here for a while when I was growing up about sixteen years ago or so. My father was a minister at one of the local churches. I'm Tony Adams."

"Ah, it's nice to meet you, Tony. So you don't live here now?"

"No sir. My father was called to another church, so my family moved to Charlotte. That is where I live now with my sister and nephew."

"Oh, I see. And is your father still at that church?" the kindly man asked, noticing the immediate grimace on Tony's face.

"Unfortunately, not. My parents were killed in an automobile accident several years ago."

"I'm sorry." Charles touched Tony's shoulder lightly. "I'm sure it's hard to lose your parents so tragically and at such a young age. After all, you're still a young man."

"Thanks, Mr. Lefrere. Sometimes I don't feel young, but I'm twenty-nine."

"Call me Charles."

"Lefrere. Is that Spanish or French?"

"French. My ancestors were mainly French. It means brother – literally, the brother. So then, what brings you back to our area?"

"Well, my friend, Alex, Alexandra, and I are both English instructors at a small college where we live. We both enjoy writing and are beginning a collaborative project – hopefully, a long essay or maybe even a book. We're beginning research on the Hutchins's murders that happened four years ago. Are you familiar with them?"

"Why, yes I am, Tony. I'm pretty familiar with the case. It was very unfortunate, very sad. It rocked the whole community when it happened. There's still a lot of anguish and animosity that prevails. My heart goes out to the families and all those who were involved in the tragedy."

"I know what you mean. Well, I'm interviewing one of Hutchins's cousins, Glenn, this morning. I'm supposed to be at his place around 10:00. I got in town early, so I decided to browse through some of the old newspapers they keep here."

"Good idea," Charles agreed. "I'm sure you'll find lots of information to shed some insight." He looked around the empty library except for the middle-aged librarian, who was busy at the desk. "Is your friend joining you?"

"No. Alex is spending the day with her mother – doing girl stuff, like lunch, nails, shopping, you know," he shrugged. "She'll be coming with me from now on though. I scheduled this interview at the last minute, so she already had plans made for today."

"I see. Well, I wish you lots of good fortune in gathering your information," he replied with a kindly smile.

"Hey, uh, Charles. Didn't you say you were familiar with the case?"

"Yes, Tony. I did. Actually, I'm well acquainted with Mr. Hutchins. I consider him a close friend."

"James Hutchins? You're kidding!" Tony wondered about his good fortune to run into a friend of Hutchins.

Lefrere frowned slightly in response to Tony's overt reaction. He leaned forward and locked his hands behind his back. He waited expectantly, patiently trying to understand Tony's exuberance.

"I meant, wow! Imagine running into you: a friend of Hutchins. What are the odds of this happening? Would you be willing to meet with Alex and me, say next Monday, here at the library – around 9:15? We'd love to 'pick your brains' if you've got the time."

"Sure. I don't see why not. I'm retired but still dabble a bit at my old occupation which was freelance photography. It's my hobby now and fills my time, but I think next Monday would work out fine. Yes, I'd be happy to meet with you and Alex here. Tell me, if I'm not being too presumptuous. Is she a *special* friend?"

Tony wasn't clear on what he was asking, so he repeated the question in his mind. The older man chuckled.

"Oh! Oh! Now I know what you mean!" Tony was blushing. "We went to school together – for our master's degrees in English. We had lots of classes together and became study partners. I think she's gorgeous, a little spoiled because she's an only child, but the most beautiful woman I've ever known."

"Hmmmm," Lefrere said with a smile. "And does she feel the same about you?"

Tony's shoulders drooped as he peered at the floor. "I don't think I have a chance. She's popular, her parents are wealthy, and she has lots of friends. I don't think she'd ever see me any other way than as a friend."

"You never know, young Tony. Follow your heart. It's the best road sign."

"Yes, sir. Well, then, Mr. Lefrere, I mean, Charles. I must go. Thanks so much. I don't want to be late for my interview. We'll see you here next Monday! Thanks and have a good day!"

The old gentleman chuckled again, nodding his head. They shook hands once more and bid their good-byes. Tony could hardly contain his excitement. He couldn't wait to drive back to Huntersville to tell Alex about meeting Charles Lefrere. Hopefully, he'd have even more to share with her after his interview with Glenn Hutchins.

Glenn Hutchins opened the front door of his home and invited Tony to come inside. After polite "small talk," Tony asked him to share whatever he would about James and the events of May 1979. Glenn, a first cousin of Hutchins, had retired in 1988, but he currently worked at a part-time job at the local community college.

"Uncle Lester and Aunt Lucy were James's parents. We all were raised by our parents who were sharecroppers on an old farm off I-40 between Marion and Asheville in the Rock Corner section. We grew wheat, cotton, and corn and had chickens, hogs, and cows. As Billy, my cousin, James's brother says, 'We didn't have too much money, but we never did go hungry. My momma always made pies and cakes. We were poor, but we had plenty to eat and enough clothes to wear.' I think the stress and strain of having to feed seven other mouths besides his own got to Uncle Lester, so he drank. My uncle was a good man. But if you got him mad, well, you had your hands full. And if he drank, back then, society turned its head the other way, accepting it was okay for him to clout Aunt Lucy or chase her with a gun."

"Now, our Grandpa Bryson Hutchins wasn't a tall man. He was about 5'5". You might think you were a bully until you met him," he chuckled. "He was as mean as a snake even though he never took a drink."

"We were a large family. My brothers and sisters were, well, let's see. First, there was Frances, me, Ray, Mary Sue, Amer, Arthur, Annie, Beverly, Joseph, Arnold, and Charles. And my mother will turn ninety this year. She lives in a rest home."

"Did James have siblings?" Tony asked.

"Yeah. Let me think. There was Lewis, then James, then Sarah May, Billy, Jolly, and finally Grady. That's all I can think of. They're scattered all around now."

"Tell me more about James." Tony was scribbling fast.

"Well, you can ask his brother, Billy. Billy tells everybody, 'James always liked guns, ever since he was a boy. He could shoot the head off a turtle or drive a ten penny nail into a tree with one bullet.'"

"No one was better than James, except me. I could outshoot James with a rifle," Glenn announced proudly with a faraway smile. "We'd line up matches on a fence, and we could shoot off fifteen out of sixteen of the match heads. As boys, we practiced shooting a lot with .22 rifles and shotguns. He kept those pistols in his overalls. He could drive a ten-penny nail into a tree with only one shot. I saw him do it many a time. Billy told me he had a gun rack with rifles and shotguns hanging over his bed. He said he used these for hunting and taking care of family problems."

"James was a good ol' boy and would give you the shirt off his back until you crossed him. When he had no money to buy Charlotte a prom dress, he sewed one himself. She wanted to be a cheerleader but couldn't afford a uniform, so James sewed her one. But if you made him mad, it was best to let him sit down and cool off. I've seen him tremble with anger. According to what I heard, he'd warned Huskey, 'If you ever set foot on my property, I'll kill ya.' Unfortunately, four or six months later, his promise came true."

Tony wrote as fast as he could to capture Glenn's recitation. He could tell this hadn't been the first time Glenn had shared his version of the story.

"Did he attend church, Mr. Hutchins?" Tony asked.

"You can call me Glenn. Well, let's see. The majority of the Hutchins were raised in the Baptist denomination. He attended church some in the little place where we were raised. But I think most recently he'd attended Wilson Baptist – don't quote me."

"Charlotte mixing up those drinks with vodka was bad" he said. "She was a minor. She had no business drinking at her age. James made a bad decision. On top of this, he left her with the bottle. They hadn't agreed on the amount to use, and then when she poured in the whole bottle, they began fussing. One thing led to another, and he started hitting them. Then she ran across the road and called the sheriff's department. And you know the rest."

"Rumor says Huskey told the other officers, 'I'll go up there and settle James down quick.'" Glenn paused. "Owen Messersmith and Roy Huskey were known to run around together. I believe in my heart if someone else had shown up, it wouldn't have happened."

Glenn paused again to collect his thoughts and change the subject.

"Now let me tell you one thing about James. He could walk around all over those woods, and you couldn't hear him. He stepped over several deputies that night, and they didn't even know it. James could have easily killed two or three of those deputies that night, and they wouldn't even have expected it."

He continued, "Grady and Billy were at the command post during the night. According to them, the prevalent attitude was they didn't want him brought out alive. I don't know if they were scared of him. They definitely were not on his side."

Glenn stared into Tony's eyes, pausing before he began talking again. He said sadly, "Pete Peterson was a good friend of mine." He lowered his gaze to the floor. "He was a good ol' boy and a good highway patrolman. He was well-liked around the community. I told James, 'If you hadn't killed that man, I'd have tried to help you get out of this.' I don't know if he [James] even knew him [Peterson]."

"I told James, 'You're gone,' and he said, 'I know it.' James was hurt about what he'd done after he came to his senses. He knew he was a goner. After the trial, he said, 'I'm gone; I didn't have a chance over there.'"

After Glenn stopped talking, Tony probed further. "Can you tell me about any other troubles he had."

"They say he shot a truck-driver near Gallup, New Mexico, while he was in the service. He had been an Air Force policeman in Las Vegas but decided he was going home to see his family. He began hitch-hiking, and a driver picked him up. He claims the driver tried to rob him, so he shot him. He told police he wrapped the body in a blanket and left him under a bridge."

"Didn't I read something about his first wife, Vandora?" Tony asked.

"Well, first of all, his first wife, Vandora, is dead. But James had been drinking some and ended up shooting her second husband, Junior Crane, five times in the stomach. Now Junior is a big ol' boy - about 6'2' and weighs around 220 or 225." He stopped talking and allowed Tony time to write.

"How big is James Hutchins?" Tony asked.

"About 5'11 and slender."

Tony continued. "The papers say Mr. Crain survived the blasts, and as a result, Hutchins spent eight months in jail. He also paid a $200 fine."

"Yes. That's all correct."

"Mr. Hutchins, I mean, Glenn, they say he could shoot the ashes off a cigarette without damaging the cigarette. If he'd wanted to kill Junior Crain, he could have, right?"

He smiled.

"Maybe, it was an act of restraint," Tony added.

There was no comment.

"When Vandora and James were married, he was stationed out West. She decided to go visit him, but she knew James had a terrible temper if he got to drinking. Vandora thought he was sweet when he wasn't drinking. Otherwise, she was terrified of him. So she invited her sister to go with her. When they arrived at the hotel where he was waiting, he pulled her down onto his lap and seemed genuinely glad she was there. But after a while, she saw a change come over his face, and he started strangling her. That's when her sister jumped on him and started dragging him backward."

"Some say his own family didn't approve of him and didn't have a great deal to do with him. Is this true?" Tony asked.

"That's what some say," Glenn replied, squinting into the afternoon sun.

Chapter Twenty

The Gift of Compassion

"Bear one another's burdens and so fulfill the law of Christ."

Galatians 6:2 (NIV)

ALEX WELLS / TONY ADAMS

When Tony arrived at Alex's hotel, he could hardly contain his excitement. Alex finally answered the door after his fourth knock. Even in the dark afternoon light, she looked terrible. Her eyes and nose were red and swollen, and her dark hair was a mess.

"Harp, are you okay?" he'd asked with noticeable concern.

"Oh, hey, Tony. Come in." She stood to the side, so he could pass.

He was disappointed she hadn't called him by his pseudo name, Truman.

"I really don't feel like working on the book, if this is why you're here," she warned. "I'm not feeling so, uh, good."

"Are you sick? Is there something I can get for you? Do you need anything?" Tony asked.

"No, I'm not sick, but thanks. I have everything I need."

"I did come by to tell you about this man I met in the library. He has first-hand knowledge about the case we can use for our book."

"That's good! But can we talk about it tomorrow?" Alex managed a smile.

Maddie, Alex's silver Yorkie ran to Tony with a toy in her mouth. She wanted to play fetch. Tony bent to pat her. "Hey Maddie. What'cha got there? Looks like your stuffed frog has seen better days."

He tugged it from her clinched teeth and tossed it. The dog bounded across the room, gathered the toy, and returned. Tony tossed the toy once again, then he turned to Alex. "Where's Abbie?"

"She's at the Vet's for the night. She got spayed today, so they're keeping her overnight. I can get her tomorrow around noon."

"Is this why you've been crying? Is she okay?"

"No. Abbie is fine. She's a little trooper – not afraid of anything. She'll be fine."

Tony shifted his feet uneasily.

"Want to sit down?" Alex asked reluctantly. She preferred to be alone.

"Sure!" Tony plopped down on the orange sofa. He was glad she'd asked him to stay.

"Want a soda?"

"No, thanks. Well, yeah, I'll take one. I didn't stop on the way back from Rutherfordton, so I am a little thirsty."

Less than a minute later, Alex returned with a glass of ice and handed him a bottle. "Here you are."

Tony poured the liquid into the glass and took a long gulp.

"You were thirsty."

"I guess I was." He stared into the glass before probing. "Alex, tell me what's wrong. Maybe I can help. I'm a good listener."

That was the final crack that broke her dam of pent-up tears. She buried her head in a green throw pillow and cried forever, it seemed. Feeling ill at ease and awkward, Tony sat silently, wishing he could leave, until her sobs waned. He longed to hug her, but he didn't want to cross the thin line of friendship and set up a barrier that would damage their collaboration. At last, she lifted her wet face and tried to smile.

"I'm sorry, Tony. I didn't mean to do that, but I couldn't help it."

"It's okay, Alex. I didn't mean to intrude," he apologized.

"Oh,Tony!" She slid closer to him and rested her head on his shoulder. "My heart is broken in two, and my father is the one who broke it."

The phone rang, but Alex didn't answer it. After it rang ten times, it stopped. Then it began ringing again.

"Alex, hadn't you better answer your phone? It might be important."

She trembled. "I can't answer it. I don't want to talk to anyone."

"Do you want me to answer it for you? I'll tell them you're busy or not here."

"No. I'll call the front desk and ask them to hold my calls," which she did.

Afterward, Maddie jumped up on the sofa and laid between them. When she rolled onto her back, Tony stroked the dog's stomach. "Do you want to talk about it? Do you want to tell me what your father did?"

"Oh Tony!" she began crying again, so he endured the discomfort once more.

Alex dabbed her eyes with a clump of wet tissues and blew her nose loudly.

"I'm sorry, Tony. My father, uh, my father is having an affair with his next door neighbor -- sleazy Mrs. Walters. I never liked her from the start. She's a widow and apparently after my father."

"How do you know?" he asked in disbelief. Tony liked Rob a lot and always marveled at how happy he and Betsy seemed. He thought they had the "model marriage" and thought Alex was lucky to have come from a home with so much love and devotion for each other.

"Mama and I had lunch at the cute little restaurant I've taken you to. You know, Café 100. I had my usual and Mama wanted something different. Well, anyway, I was taking lunch to Daddy, something Mama asked me to do because she was worried he wouldn't eat anything for lunch. He was working from home today. She says he's been doing it a lot. Now I know why. Her women's club meeting was today, and since she hadn't bought groceries this week, she asked me to get him a take out. She paid for it. I drove to the house, singing to the radio. I had the tops off because it was such a wonderful spring day."

Tony thought, *I hope her writing and organizational skills are better than her oratory skills. This story is hard to follow.*

"Well, anyway, when I walked in, uh uh, walked in to my parent's house, I thought it was strange the television wasn't on, even though I'd heard voices and thought it was, but he wasn't in the den where he normally worked. Instead, I heard laughter coming from the kitchen and assumed he was watching television in there. When I walked in, I found them together in the kitchen. They didn't even notice I was there. She was backed up against the refrigerator, and Daddy had his hands on her hips. It made me sick to see the way she was looking at him. And on top of this, she had her arms around his neck. I think they were getting ready to kiss."

"Whew!" Tony whistled. "That's bad. What did you do?"

"I was so shocked, I fell to the floor and started screaming at them. I have no idea what I said, but I got out of there quickly. He ran after me and was standing at the door when I left, but I didn't look back. I never want to see him again for the rest of my life. How could he hurt my mother this way? How could he do this to us?"

"Does Betsy know?" he asked.

"Poor Mama. My poor mama. It will break her heart."

"So I discern from your answer Betsy doesn't know – yet."

"I won't tell her. It would break her heart into little pieces. She loves my father so much. I thought he loved her, too. Was I wrong! I wonder if Mrs. Walters is his first. I thought he was beyond reproach. I can't believe my father would do this. I didn't think my father was like other men. I guess all men are cold and calculated liars who can't be trusted."

Tony shifted positions on the couch, moving slightly away from Alex.

"Anyway, what could I do afterward? I didn't want to see my mother because she'd know I'd been crying. I've cried all afternoon. Especially, when he came knocking at my door."

"He came here?" Tony asked.

"Yes, but of course I didn't answer the door. I called the front desk and asked them to have him leave. Before they came, he whispered outside the door, 'Alex, I'm so sorry. Believe me. I'm sorry. I need you to forgive me, honey. Nothing happened. I promise. And nothing ever will. Please forgive me. I love you, honey. I love you, and I love your mother. I'm sorry.' I heard the front desk clerk when she came and escorted him away."

"Then maybe nothing did happen, Alex. Maybe you prevented it from happening."

"I hope so. But it doesn't make it any better. I don't know whether to believe him or not. How can I trust him after this? How can Mama ever trust him again?"

"Maybe she'll never find out."

"And is this supposed to make it better? So I called and cancelled my facial. I'd been looking forward to it all week long. I told the receptionist to tell Jennifer, the aesthetician, to tell Mama I had menstrual cramps and needed to reschedule it for another day. I'd come to the hotel to rest."

Tony cleared his throat. He felt ill at ease whenever he saw his sister's box of tampons or pads under the hall bathroom's cabinet whenever he volunteered to give Johnny a bath and had to search for the bubble bath. Women's things made him uneasy. "Will she believe the excuse?"

"Of course. All women use it as an excuse when they don't want to face something."

"Do you?" Tony asked. He was trying to be a good friend and respond the way a girlfriend might.

"Do I what?" Alex asked irritably.

"Do you have, uh, menstrual cramps?" As soon as the last word left his lips, he regretted it.

"No. Fortunately, I don't have to endure that, too – at least not right now."

"Oh," he felt inadequate to say more.

She paced the room and slumped into the nearest chair. "Anyway, I can't let my mother's heart be broken. And I don't want to be around him, so we need to get really busy researching and interviewing people. I want my calendar to be booked so that I'm never here when the phone rings or when they knock at my door."

"Don't you think your mother will figure out something is wrong? As close as the three of you are, she'll know something's up if you don't visit them."

Standing suddenly, she walked to the nearest end-table and turned on the lamp.

"Well, I'll figure out how to handle Mama. I don't want to hurt her too." She began pacing again.

"Do you think he'll confess?" Tony busied himself by scratching the dog's stomach.

"He should, but I doubt it. If we were married, and you did something like this, would you confess to me?" Alex's hands were on her hips; she leaned forward. She looked like a drill sergeant.

Tony stopped rubbing and stared blankly at Alex. He wondered why she'd used them as an example. Was there hope? But his pause had been interpreted as a different meaning to her.

"I'll answer it for you," Alex stated matter-of-factly. "Of course you wouldn't. You're one of them."

Chapter Twenty One

The Gift of Memories

"I can only note that the past is beautiful because one never realizes an emotion at the time. It expands later, and thus we don't have complete emotions about the present, only about the past."

Virginia Woolf

ALEX WELLS / TONY ADAMS

Alex and Tony sat on one side of the library table across from their new friend and newly discovered walking encyclopedia, Charles Lefrere. In the few hours, they'd talked with him, Alex had developed an insatiable crush on the debonair fifty-five year-old, whom she found exciting and intriguing. This was the gentleman Tony had met the week before when her world had come crashing down. She pushed those memories and heartaches aside to focus on Lefrere. Their shared goal for today was to "pick Lefrere's brain" of facts and details surrounding his friend, Hutchins, and the murders of 1979. But Alex was content hearing about all his travels to Greece and winters in Switzerland. She loved his poetic way of describing the Vikos Gorge with its steep rocky slopes and medicinal herbs. She could almost picture the rare flowers growing along the banks of the Voidomatis River. Charles's narration about Switzerland was illustrative and descriptive. He made it come alive, so much so she visualized the panoramic view of Lake Lucerne and its snow-capped mountains as he had. He talked about mulling through the various watch and souvenir shops alongside the quaint, picturesque lake.

This freelance photographer had come to Rutherford County in the early '70s. His magazine had assigned him to capture the region's landscape and features. He was instantly infatuated with the natural beauty of the rolling hills, the quaintness of the towns, the beautiful simplicity of the pastoral scenes, and the genuine friendliness of the people. "I loved the 'small town friendly' feeling the people embraced." So, the confirmed bachelor had fallen in love and decided to put down roots in the county. A few years later, he'd met the guarded James Hutchins and became one of his few friends and confidants.

Finally! He's getting around to Hutchins, Tony thought. While he enjoyed Lefrere's adventures and found them fascinating, he preferred hearing more about Hutchins and May 1979, which was the reason why they were here in the first place. It seemed Alex had somehow forgotten. He watched her face; she was completely mesmerized by the older man and wore a weird-looking grin on her face while Lefrere babbled about all of his travels to Europe and Asia. As if Charles could read Tony's mind, he changed subjects.

"Well, we're not here to talk about me. You folks need my help for your research. So you're hoping to make this into some sort of book?"

"Yes," Tony eagerly answered. "We're thinking a true crime book or story – depending on how much material we gather. Also, we haven't decided on a perspective or what our purpose may be, but we can decide as we go along or after our research is over."

"It sounds fascinating. Sort of like how I tell a story with my pictures. I'm not always sure what the object or the theme will be until I come upon it."

"That's what I'm thinking," Tony agreed.

"Tell us what you know, Mr. Lefrere," Alex said with a smile.

"Call me Charles, please." He returned her smile.

"One cloudy Saturday morning in the fall of 1977, I was meandering along a lonely path in the woods. Surely it had been trampled along by deer and other indigenous wildlife over the years. That's when I heard gunshots. And crazy me, I dismissed any danger befalling me and headed in the direction of the blasts. As I got closer, I began calling, 'Hello! Hello!' I didn't see anyone at first until I felt the hair stand on the back of my neck. That's when I discovered a leery James Hutchins within six feet of where I stood. I hadn't heard him approach but realized he'd been target practicing until I'd interrupted his momentum with my calls. Once I introduced myself, and we chatted for a few minutes about the weather and such, he seemed to relax. After a while, he expressed curiosity about my camera bag and equipment I was carrying. Of course, I was pleased to show him my camera and explain the different lenses and filters I used. He mentioned his son was hoping to get a camera for Christmas, but he didn't think he could afford it since he'd been out of work for a while."

"When our conversation began to lag, as he seemed to grow quiet -- a man of few words, I mentioned I'd decided to return early the next morning to take some sunrise shots. His short answer was we'd probably run across each other again in the future. And we did the next day. But this time, he reciprocated his interests by showing me his rifle and two .44 Magnums he had concealed in his overalls. After he explained the different calibers and showed me how to load the rifle and the handguns, he displayed quite a feat of shooting expertise. I quickly realized how skillful and steady his aim was. To my amazement, he drove a ten penny nail into a tree with one bullet."

"So you saw him do it!" Tony almost leaped off his chair. "Alex said I was exaggerating, or Glenn was not telling the truth."

"No. It was no exaggeration. I saw it with my own eyes. He even offered me his pistol so I could try, but I declined. I'd never held a pistol before, and I didn't want him to discover how incompetent I was. I probably couldn't have hit the tree, and it was a huge poplar with a wide girth." He laughed.

"He had been in trouble before," Tony added. "Did he share any of this with you?"

"Yes. Over the days and months, we began meeting up at different places in the woods – him hunting or target shooting, with me taking pictures. And there were times when I secretly hoped for our paths to cross. I'd watch him target practice, and then he'd hike along silently while I took pictures. Strangely, looking back on it these days, it was as if he were protecting me. After a few of these meetings, he began to confide in me, telling me about his life."

"James said when he was twenty-five, he joined the Air Force during the Korean War under a special program and was trained as a rifleman. By April 1954, he and his first wife were having problems. She was pregnant with their second child. He became homesick and wanted to go home and straighten things out. Unfortunately, he'd gone AWOL. While he was hitch-hiking through New Mexico, a truck-driver picked him up. According to James, the man allowed him to drive the truck so he could get some sleep. Afterward, James said the truck driver tried to rob him and threatened to kill him, so out of self-defense, he shot and killed the man. Panicked, he wrapped him in a blanket from the sleeper compartment and placed the body under a bridge. An Oklahoma trooper pulled him over for speeding and arrested him when he noticed there were bloodstains on the front seat. He was charged with first degree murder, but the charge was dropped to voluntary manslaughter later because of insufficient evidence. Vandora, his first wife, sold their stove so she could go to the trial. He was convicted and served four years in a New Mexico prison. A psychiatric report would later say the time Hutchins served in prison warped his mind. They returned him to military custody and discharged him for bad conduct."

"Wait a minute! Tell me again what he was driving," Alex asked. "I'm sorry to ask."

"He was driving the dead man's truck," Charles answered. "He claims the man asked him to drive, so he could sleep. James had agreed and probably welcomed the quietness – not having to carry on a conversation. After all, every mile was bringing him closer to his home in North Carolina."

"I'm sorry I asked. What a dimwit!" she said. Tony frowned and shook his head.

"Supposedly, the truck driver woke up and had concocted a plan to rob James. And he threatened to kill James. So James ascertained this was self-defense; it was either the truck driver or him."

"I've gathered some more information from the articles in newspapers. According to a friend who grew up next to Hutchins, he was quiet and a loner, who preferred going hunting instead of going to school. And his brother said he was always 'high-tempered.'

"But tell us more about Endora," Alex requested.

"You mean Vandora, Alex," Charles chided.

"Yeah," Tony agreed. "Glenn gave me a little information. Did they divorce?"

"Yes," Charles said. "By the time he'd served his time, she'd divorced him, sometime around 1959 I think. She's described by many who knew her as being a good, hardworking woman who lived a hard life. In December of 1966, James was charged with assault and battery with the intent to kill for attacking her husband."

"Junior, uh, somebody, right?" Tony asked.

"Yes. Junior Crain. You've been doing your homework, Tony," Charles replied.

Tony gave a quick smile and grew serious again. "Didn't he shoot him five times in the stomach?"

Alex gasped. "What?"

"Yes, with a .22. But the man survived," Charles reassured her. "James was mad because he didn't like the way Junior was disciplining James's and Vandora's two older children – Shirley Jean and James, Jr."

"I didn't understand this part," Tony stated. "So did he have two other children with Vandora?"

"Yes. They were his two older children – Shirley Jean born in 1952 and James William, Jr. born in 1954. Then, as you already know, he had three younger children with Geneva. He met Alice Geneva Murphy in August of 1959, and they were married two months later when she was eighteen years-old. Shirley would have been around twenty-seven and James William, Jr. would have been around twenty-five when the murders happened."

"Right!" Tony alternated between writing and flipping pages. "According to public records, Charlotte Iona was born in 1961. James Vance (Jamie) was born in 1963. Lisa Ann was born in 1965."

Alex was having difficulty digesting the story and whistled loudly, "What a winner! Oh my, gosh, Tony! What have you gotten us into? This guy is a looney. This man's a murderer who deserves to die."

"Wasn't he also charged with shooting an unarmed man after that?" Tony asked.

"Yes. But I believe those charges were later dropped. And there were other skirmishes with the law, things like driving under the influence, driving with no inspection, traffic violations, assault, driving with a suspended license, and driving with an improper registration. Even though some may think of James as being simple, I believe he is a very complicated man. Sadly, he was unmistakably guilty of many things."

"You can say that again," Alex moaned. "I think we need to forget about...."

"Allow me to continue, Alex," Charles interrupted. "James was never proud of anything he did. It took a long time for me to gain his trust and for him to open up. This man is a very personal man – he never liked the limelight. He wasn't a bragger. He basically demeaned himself and his past. He carried around a lot of shame."

"But Charles, if he didn't like the limelight, all of his wrongdoings did – they placed him in the limelight over and over again," Tony added.

"I agree, Tony. That's an interesting point." When Charles nodded, a tuft of white hair fell across his brows. Alex thought it softened his forehead and made him look younger. "You could compare it to a troublesome child who, in the end, misbehaves to gain his parents' attention. That's how you could equate it."

"We do know from Glenn, his cousin, that James's childhood was less than savory with his drunken father chasing his mother around the house with a gun."

"What? How sad!" Alex exclaimed.

"Yes indeed." Charles cautioned them. "Now, some of this came out at the trial. Please don't misunderstand. In no way am I making excuses for James's actions or behavior, but I think you should know this. When James joined the service, he read like a third grader. His intelligence quotient was 88, equivalent to that of a twelve or thirteen year-old. A psychiatrist testified at his trial that James thought people persecuted him. Perhaps this is a result of the relationship he'd had with his father. He compared himself unfavorably with others, feeling inferior and inadequate. Again, this was probably reminiscent of his childhood. Obviously, he had no self-esteem – rebuking himself afterward for his actions. A psychiatric report diagnosed him as a 'paranoid psychotic' who could function well in his family and at work, 'but he suffered delusions about law enforcement officers – especially when drinking.'"

"But never making better judgements before committing his actions," Alex added. "It's like he didn't learn from his unsavory behavior. It's like he didn't mind spending time in jail and prison. He kept on getting in trouble with other crimes and misdemeanors. Sort of like he was above the law and dared to be caught. A prime example is buying liquor for his minor daughter on her graduation night. That's against the law. And then he'd agreed to let her serve it to other minors. That's against the law. I call this being defiant."

"We know he was pretty decent until he started drinking," Tony inserted. "One of his managers said he was a good worker, a hard worker. He remembered Hutchins as being quiet, but he never noticed anything wrong with him."

"Right, so if Hutchins knew it made him bad, why did he keep on drinking?" Alex asked.

"Maybe drinking was his only way of escape; a way of not being caught up in the stress and emotions of everyday life. A way of not feeling," Tony added. "I'm no psychologist, but it was obvious he had an addiction problem." Tony suddenly thought of Terri.

"Alcohol made him stronger, sort of like giving him a backbone," Alex suggested. "But it's like he'd get all wrapped up in destructive emotions that obscured reality. He lost any sense of reasoning, and didn't understand why he had to pay the consequences."

"Maybe because emotions were already high that day, like being happy to have the day off, being proud his daughter was graduating, and wanting to celebrate with his family, Charlotte triggered the negativity by becoming defiant and verbally combative about the punch. When she kept talking back to him, her insolence along with the beers bolstered his rage. I can imagine his feelings were hurt after all he'd tried to do for her to make it a special day – allowing a party, driving to Chesnee, and taking the day off from work. To him, she was being unappreciative and spoiled," Tony offered.

"Yeah, so he *reacted* to all the environmental stimuli and became irrational," Alex said.

"That was his modus operandi. His bad temper never allowed him to pause and reason before reacting," Tony agreed. "He'd always felt like the only justice he could count on was *vigilante* justice."

"Imagine if everyone felt this way," Alex sighed. "There'd be no need for law enforcement. We'd all be carrying guns and having gunfights in the *OK Corral*."

They were silent, lost in their own thoughts for a few minutes before Tony spoke again. "He was a man who struggled all of his life. He struggled internally with his drinking, his violence, and the aftermath his impulsive behavior left behind. And he struggled externally by always battling to stay free, to escape, to search for a meaningful life. And he struggled to keep from being executed."

Charles had been listening to their speculative banter. He added, "This is interesting. Another window into who James was is how his wife, Geneva, described him. She said he was the kind of man who thought whatever belonged to him was his to do with as he pleased."

"Wait a minute. I have her quote somewhere in my notes," Tony inserted as he flipped through his legal pad. "I found it in several newspaper articles. Here it is. Geneva said, 'My husband was the kind of man who thought that what was his, was his – and he could do anything he wanted with it. If he wanted to beat his wife, that was his business. Nobody had the right to interfere with that. When those lawmen came up there, to him they were trespassing. It was his house and his business."

"Wow!" Alex groaned. "She sounds like a blast from the past. Do women really think this is acceptable nowadays?"

Neither man answered.

"Well, I can tell you this. I do not belong to anyone but me, and I'm not marrying any man who thinks I'm his property, and he can do whatever he pleases with me. No sir."

Charles cut his eyes in Tony's direction and smiled when he met Tony's wide eyes. Tony changed the subject.

"Here are some notes about what you said earlier. They married in 1959 when she was eighteen, and he was thirty. Wow! That's a big age difference."

"Yes, I think it's correct. One person described Geneva as being 'one of the finest people I have ever met.' Others described her as 'sweet, soft-spoken, and someone who believed in prayer."'

"I'd say!" Alex interrupted. "No doubt those prayers are how she survived being married to him all those years."

"Another couple is quoted as saying they were neighbors when the Hutchins used to live in Forest City. He supposedly never left the house alone, and he kept a tight rein on his children. These people were fond of the family. They went on to say he helped his wife with domestic chores and often helped an elderly couple who lived next door. The woman is quoted in the newspaper as saying, 'James, I think, had a lot of good in him as well as the bad. Everyone has good in them if you look for it.' The woman admitted she knew he drank and Geneva wasn't happy about it and knew she couldn't do anything about it, but she said when he did drink, he stayed home. All Geneva wanted was a happy, decent home to raise their children. So when he drank, they tried to stay out of his way."

"Here's something I found in a local newspaper this morning," Alex added. "His brother, Billy, was quoted as saying 'his brother was an alcoholic. On pay nights he'd get him a fifth and that would last him the whole weekend. Maybe sometimes he'd get two fifths. He preferred beer and Country Gentleman bourbon.' And another neighbor described the children as being well behaved."

"Interesting," Charles said thoughtfully. "Well," Charles said, standing, "I need to leave."

Alex jumped at the chance to give her newest hero a big hug. Tony shook Charles's hand. "Thanks for your time, Charles. We enjoyed learning more about Hutchins through your eyes. He's becoming a real person to me now."

"How do you mean?" Charles asked curiously.

"We all have our demons, I guess. We're all less than perfect in our own way. Some of us have a better foundation than others to build upon. I don't know. I'm sorting out all of this in my mind."

"I agree, young man," Charles chuckled and clapped him on the back. "But in the end, it's all about the choices we make. Have a productive day, drive safely, and may God bless you both!"

"And may God bless you, too!" Tony called after his back, which was disappearing behind the closed door into the sunlight.

"He already has," Charles called.

The librarian stared at them.

Alex put her fingers to her lips and apologized, "We're sorry. We'll be quiet." Then she turned to Tony, shrugging her shoulders and raising her eyebrows. "Is he getting all religious on us?"

"Don't think so; I think he always has been."

Chapter Twenty Two

The Gift of Weaknesses

"That is why, for Christ's sake, I delight in weaknesses, in insults, in hardships, in persecutions, in difficulties. For when I am weak, then I am strong."
2 Corinthians 12:10 (NIV)

TONY ADAMS

He couldn't unlock the door fast enough. Johnny's cries were piercing. "Mommy! Mommy!" he wailed.

Tony slammed the door open, banging the wall, and ran straight in the direction of his nephew's voice. When he entered the bathroom, he saw naked little Johnny sitting in the middle of the tiled floor. Blood streamed from his chin down his chest and onto his legs and floor.

"Unky Tony! Unky Tony! It hurts!" Hurriedly, Tony scooped the tiny boy in his arms, and grabbed a nearby towel to stop the bleeding, which seemed to be coming from a gaping cut under his chin. Tony sat on the edge of the tub and hugged his nephew tightly to his chest. He made a rocking motion until the crying stopped.

"Hey fellow, what happened?"

Tony peered around, taking in the scene. Obviously, he deduced, Johnny had tried to draw his own bath as water filled the tub half-way. *Too deep!* He thought. Tony reached down and dipped his finger into the water to test the temperature; it was really hot. *I thought I'd told the maintenance man to lower the thermostat on the water heater. If he'd gotten into this water, he'd have been burned badly. Thankfully, he'd traded a bad burn for a busted chin. I'm sure this will require stitches.* He saw a trail of blood leading from the edge of the tub into the bath water.

"Let's get you dressed. Here, hold the towel to your chin while I go and get you some clean clothes."

Toys were strewn all over the floor, and the bed wasn't made. A half-eaten pop-tart and an empty glass of milk was on his *Star Wars* table. His clothing drawers were almost empty. Evidently, his sister had not had time to wash clothes or make the bed or feed her son or bathe him. *Speaking of Terri, where is she? I'm sure she's in the same place she usually is.* He found one clean shirt and a pair of jeans. Tony scrounged around until he located a pair of matching socks. There wasn't an undershirt. Luckily, there was a clean pair of Darth Vader briefs. When he returned to the bathroom, Johnny was still standing in the spot where he'd left him. Big Bird was lying on the floor beside the toilet. Fortunately, he wasn't blood stained. Johnny would want to take him along to the hospital.

After Tony dressed his nephew, he lifted him into his arms and stuffed a clean towel under his chin. The bleeding had slowed, but as he'd already surmised, the gash was gaping open, so he'd definitely need stitches. We need to go see the doctor, okay?"

Johnny's bottom lip poked out and quivered. His dark eyes swam in drowning tears. He began to cry. "Don't wa...want...to...to...see ...doctor."

"Hey, I need you to be a brave boy, okay? Can you do this for me?"

He whimpered.

"Want Big Bird to go?" Tony asked.

Johnny nodded.

"Okay, buddy. He's going with you to see the doctor. I'll be there, too. I won't leave you."

Johnny sniffled. Tony kissed his forehead.

"Afterward, we'll go to McDonalds and get some supper. Will that be okay?"

"Chik-en nuggets?"

"Yeah. You can have all the chicken nuggets you want. We'll even have an ice cream sundae, too. Does this sound good?"

"Uh huh." Johnny nodded.

As he walked out of the bathroom, he stood beside his sister, who was curled on her side and sound asleep on the sofa. An empty bottle of cough syrup was stuck to the end table where the remains had dripped. Half a bottle of chardonnay and an empty glass stood beside it. Then there was the familiar medicine bottle he hated: Valium. How was she getting so many bottles of Valium? Obviously, she'd slept through the crisis.

Not any longer, Sis. Tony thought. *Not any longer. This baby isn't going to be neglected. I hope you're awake and sober when I get home. We're going to have a heart-to-heart talk.*

Terri watched from the doorway as Tony covered her son with a sheet and *Star Wars* spread. He bent down and kissed his head and ran his fingers through his hair. Tucked closely under his bandaged chin was Big Bird, his faithful companion.

Thank God for Big Bird, Tony thought.

The Emergency Room doctor had pretended to stitch up the stuffed animal's chin. That had fascinated Johnny and made him more receptive to having his own chin sutured. When the doctor began, and Tony saw the needle, he felt queasy. All the blood figuratively ran from the top of his head and pooled at his feet. A sympathetic nurse guided him to a nearby chair and instructed him to put his head down while she held the little boy's hand. In the end, Johnny had every reason to cry, but he'd been brave, and only cried a little in the beginning. The nurse and doctor had kept him busy by asking lots of questions about Big Bird.

Afterward, Tony was encouraged by his appetite. He'd eaten his favorite meal of fries and chicken nuggets. And he'd been allowed to have a soda and chose both an apple pie and a chocolate sundae. He certainly deserved it.

"Don't you want to kiss your son goodnight?" Tony turned to his sister and asked.

"Of course I do." She stumbled over to the bed and awkwardly knelt to kiss her son's forehead. "I love you, Baby. Mommy loves you."

As Tony closed Johnny's bedroom door, Terri headed toward her bedroom.

"Oh no!" Tony cried. "We're talking, Terri. And we're talking tonight before either of us goes to bed. If it takes all night, we're going to get some things resolved."

"You sound angry."

"I am angry, Terri. I think I have a right to be."

"Well, I'm sleepy, Tony. I'm not in the mood. I don't feel well."

"Of course you're sleepy and don't feel well, Terri. You're high off of cough syrup and half a bottle of wine. And who knows how many Valium you've taken today. You didn't even hear your son screaming."

"I doubt he was screaming," she slurred.

Stay in control. Stay calm, he told himself. Tony lowered his voice. "Terri, we have to do something for Johnny's sake. What happened tonight is as much my fault as it's yours."

"How can it be your fault?" she asked.

"Because I haven't done everything possible to protect Johnny. I haven't done everything I need to do for you. You're my sister, and I don't want anything to happen to you. After tonight, things are changing around here. I'm taking control."

"How? What do you mean by that?"

"I'm putting my foot down. I'm enrolling Johnny in daycare tomorrow, and I'll pay for it. And you're going to see a doctor. You're depressed and medicating yourself with any and all medications you can get your hands on – prescribed or over the counter. On top of this, you're drinking way too much."

"You saw I only had cough syrup. I didn't take too many Valium, and there is half a bottle of wine left. Go look if you don't believe me."

"Sis, I know you better than you know yourself. Remember? We're twins. You drank a whole bottle of cough syrup; I purchased it yesterday for my cough. I hadn't even opened it. And you drank a bottle and a half of wine. You're getting sloppy with your hiding places. I found the empty bottle stuffed under the trash bag in the bin. So there is no need to lie to me."

"Tony, please leave me alone. I can't talk now. I'm too tired. I'm going to bed."

"Okay. That's fine, Sis. But tomorrow morning, I'm going to enroll Johnny in the church daycare. I'm calling my medical doctor to schedule an appointment for you."

"Whatever. We'll see," she said turning on her heels.

"Yeah, we'll see. And if you don't get help, I'm calling Mark. Johnny is his son, too."

She whirled around on her bare heels and screamed at the top of her lungs. "No you're not calling Mark! He walked out on both of us. He doesn't care about his son or me. Leave me alone."

"I love you, Terri. You're my sister, but you need help, and this time, you're not going to talk me out of it. You've got to get your life together. Get a job. Take care of your son. Find another man to love."

"I don't want another man! Men only cause pain!"

Hmmmm. He thought. *Where have I heard those remarks lately? We must be a terrible species.*

She slumped to the floor and buried her head in her arms. "Tony!" she sobbed. "Tony, help me! I don't know what to do. It's easier to sleep my life away than it is to face every day. I have nobody!"

"That's not true, Sis. You have me, and most of all, you have a little boy who loves his mother. You would have been so proud of him tonight, Terri. He got four stitches, and he hardly cried. He's a little trooper. Precocious – so smart. So smart he scares me. He was trying to run his own bath before he banged his chin. The water was too hot, Sis. Thank God he fell and banged his chin, or he could have had serious burns on his feet and legs."

"Mommy!" Johnny had gotten out of bed and ran to his mother and crawled into her lap. Tony adored the pitter-patter of his bare little feet on the hardwood floor. "Mommy. Why are you crying? Are you sad? Are you sad at me?"

"I'm okay, Johnny. Mommy's okay. Mommy's not sad and definitely not 'sad at you'" Terri smiled. She stroked his dark hair. "Mommy is so sorry you got hurt. It's my fault you were hurt, and I'm so sorry. I'm so sorry." She rocked him in her arms. "Mommy is going to get better, I promise. Okay?"

"Okay," he whispered and kissed her wet cheeks.

"Let's get you back into bed," Tony suggested, while reaching for him.

"Goodnight, Baby Boy," Terri cooed. "Mommy loves you."

"Love you too." Johnny waved goodnight as he and Tony disappeared.

Terri knew she needed help, but now was not the time to discuss it. Between now and tomorrow morning, she'd have to figure out some way of delaying Tony's plans for her.

Chapter Twenty Three

The Act of Struggling

"I urge you, brothers and sisters, by our Lord Jesus Christ and by the love of the Spirit, to join me in my struggle by praying to God for me."

Romans 15:30 (NIV)

ALEX WELLS / TONY ADAMS

Somewhere in the distance, Tony heard a loud, irritating sound. In his deep sleep, he reached for the alarm clock and slammed his palm on the buzzer. But it kept on – an irritating clanging sound. He opened his eyes, realizing it was the telephone. He reached for the receiver. "Hello?" he yawned.

"Tony? It's Alex. Are you busy?"

"Not at the moment. What time is it?" he said sitting up quickly.

"9:15. Why? Did I wake you?"

"Well – uh – yeah. Did you say 9:15?" he asked while jumping to his feet and searching the closet for a pair of pants and a shirt.

"I'm sorry. Yeah, it's 9:15. But I had to talk to someone."

"It's okay. Shoot."

"My father keeps leaving messages for me to call him or come by the house to talk to him. Every time I go to the front desk, they have a stack of phone messages for me. Some are from the contractors working on my house, but the majority of them are from him. Mama's called and left one or two messages. This is aggravating. Why won't he leave me alone?" she groaned.

"Because he's your father, Alex, and regardless of what he's done, he still loves you. It sounds like he's remorseful and is trying to make things right."

"Well, if you're going to take up for him, I'm going to hang up," she pouted.

"I'm not taking up for him. He was wrong to do what he did, and it sounds like he is trying to show you he's sorry. But you aren't giving him a chance. And whether you want to admit it or not, you still love your father. He definitely loves you regardless of what he's done. He made a mistake, Alex. We all make mistakes. Obviously, if he's still home, then he has either told your mother, and she's forgiven him, or he hasn't confessed and hopes you won't tell her."

"That's rotten. And you're rotten for taking his side. Goodbye."

He shook his head. *Women! First Terri and now Alex. I can't win.*

The apartment seemed quieter than usual. Tony tiptoed down the hall, thinking everyone was sleeping in. When he peeked into Johnny's room, the bed was empty. He hurried down the hall to see if he was in bed with his mother. Terri's bed was empty, too. Alarmed, Tony rushed into the living room and kitchen combo. No one. Where were they? Panic gripped him. He whizzed around in a full circle. On the coffeemaker was a note. His name was printed on the outside of the envelope in Terri's handwriting. He hastily tore it open.

Dear Brother,

Please don't be angry with me, but understand I have to do things my way. My heart is broken, and I've got to find a way to heal myself. Johnny is my responsibility, and I'm sorry for not being a better mother and sister. I love you two more than you know. You're the most important two people in my life now that our parents are gone.

I agree Johnny needs better care, so I'm leaving him with you. You're good with him. He loves you, and you love him. I've watched the two of you together, and until I'm on my feet, I'm trusting you with the welfare of my son.

I am taking him to the church daycare and enrolling him this morning as you suggested. It was important for me to say my goodbyes to him there. Please remind my son every day and every night I love him.

I'll find my way home somehow. I don't know how long it will take. Have faith in me. I love you.

Sis

Tony was stunned. *How could Terri do this? Where could she have gone? Terri was in no condition to take care of herself, much less try to heal herself. She needed a professional, a doctor. She wasn't thinking clearly. What would she do for money?*

Suddenly, reality came rolling in like thunder, surrounding him in a thick hazy darkness. Now, his nephew's welfare was solely his responsibility. He'd been wrong to threaten Terri last night he'd go to Mark. Mark didn't want him because his new girlfriend wasn't fond of children. Mark's parents had basically disowned him because of his philandering behavior and his disownment of Johnny, their only grandson. Johnny seemed like his own child; there was no way he'd ever give him up to anyone but Terri.

He had fallen in love with his nephew even more than he could imagine. There had been too many nights when he'd arrived home only to find his nephew sitting on the floor, playing with his toys while his mother was asleep on the sofa. He'd had the responsibility of bathing him and feeding him supper and putting him to bed. While he was thankful conditions for Johnny were going to change, Terri's conditions had gotten worse. She would be out of his sight but not out of his mind. He'd wanted to help her get better. He'd be worried sick until his sister returned – safe and sound. But she had told him to have faith in her and promised to find her way back – doing things her way. He had to believe maybe she could. Johnny had to be his first priority until she did.

Overwhelmed, he stumbled to the telephone to call the daycare. He needed to confirm Johnny was safely there. He was. Then Tony asked about the pickup time. Finally, he asked if Johnny needed anything for his first day. The lady on the phone seemed kind and told him "his wife" had brought Big Bird, but they didn't like the children to bring their own toys to the daycare. She explained they didn't want the toys to be damaged, lost, or fought over by the other kids. Johnny's mother had brought him the required change of clothes and a blanket. His snacks and lunches would be included in the weekly cost. Tony thanked her and hung up.

Relieved Johnny was in a safe place, Tony sank to the floor and allowed himself to cry.

Chapter Twenty Four

The Act of Humility

"Finally, all of you, be like-minded, be sympathetic, love one another, be compassionate and humble."
1 Peter 3:8 (NIV)

ALEX WELLS / TONY ADAMS

Tony and Alex were meeting Charles around 11:00 a.m. at the library before their first interview with some of the Rutherford County sheriff's department officers. Tony had been unusually quiet on the ninety minute drive from Huntersville to Rutherfordton. That morning, after arriving at the library, he had remained silent, and Alex had noticed him scribbling lots of notes. After an hour or so, he'd opted to leave her at the library while he walked down the street for another cup of coffee. Obviously, he didn't want her to accompany him because he didn't invite her. He promised to return before Charles arrived. Alex thumbed through his legal pad, reading some of the handwritten notes. Then she flipped to a page about drugs.

A depressant drug is Ethanol, which includes the alcohol in beer, wine, and liquor. It should be given special consideration because it was the leading cause of death by drug overdose – especially when the deadly combination of alcohol and other depressants were ingested. This was known as the "synergistic effect," causing bodily functions to slow down. One half of all murders and one fourth of all suicides can be attributed to alcohol.

Another depressant is Benzodiazepines – something like the widely prescribed and distributed Valium. By 1970s, more than one half of all prescriptions written were for these types of drugs. The rise could be attributed to the fact that the treatment of anxiety disorders historically were treated with barbiturates. Benzodiazepines were considered safer due to the lower amounts of the drugs needed to cause sedation – much lower than the amount needed to cause an overdose. All drugs are dangerous; inherently, danger can come from the length of time it takes for the compounds to be eliminated from the body. Dependency is possible; because the dosage levels are low, people may mistakenly take more. Withdrawal can be severe.

Opiates are narcotics. They are prescribed to relieve pain. There is a high potential for abuse. Demerol is common one. Opiates are highly addictive, both physically and psychologically. As the drug is taken, tolerance levels build rapidly. When the person is withdrawing, use can be increased because of the physical and psychological withdrawal symptoms that may be experienced. Withdrawal usually begins within four – six hours after the last dose is taken. Individual may experience uneasiness, diarrhea, abdominal cramps, chills, sweating, nausea, runny nose, and watery eyes. The severity of the symptoms will depend on the amount taken, how often the drug was taken, and how long. Withdrawal symptoms peak around 48-72 hours and subside within seven to ten days. Afterward, sleeplessness and drug cravings may persist for months. Women, in particular, can suffer from anemia, heart disease, diabetes, pneumonia, and hepatitis during pregnancy and childbirth.

Alex wondered why Tony seemed so interested in all these drugs. She was confused and couldn't wait for him to return and make this clear. Did he believe Hutchins was on drugs? She'd also be sure to ask Charles what he knew about any drug abuse Hutchins may have had.

Addiction is subjective – based on the individual's metabolism, the length of time the person has used the drug, and the dosage taken along with other factors. People mistakenly believe that prescriptions won't cause dependence. Physical and psychological dependence can occur. Withdrawal is dangerous; no individual should attempt to discontinue use without medical supervision. ***More people have died from Valium withdrawal than from Valium overdoses.***

Alex noted the last fact had been underlined and highlighted. She didn't remember Hutchins being on Valium – just drinking alcohol. Maybe Charles had told him otherwise.

Withdrawal symptoms can take up to three days after the last dose due to long half-life of compounds. Onset of withdrawal symptoms can be craving the drug, having severe anxiety, sleep disturbances, and hallucinations. The peak generally occurs between the first and third week after use of the drug is discontinued. Drug craving and more subdued physical symptoms may occur for months after the last dose is taken.

After reading his notes, Alex didn't have to wait more than ten minutes for Tony to return. His disposition seemed more pleasant. Maybe caffeine was what the doctor had ordered.

"What have you been doing?" he asked. "Have you found any new information?"

"Not really. I've been reading your notes. What's this about drugs? I know Hutchins was an alcoholic. All accounts say he wasn't abusive when he wasn't drinking. It was like the alcohol changed his whole disposition from being a nice, kind man to being violent and raging. Did you find out he was taking other drugs, too?"

"No. All I know about is the alcohol, like you. But I found that information interesting and decided to take some notes." He avoided her eyes.

"Oh, okay," she replied. "Tony, are you mad at me for hanging up on you yesterday? I know it was childish. I'm sorry."

"Of course not. I'm not upset about it, but I do agree, it was a rather immature way to act. But I accept your apology."

"So you forgive me?" Alex teased.

"Of course, I forgive you," he said with a half-smile.

"Good. Thanks. Here comes Charles. Get your notepad ready," Alex warned him. "And don't forget, we have an interview at 1:00 at the Sheriff's office."

After greeting Charles with warm hugs and handshakes, they got down to work learning more about Hutchins.

"So, Charles, how long had they lived where the murders took place?" Tony asked.

"I think they moved from Forest City in 1974. James had been eager to return to Rutherfordton where he'd been raised. People say he became a good neighbor, helping others living around him. He fixed up the rental house by installing paneling and new floor tile. He raised chickens and planted a garden. He was proud of the land and the fields around his house. He liked being out in the country, like where he grew up as a boy."

It was a sunny afternoon when Alex and Tony met with Lieutenant Mike Summers, Detective David Philbeck, and Patrolman Dan Good at the Rutherford County Police Department. After shaking hands and explaining they were hoping to write a true crime novel about the Hutchins's murders, they were invited into a meeting room and sat across from the three officers at a long table. Tony opened his note pad and began the interview by asking Lieutenant Summers if he knew Hutchins personally.

"Sure. I knew who he was. I gave him a ticket once for having an expired inspection sticker. Then I cited him again for an improper registration, things like that. He had other traffic violations over the years. Hutchins was known to have a hot temper."

"Did you run across him any other times?"

"No. I know he was cited several times by the Sheriff for driving violations and complaints about him driving penny nails in a tree. We'd all heard about him killing a truck driver years ago and being charged with voluntary manslaughter. Then there was the time he'd shot Junior Crane in the stomach five. Fortunately, Crane survived."

"Did you work with Officer Messersmith?" Alex asked.

"I sure did."

"How would you describe him?" She took notes.

"He was such a nice guy. He didn't have to become a policeman, but he wanted to. He was assigned to the Lake Lure and Chimney Rock area. He was a quiet individual -- someone you enjoyed being around; you could talk to him all day long. Once he and I got called to the fire department in Union Mills. The report was there was a couple of guys there fighting with knives and who were believed to be carrying guns. Fortunately, by the time we arrived, the ruckus was over and the guys were gone. Owen smiled then; he smiled all the time."

"What about Peterson?" Tony probed.

Summers frowned. "I was leaving the grocery store when I found out what was happening. We had blind communications back then – 'scanner hop.' I heard Pete talking to the dispatcher. He was chasing the suspect on Goodman Edwards Road. G235 was his call number. I remember G248 was Dan Good's."

Patrolman Good acknowledged him with a nod and smile.

After a short pause, Detective Philbeck said, "I had heard screaming over the radio. Somebody was calling for help because a policeman had been shot. I found out later that Charlotte Hutchins had called the Sheriff's department from a house across the street."

"Patrolman Good, what was the manhunt like?" Alex asked.

He sighed. "Not pleasant. It was like a three-day night. I was with two other troopers, Larry Davis and Bill Hines and a dog handler from McDowell County, James Boyce. He had a dog, a bloodhound. It was getting dark once we found the car. So we started into the woods with the dog and walked hills and really small mountains for a long time. I think it was five to six hours. Around midnight, we started up a steep hill and heard him call out, "Who is it down there?"

We told him we were a bunch of old coon hunters. At this point, he didn't shoot; but we laid flat on the incline.

"Later on," Patrolman Good continued, "he figured out who we were. So we told him who we were. That's when he asked, 'How's that [GD} trooper I shot?' We tried to use psychology on him to get him to surrender. So we told him we didn't know. He yelled back, 'I blew his [GD] head off. I shot Roy and Messersmith because I was tired of you SOBs coming to my house.' We talked to him – having several conversations between then and daylight when we finally got him."

"But he had stopped talking around three or four in the morning. When it was getting daylight, and we could see the sunlight coming over, Bill Hines lit up a Lucky Strike cigarette. He said, 'Boys, I've taken all I can. I've got to have a cigarette.' Hutchins had worked his way down the hill close to us; we never heard him. As soon as Bill struck the match, Hutchins shot both barrels of his .12 gauge shotgun at us. He missed us by two feet. He meant to kill us, so we fired back at him."

"Wow. I'm sure it was scary." Alex agreed.

He nodded his head. "That's when they sent in the SCLED dogs."

"What does the acronym SCLED stand for?" she asked.

"South Carolina Law Enforcement Division. They put bells on their bloodhounds. They were allowed to turn the dogs loose. It seemed so ironic he wasn't afraid of us and our guns even when we fired back at him. The dogs with the bells are what scared him. He yelled for us to get the dogs away from him. He was afraid of the dogs more than of us. So I told him to throw out his guns." He did, and I handcuffed him."

"Did he struggle?" Tony asked.

"No. He just complied with no resistance."

"How big is Hutchins?" Alex asked.

"I'd say about 5' 11," slim built."

"How far into the woods were you?" Tony asked.

"About a mile and a half. On the way out, he said nothing. I took him to where our cars were parked. They put him in an SBI car. I never talked to him any more."

"You knew Roy Huskey, I'm sure, didn't you?" Alex asked Patrolman Good.

"Yes. Roy was a character. He talked all the time; he was different from Damon. He liked to rub people the wrong way, like nicknaming Mike a 'damn Yankee.'"

They laughed at the memory.

"He could be a hard person to get to know, but once you did, he was nice to know. Roy was good to me," said Summers.

"And Peterson?" Alex asked.

"We drank coffee together," Summers replied. "He was a 'Trooper's Trooper.' He could have been the poster boy for the N.C. Highway Patrol."

"He was top of the list," said Philbeck. "We jogged together at times. That rascal would turn around and start running backwards and would continue hollering at me. He was in tip top shape. It was sad he was only thirty seven years old when he died. I don't know if Hutchins knew Peterson or Messersmith."

After everyone stopped talking, a solemn Patrolman Good said, "Pete Peterson was my best friend. I was in Vietnam. I saw lots of dead bodies. I was awarded the Purple Heart. But one of the worst things in my life was losing Pete."

"Do you want to witness the execution if you're able?" Tony asked.

"I don't," Good replied. "I've chosen not to."

Mike Summers didn't hesitate. "I do. I want to witness the execution."

Chapter Twenty Five

The Act of Searching

"If you want to understand today, you have to search yesterday."

Pearl Buck

ALEX WELLS / TONY ADAMS

The following week they had a scheduled meeting at 4:30 p.m. with Officer R. H. Epley (Firpo) at his home. Alex and Tony's first knock was welcomed immediately by the officer who invited them into a warm and comfortably furnished living room. They sat side-by-side on a sofa facing the man who sat in his favorite overstuffed arm chair. Tony asked him to talk about whatever he could remember regarding the people or the events of May 31, 1979.

"Roy told it like it was. He was what you could call 'outspoken.' My first experience with Roy was at the race track between Spindale and Forest City. He was out there running a crane. I climbed up and put my arm around him, and he rode me around in the crane."

"On May 31, 1979, we were at the gas pumps outside the jail a little before 6:00. It was Messersmith, Roy, and me. Messersmith and I had finished our shifts, but Roy was coming on at 6:00. The dispatcher, a young black girl, came outside and told Roy there was a telephone call for him."

"She said, 'Roy, I gotta phone call. Some girl with a problem wants to speak to you.' He disappeared inside for a few minutes."

"When he returned, he said, 'Hutchins is up there showing his ass. Stop by there with me,' so Messersmith told him he would. I left and drove home. My wife was cooking fish for supper. We had the scanner on. That's when I heard 'Officer has been shot' and immediately headed back to Rutherfordton. The dispatcher told us she had been trying to get through to Asheville for help. I later learned that Patrolman Wayne Spears had been behind Peterson and was trying to catch up when Peterson was shot."

"I helped put people in key positions. We knew where Hutchins had entered the woods. There were armed forces from everywhere. Ray Dixon is the one who set up the command post before Tom McDevitt took over. 'Containment of the suspect' was the number one thing -- it was our priority."

Tony and Alex respectfully remained quiet and allowed Epley to continue.

"Forrest Thompson is the one who radioed Damon Huskey and told him Roy had been shot. We called Ellenboro to request bloodhounds. There were several officers in the woods that night. The 'Snoopy' helicopter from Charlotte was flying around with a sniper in the helicopter in case they got sight of him. They were Boyce, Davis, Hines, Good, and Hollifield from McDowell County. Around four o'clock in the morning, they made contact. Hutchins shot over Bill's head."

"The SCLED dogs, the bell dogs, from South Carolina were standing by. After Bill returned fire, he sent a radio communication for them to send in the dogs; they were ready. A man named 'Hoss' led the dogs into the woods to circle the suspect and retrieve him. After the dogs located him, it wasn't long before he surrendered. I was at the command post when they brought him out. Later on, they gave one of the bell dogs, Gracie, to Sheriff Damon Huskey."

"Hutchins's first appearance was in the Forest City Police Department before Judge Hollis Owens. I opened the court, by saying 'Everybody please rise.' He rose. Afterward, Hutchins sat there and stared at me. I stared back at him. He had this dead look like he could look right through you – like he was mad at the world."

"How big is he?" Alex asked.

"Medium build – not large, not skinny."

Tony finished scribbling notes onto the yellow legal pad. "What do you know about Hutchins?"

"I worked at Stonecutter's from 1967-1972 before I joined the Sheriff's Department in 1972. I was made an assistant supervisor in1969. His wife, Geneva, worked there, too. I often heard her talking about James, but I can't remember anything she said about him. I do recall Geneva had a bad eye."

When the conversation had dwindled for a little while, Alex asked, "What did you think of Messersmith?"

"He was a good man. Easy going, a good ol' fellow who wouldn't hurt a fly. Everyone loved him. He was a fantastic man. I personally loved him to death. He was the kind of man who says 'please.' So after the first shots, Owen pulled in the driveway and stepped out of the car. That's when he was shot through the car and his side. Hutchins was standing on the screened-in porch when he shot both of them. I do know Roy was left-handed. Hutchins shot the first time and hit the car; then he shot again, striking Roy in his right arm. The third shot he fired struck Roy in the head."

"And Peterson?" she asked.

"Peterson was a training officer. He knew what to do under these circumstances. He opened his door, drew his pistol, and kicked back so he could get behind the car's engine. They're taught to get the heaviest piece of equipment between them – the engine block. He didn't get down quick enough or low enough. Peterson was a joy to be around."

"This was like losing family members because we work so closely together. They were given law enforcement funerals. Roy's funeral was at Crowes, and he's buried at Sunset. Owen was buried in Buncombe County around Lake Lure and Chimney Rock. He's buried on the side of a mountain. Peterson, I think, was buried around Asheville – maybe Old Fort or Montreat."

"Are you hoping to witness the execution?" Tony asked.

"No. Luke Roberson and Ray Dixon hope to go to the execution."

There was a long pause before he spoke again. "I will tell you this. May 31, 1979, is the last day my wife cooked fish for supper."

For a lot of people, the world's glimmer of innocence was dimmed, but not extinguished. It was their love and memories to the fallen, which stoked the fires again.

Chapter Twenty Six

The Gift of Time

""There comes a time when the world gets quiet and the only thing left is your own heart. So you'd better learn the sound of it. Otherwise you'll never understand what it's saying."

Sarah Dessen, Author

ALEX WELLS / TONY ADAMS

It was January 6, 1984. During the darkened, cloudy night, a light dusting of white snow had covered the dormant trees along the road's right-of-way and on the brown grasses and weeds in the yards and fields they passed by. Alex had wanted to postpone their visit with Charles, but Tony kept stressing the importance of taking advantage of their Saturdays, which was the only time they had to devote to their writing project now the holidays were over and the winter semester was beginning in seven days. Besides, Hutchins was scheduled to die in a week. They stopped at a nearby convenience store to buy cups of coffee to warm them until the library was in sight.

"So I want you to know Mama is thrilled you asked her to babysit Johnny again today. She adores him, and I think he adores her too. And don't get mad, but I think she plans to clean your place while she's there – you know, vacuum, dust, bathrooms, cobwebs, dusty baseboards, all of the above."

Tony groaned. "I wish she wouldn't do that."

"Why? Are you afraid she'll see things you don't want her to know about?"

"What? What?"

She smiled slyly.

"No. I have nothing to hide. Remember, I'm a virtuous surrogate father now. I don't have time for dating or romantic dinners. All of my attention belongs to my nephew. And actually, I like it that way. We have fun."

"That's so sweet," Alex cooed.

"I don't want Betsy to think she has to clean my house whenever she comes to babysit. That's not my expectations. She's doing me a big favor by keeping him on a Saturday, so we can continue working. I'm sure they have other things to do."

"I wouldn't know about that. But Mama knows you don't expect it. She does it because she's fond of you and because she can't stand a dirty house," Alex laughed.

Tony feigned hurt feelings before responding, "My house may be dusty, but it's not dirty. I keep a cleaner house than most guys my age. You should have seen my college dorm. Now it was dirty. My roommate didn't know how to hold a broom or what a closet was. He definitely didn't know how to use a washing machine. After a while, I gave up. He was a lost cause. That's the only time I've ever lived in filth."

"Yuk! Well, I've been sure not to give her the new key to my house, or she'd be rearranging my furniture. I had all the locks changed after I moved back in. Surprisingly, she hasn't asked for a key yet."

"Oh! Well she will."

"I know," Alex agreed. "As long as she doesn't give it to Daddy. And by the way. I'm so happy to be back in my home. You didn't even ask me about it."

"I'm sorry, Alex. With the holidays and Christmas vacation, I haven't seen you a lot lately. I had a lot going on during the holidays. Did I even tell you that Johnny and I went to my cousin's house in Wilmington for Thanksgiving and stayed the entire weekend? They have a nice home and two kids of their own. Johnny had a ball playing with them."

"Then before I knew it, I was playing Santa Claus, which was a new experience for me. I can't tell you how many times I rushed to the store to find a toy he mentioned he wanted. Every day, the kid came up with something else he wanted Santa to bring him. And with his mother gone, I wanted him to have a good Christmas."

"Did you hear from Terri?" Alex asked.

"Yeah. She sent me a Christmas card and a box for Johnny. It had an *E.T.* doll and some VHS tapes in it, which he loved. But the poor little fellow kept expecting her to walk through the door on Christmas Day."

"What about his father? Did he hear from him?"

"No. But he does keep sending his monthly child support check, but I don't open the envelopes. That's between Terri and him. Besides, I don't need his money. I can take care of Johnny all by myself. I can't figure the guy out. He was beside himself when Johnny was born. He was one of the proudest fathers I've ever seen. But now?"

Alex fell silent. *You're a good man, Tony. Johnny is fortunate to have you. Terri is, too.*

"Hey," he said. "I'm sorry about your New Year's Eve Party. I had planned to come, but Johnny was running a fever, so I didn't want to leave him with a babysitter."

"No problem. But you were missed," Alex said. "We did have a great time."

"Who was there? Did your father come?" Tony asked nonchalantly, hoping he wouldn't hear Cullen Park's name mentioned. He considered Cullen a rival for Alex's affections.

"Of course he didn't come. I didn't invite my parents. After being forced to be around them at Thanksgiving and Christmas, I needed a break."

"So you and your dad still haven't made up?"

"No! I've told you. That isn't going to happen. Apparently, he's fooled my mother, but he can't fool me. I caught him red-handed; remember, I know the truth. It was difficult to keep up a civil front with him, but I didn't want to have a scene in front of Mama and our relatives. So, I was a good actress. I'm determined for Mama not to know."

She folded her arms and stuck her nose in the air. Then she continued.

"We have all our relatives over for Thanksgiving dinner. Whenever he'd get close to me, I'd move away and find someone to talk to. But when Mama asked me to help her clean up the dishes after everyone left, I was worried he'd try to take advantage of the situation. But he stayed in the den and watched television. When I was leaving, they both walked me to the door and kissed me. I kissed Mama back but not him."

"How did you handle Christmas?"

"I accepted an invitation to have Christmas dinner at Ashley's house. She wasn't going home for Christmas, so she had invited me and two other girlfriends she'd known from college, so it worked out perfectly. Mama was hurt, obviously, because it was our first Christmas apart. I admit, it did feel a little sad for me, too, but I didn't want to be around him."

"Wow, Alex. I hope I never offend you. You can surely carry a grudge."

"It's not like he bought me the wrong present or told me a white lie. That denotes a grudge. My father was unfaithful to my mother. He recklessly disregarded our family unit. He didn't care if his selfish actions destroyed her OR our family. I'm sorry, but I can't forget it nor forgive him."

"So did you go at all?"

"Yeah. I took the dogs over Christmas morning. Mama always fixes grand-dog stockings for Maddie and Abbie. She started doing this for my first Yorkie, Neely. And of course, she'd fixed her famous sausage, egg, and cheese casserole and champagne mimosas. But I couldn't eat. My stomach was in knots, so I lied and said I'd already eaten. I waited in the den and played with my puppies while they ate. Even the Christmas music didn't cheer my disposition. There were presents under the tree for me, but I could have cared less."

"How'd you handle it? I'm sure it was really awkward."

"Well, I'd gotten joint gifts for them instead of separate gifts like I normally do. After all, how was I going to buy gifts for her and not for him? She'd definitely known something then. He'd gotten Mama a beautiful diamond tennis bracelet, so she was thrilled with it. I was glad because it took the focus off me for a while. Mama had gotten him a new set of golf clubs, which he'd been wanting for some time, so he seemed really pleased about those. She told me he'd been hinting for months like no one could figure out what he was doing." Alex giggled. "He's so transparent."

She blew warm air onto the window and drew a heart around her name before continuing. "Then Mama asked me to open my gifts. It was so uncomfortable; I really didn't want to. The air was as thick as a mosquito net. I wanted to escape. But I opened each wrapped box dutifully, smiled, and said, 'Thank you' like a big girl. I even smiled in his direction once or twice. Afterward, I told them I needed to leave and get ready for Ashley's dinner. Mama carried the Yorkies to the car, while he carried my stack of gifts. When Mama and I hugged, she had tears in her eyes. Well, it almost did me in! Then he bent down and kissed me on the cheek and said, 'Merry Christmas, Baby. I love you.' As I drove out of the driveway, I could see him standing there in the rearview mirror watching me. That's when I started crying for the past and what used to be."

Tony thought Alex was really cold. He felt sorry for her mother – and yes, even her father. But this was his own opinion; he had to respect her feelings even though he felt the need to talk to her again. "We're almost there, Alex. We're a few minutes late; Charles will be waiting."

"Okay." She paused. "Oh, you asked me who was at my party. Let's see, it was Ashley and her new boyfriend, Chase Peters; Chesney Cain, the new instructor in the math department, and his girlfriend, Elaine; Zac Daniels and Caite Gray; and Natalie and Edward Avery. I think that's everyone."

Tony released a slow breath.

Then she quickly added, "Oh, I forgot. Cullen Park came late."

"Really? So he showed up." Tony's quick elation deflated quickly.

"Yes. He got there late but in time for the count down and kiss," Alex stated. "Why?" She secretly hoped Tony was jealous.

"Just curious. So he kissed you?"

"No. He kissed his girlfriend. She seems like the jealous type, so he didn't kiss anyone else. Besides, they only had eyes for each other, which is probably why they were late."

Tony was elated; but he asked cautiously, "Then who kissed you?"

"Well, because you weren't there, Ashley asked Chase to. Chesney did, too. Then we all hugged and sang 'Auld Lang Syne.'"

They were quiet for the last five miles. When they arrived, as predicted, Charles was waiting inside the library at a table. After exchanging quick greetings, Charles said, "Have a seat, both of you. I have news."

Chapter Twenty Seven

The Gift of Friendship

"If I had a flower for every time I thought of you…I could walk through my garden forever."
Alfred Tennyson

ALEX WELLS / TONY ADAMS

Charles seemed gloomy when he shared his news. "They moved James from Death Row this morning."

"How do you know this?" Tony asked.

"Let's say I have my sources," Charles replied. "That's where he's lived all this time along with thirty three other condemned men. He got his first glimpse of the morning sun – the outdoors – in years when they escorted him to an area with four holding cells, outside the Death Chamber. He'll be in one of those cells until his execution in a week, at 6:00 a.m. on January 13.

"So it's still scheduled?" Alex asked quietly.

"Yes, yes it is," Charles said sadly. "His attorneys are working on some more appeals to try and prevent it or delay it. We'll see what happens. As you'll recall from your notes, the execution date of January 13, 1984, was set this past September 8. It has never gotten this close with all the appeals and change of dates. But they will ask him to choose his preferred method of execution today."

Tony stopped writing and stared at Charles. "How do you know all of this?" Charles waved off his question.

"And what are his choices regarding execution?" Alex asked.

"Lethal gas or lethal injection," the photographer stated.

"Do you have an idea of what he'll choose?" she asked.

"Yes. He'll want lethal injection."

Tony scratched his head. "You and Hutchins must have had some deep conversations during those visits you've made to the prison."

Charles smiled.

Alex was thoughtful; then she said, "Isn't it ironic he gets to choose his method of execution, and he's the bad guy, but Huskey, Messersmith, and Peterson didn't get to choose their preferred method of dying; and they were the good guys."

Charles and Tony didn't share their agreements aloud; they nodded their heads.

"And another thing I've been thinking about. Why with his record – killing a man back in the '50s and shooting Junior Crain and possibly others – why was he able to have guns? What's wrong with our gun laws these days? Can you answer that one? It seems to be if you're a convicted criminal – especially if you've shot people – you should not be able to possess guns."

"Point well taken," Charles stated. "I've often wondered the same thing."

"Me, too," Tony added.

"Want to come in and have a soda?" Alex asked Tony when they pulled into her drive way? "You haven't seen the house since I got moved back in." She removed her sunglasses and squinted at the sudden glare.

"No thanks, Alex. I'd better not. I have to get home and relieve Betsy. I'm sure she's tired and needing to get home to have supper with your father. Plus, I can't wait to get home and see my spic and span condo. Between caring for Johnny and cleaning my pad, she has to be worn out."

"Okay. Tell Mama I said hello, and I love her."

"I will. Hey, we got a lot done today. Thanks!"

"Sure. We're really gathering a lot of good information. Do you believe he'll be executed next week?"

"I don't know. He's dodged the bullet – no pun intended -- several times now. I don't know. Maybe his attorneys can pull another rabbit out of the hat."

"Maybe. Well, see you. See you in the lounge Monday morning before my first class. Okay. Call me if you get lonely," she said with a grin.

He beamed. "Will do."

As he backed out of the driveway onto the street, she watched until his car disappeared. *I wish he'd ask me out sometime, other than working on this book. Maybe he's not interested. Maybe it's because he has Johnny now. Maybe I should have invited him and Johnny over for supper. Hey! That's an idea! I'll call him tomorrow and suggest he bring Johnny over while we transcribe our notes. I'm so smart!*

Humming to herself, she walked to the mailbox and pulled out a stack of white envelopes. Thumbing through the boring pile of junk mail, she noticed a strange envelope. *Why am I getting something from the North Carolina Department of Correction?* Curious, she used her finger as a letter opener and pried open the folded letter. It was addressed to her. As she read, her eyes grew bigger and bigger. She was amazed.

The execution of James Hutchins is scheduled to be carried out at Central Prison in the Death Chamber on January 13, 1984 between the hours of 6:00 A.M. and 6:00 P.M. You have been selected to serve as an official witness to the execution and to sign the execution register indicating the execution was carried out in compliance with G.S..15-137.

This letter as well as some form of identification will serve as your authority to attend the execution on the date set forth above. In the event you are unable to attend please notify me immediately so an alternate can be selected and notified.

I will notify you on Wednesday by phone of the exact time you should arrive at Central Prison. In the event you do not hear from me by Wednesday at 3:00 P.M., please call me at Central Prison so we can confirm the exact time of the execution. My phone number is 53-0130.

If a stay of execution is granted, you will be promptly notified by my office.

I appreciate your volunteering to serve in this official capacity and if you have any questions, please do not hesitate to call me.

The letter was signed by the warden.

Alex's heart was pounding. She felt like a noose had been applied and was choking off all air supply. How had this happened? She was confused. Had Tony failed to tell her about this? Why wouldn't he have mentioned attending the execution to her? How could you forget something like that? She checked her watch; it would take another twenty minutes for Tony to drive across town to his house. That's when she'd call him and get some answers. She'd also confirm he'd received a letter, too. After gathering her breath, she rushed inside to be welcomed home by the excited chorus of her two Yorkies.

With quick motions, she jerked off her coat and woolen scarf, and hurriedly hugged each dog to her chest. "Hey Maddie! Hey Baby! How's my girl?" Then she did the same with Abbie. They finally calmed down when she gave them each a doggie treat and went back to their separate doggie beds. She tossed each one a couple of treats for good behavior and gave each one a new rawhide bone before rushing to the phone. Dad would know what to do. She'd call him. In the midst of dialing her parent's number, she halted, feeling heartsick and disappointed and empty. She replaced the receiver, dropped to the wooden floor, and sobbed.

Forty minutes later, her phone rang.

"Hello," she said.

"You're not going to believe what I just got in the mail," Tony yelled.

"You're hurting my ears, and yes, I can believe what you got because I got one, too. Did you forget to tell me about this?" demanded Alex.

"Forget to tell you what?"

"To tell me you'd volunteered us to witness the execution. And why did it take you forty minutes to call me?"

"Of course I didn't forget to tell you! I didn't do it. I thought you'd done it and had forgotten to tell me. And as far as taking forty minutes, it took a while for your Mom to leave. Johnny was crying after her, not wanting her to go."

"Oh. Okay. Well then, how did this happen, Tony?"

"Alex. I don't know. Maybe one of the folks we've interviewed suggested this because we're hoping to write a book. Anyway, I think it's great!"

"Great! How can you say that? I'm not exactly excited to be going to witness an execution even though I believe he's a scumbag and deserves to die. They should have shot him in the woods. No one would have ever known."

Tony was silent.

"Are you there?" she asked.

"Yeah. I'm here."

"What's wrong?"

"Nothing is wrong."

"Yes it is."

He paused again. "I wish you weren't so judgmental, Alex. You're right. They could have easily shot and killed him and made up some kind of lie about why they did, but they would have known. They would've had to live with this lie and murder for the rest of their lives.

And if they had, they would have been lesser men -- no better than he was."

"What are you talking about?" Her patience was exploding. He made her feel like a child.

"You can be very judgmental, sometimes, and uh, uh, unforgiving, Alex."

"Well excuse me for living, Tony. That's who I am. Accept it or find someone else to help you write this book. I'm a little tired of this conversation. I need to go."

"Don't be angry, Alex. I don't mean to criticize you. It's just ...."

"I need to go. I said I'd never hang up on you again. Sorry. Goodbye."

Dejected and upset with himself for hurting her feelings, Tony replaced the receiver. That's when he felt a welcoming tug on his pant leg.

"Unky Tony? Can we play Chutes and Ladders?"

"Sure, little guy. Why not? Chutes sounds like a good idea."

Chapter Twenty Eight

The Gift of Acceptance

"Bear with each other and forgive one another if any of you has a grievance against someone. Forgive as the Lord forgave you."

Colossians 3:13 (NIV)

ALEX WELLS / TONY ADAMS

On Sunday afternoon, Alex invited / summoned Tony to come over and discuss their last conversation. Reluctantly, he agreed. He wasn't in the mood for a showdown, but apparently Alex was. Tony certainly hadn't meant to offend her. He fastened Johnny into his car seat and handed him two picture books, a covered cup of fruit juice, and his *E.T.* doll to keep him company. He hoped these items would keep his nephew occupied while they drove across town. He regretted upsetting Alex the previous night, but this had weighed on his heart for a long time. Tony believed in honesty, but sometimes blatant honesty could prove wrong. Maybe it had this time.

When Alex answered the door, she deliberately avoided his eyes. Instead she scooped Johnny into her arms and bear-hugged him for an exaggerated period of time. Tony removed his sunglasses, rolled his eyes, and followed behind her. *Women!*

Finally, after she'd cooed and wooed Johnny with a new VHS children's movie and plopped a plate of home-baked chocolate chip cookies beside him on the floor, she turned to face Tony.

"I think we need to decide if we're going to continue working together."

"What? Of course we are! Alex, if you're upset about what I said last night, I didn't mean anything harsh by it. It's an observation."

"Well, you hurt my feelings. It's like you're criticizing me. Isn't it bad enough I'm having issues with my father? Now you're finding fault with me," she accused.

"I am not finding fault with you. I'm stating an observation, my opinion. When you suggested the officers should have shot Hutchins while he was in the woods, it bothered me you would think this way. They are dedicated officers, sworn to uphold the law and bring him in – not a bunch of vigilantes who were out to shoot the man even though they probably wanted to for killing their friends in cold blood. Think about Damon Huskey. He lost his brother that evening. Thank God, those men stood on this side of the law."

"You know I didn't mean it. So do you think I'm confusing revenge with justice?" Alex asked.

"I think you know the difference, Alex. You're an intelligent, educated woman. But if they had inflicted harm on Hutchins because of what he'd done that day to their friends, then it would be called retribution – not being lawful, not ensuring he was tried in a court of law, not preserving his rights in a fair and equitable way. And yes, even a murderer has rights."

"You're not my professor, Tony. I thought you were my friend. You don't need to lecture me."

"I'm not Alex. But admit it. You do hold grudges."

She smirked. "I believe you should be held accountable for your actions."

"I agree. And he is being held accountable for his actions. He's been convicted, and now he's scheduled to be executed."

"And I think you reap what you sew. Only his punishment won't be like their punishment. He gets to choose how to die. They had no choice. And lethal injection is probably the most humane way of all to die."

"I agree. But knowing it's going to happen and when it's going to happen – well, I don't know how I'd be able to live with it. I dread going to the dentist every six months, and when I have to go for a scheduled filling, well ... I'd probably be having panic attacks if I were him."

Her irritation was fading. "He knew alcohol changed his personality, but he kept on drinking. If people don't reach out for help or help themselves, then no one can help them."

"That's true," Tony replied thinking of his sister.

"I don't think he wanted help, Tony."

"Well, it doesn't seem like he ever asked for it. There had to be times when he was forced to become sober, like when he was in jail all that time in New Mexico or during other stints with the law. He certainly couldn't turn to alcohol then. But whenever he'd get out again, I do believe he used alcohol as a means to escape from life."

"I think so, too. But it doesn't make what he did right. Isn't it why most addicts do what they do?" she asked. "Isn't it because they can't face reality, so they turn to something else to make them feel good, like drugs or alcohol?"

Tony swallowed hard. *Addicts. Not Terri,* he thought. *Yes, she had turned to wine and harmless medications because she couldn't face life without our parents and her husband. But he refused to label her an "addict." He couldn't use her name and label in the same sentence.*

"Alex, can I have more cookies?" Johnny asked. His plate was empty except for crumbs.

"Sure, sweetie, if your uncle doesn't mind."

"Huh? Oh, I guess two more won't hurt. But that's all. Is your movie good?"

"Um huh," Johnny said while stuffing half a cookie into his mouth.

When Alex returned to the sofa, she sat closer to Tony.

"Alex, I'm not making excuses for Hutchins. This man grew up in terrible poverty and never could escape it. We know his father was abusive to his mother, which caused him to drop out of school to work and help the family while his dad was locked up in jail. Imagine how hard it would have been for a twelve year old boy. And we know he didn't respect authority or bend to society's laws and norms. He rejected them. And on top of this, he was violent and abusive with his own family."

"But we're told he had a good side when he wasn't drinking like sewing a prom dress for Charlotte or the talks he had with Lefrere like a regular person," she added. "I want to be convinced he had a good side. Then I can believe he was more normal than such a gutless murderer. Do you think he regrets what he did, or do you think he's too callous to be regretful? I keep thinking about how he shot Peterson and then kind of bragged about killing him when the officers were in the woods to capture him – like he was proud of it. And he could have killed them. He didn't act like he cared."

"Lefrere thinks he regrets his action; he seems to know Hutchins better than almost anyone, well, maybe not his family. They had to live with him. There's a difference between being remorseful or repentant, isn't there, Alex?"

"Yes. I guess so. I've never really thought about it. To me, remorse is all about feeling guilty or regretting whatever you've done. Like my father should be. Repentant is about feeling guilt or regret and then expressing it so others know your feelings. Like my father should do."

Tony was silent and expressionless.

"But do you believe he was being stubborn when he didn't testify at his own trial?" she asked.

"No. Remember Lefrere said his attorneys didn't let him testify. They were afraid his other convictions would be raised. Besides, the prosecution would have eaten him alive on the stand."

"About this execution. I guess you want to go?" She half stated it; half asked it.

"Yes. I do. And I hope you'll come, too." He said while earnestly seeking her eyes.

"I'd still like to understand how we got invitations," she said stubbornly.

"I've been thinking. I think it was Lefrere, Alex. I think he pulled some strings. If I'm not mistaken, Hutchins can choose people to attend the execution if he wants to."

"Do you think Charles will be there, too? I hope so."

"I have no idea," Tony said. "I hope so, too."

"Tony, if you only had a few hours left to live, what would you do?" Alex asked.

To tell you that I've fallen in love with you, he thought.

"I don't know. I guess I'd gather my friends and Terri and Johnny and you together and spend all those hours, minutes, and seconds with them. We'd talk, and hopefully laugh, and then we'd pray. Then we'd talk and laugh and pray some more. How about you?"

"Did you say me?" she asked with a bright smile. "Probably the same thing." She thought of her parents and how hard it would be to say goodbye to them – even her father. A lump rose in her throat and tears stung her eyes. She fought them back by asking another question.

"Would you order a last meal?" she asked.

"Probably not. My stomach would be so upset, I wouldn't be able to eat anything."

"So when you say I'm judgmental, what do you mean? Judgmental has a negative connotation, Tony. I looked it up in the dictionary last night. It's when a person forms harsh or critical opinions about people or things. It implied being close-minded. So do you think everyone should forget about what Hutchins did? Do you think I should forget about what my father did?"

"I don't think it is possible to forget about something that has been done against you like Hutchins killing those three officers. There is no way the families or even his own family could ever forget what happened that day. But anger dissipates over time and opens the door for forgiveness to be possible. Think about your father. Are you as angry as you were that day when you walked in on him and the neighbor?"

"Yes," she answered defiantly. "No. I don't know. I'm still hurt about what he did."

"Do you believe time can heal all wounds?" Tony asked.

"I think time diminishes the pain, but I think the wound is still there. Time hasn't healed my wound."

"Have you done anything to try and heal your wound? What if your father apologized, Alex, and told you he regretted what he'd done. Could you forgive him?"

"I don't know. Besides, it's a moot point. He hasn't apologized."

"Yes he did. He said it through your motel door. He tried to tell you at Christmas. You really haven't given him a chance to tell you he's sorry."

"Am I supposed to forgive and forget and act like nothing ever happened? Just like Hutchins. So far, no one we've interviewed, even Charles, or nothing we've read has him admitting he's sorry. So are the families supposed to forgive him on their own and move on with their lives? Doesn't he have to apologize first? I believe you should apologize for your actions and behaviors. This gives the person who was wronged the opportunity to decide whether or not to accept the apology."

"I agree people should be repentant if they are remorseful."

"So once my father asks for my mother's forgiveness, then I'll let you know if I've forgiven him. Until then, we should focus on our book."

"Agreed," Tony said with a smile. "But keep in mind. You may never know if he does or doesn't apologize to her. That is between them."

She wanted to change the subject. "Now, would you like a glass of wine? I have a new Pinot Grigio."

"Better not, since I'm driving us home. But I'll take a soda if you have one."

"Coming right up," she replied.

"Oh and Alex. Something you might be interested in knowing."

"What?"

"I enjoy our discussions."

Her smirk changed into a mischievous grin, bringing an enticing sparkle to her deep brown eyes. "And I enjoy verbally sparring with you."

On the way back with the soda, she stopped to light two nearby jar candles. Their dancing shadows instantly warmed the room.

"I think we can use a little light on the subject, don't you?" she giggled. "I love candlelight. I would have enjoyed being Abraham Lincoln and doing my homework by candlelight."

"Yes, maybe," he replied. *And candlelight entices your beauty even more.*

Chapter Twenty Nine

The Gift of Mercy

"But because of his great love for us, God, who is rich in mercy, made us alive with Christ even when we were dead in transgressions—it is by grace you have been saved."

Ephesians 2:4-5 (NIV)

JAMES WILLIAM HUTCHINS

On Thursday, January 11, 1979, Hutchins's attorneys entered appeals to delay the execution scheduled for 6:00 a.m. January 13. Over the course of the day, his attorneys pursued two issues through the courts. The first one was the state's law forbidding execution of an insane person; they wanted to provide testimony as to whether Hutchins was currently insane. The second issue regarded the death-question qualification of jurors because five potential jurors had been excluded from the McDowell County trial because they opposed capital punishment.

Selwyn Rose, a psychiatrist from Winston Salem, N.C., who had been hired by the defense, had met with James for a short time during the morning before she had headed to a noon hearing in Raleigh to testify before Superior Court Judge Robert Collier. She would be quoted as saying, "Hutchins has no fear of dying and he believes he was 'going to be in a better place' and 'the sooner the better.'" She had also testified that Hutchins "is mentally ill," but "he knew the difference between right and wrong." She concluded by saying Hutchins was in a "severely paranoid state and believes every event is fixed against him" and "because Hutchins feels he shot the two deputies in self-defense, he was in the right and will go to heaven." Hutchins was also quoted as telling another doctor at Dorothea Dix that "in response to his prayers, he heard the Holy Spirit speak."

Judge Collier denied the request to delay the execution, so the defense attorneys appealed to the N.C. Supreme Court and to the chief district judge for the Western District of N.C., U.S. District Judge Woodrow Jones in Rutherfordton, but Judge Jones also denied the request to delay the execution.

After Judge McMillan of Charlotte issued an opinion, the N.C. Supreme Court held a conference in which they listened to Judge McMillan's opinion, which was "people who oppose the death penalty shouldn't be excluded from juries that decide guilt or innocence." The N.C. Supreme Court refused to grant a stay of execution.

After receiving this rejection, two of his defense attorneys made an impromptu visit to the governor's office at 9:00 p.m. Next, they prepared an appeal to the 4th U.S. Circuit Court of Appeals in Richmond, Virginia.

A stay was issued after midnight on January 13, 1979, by Judge J. Dickson Phillips. Forty-nine minutes prior to the execution time of 6:00 a.m., the North Carolina Supreme Court blocked it. Hutchins was returned to Death Row to live out another two months waiting to die.

Three days later, a new execution date of March 16, 1984, and an execution time of 2:00 a.m. was set.

Chapter Thirty

The Act of Confrontation

"Remember, confrontation is about reconciliation and awareness, not judgement or anger."

Dale Partridge, Author

ALEX WELLS / TONY ADAMS

Alex had overslept; somehow, she'd banged the ringer on the alarm clock and fell back asleep. Panicked, she jumped up. Tony was coming in a couple of hours, so they could head to Rutherfordton to meet with Charles. James Hutchins had received another reprieve from his January 13 execution. Now it was re-scheduled for March 16, and they had somehow received invitations to attend the execution. After throwing fresh coffee grounds into a filter and snapping it into the coffee maker, she loaded two slices of wheat bread into the toaster and slammed down the lower lever. That's when the doorbell rang. *Oh my gosh! Not now!* She thought.

The excited and yapping Yorkies followed behind at her heels. Alex peeked through the door's peephole. *Mama! Not now!* She groaned.

"Hello, Mama. Come on in," she said while opening the door. The bright sunlight blinded her as she closed the door.

The two women hugged and kissed each other, which was their normal greeting.

"How have you been, Alexandra?"

Alexandra? Mama never uses my formal name unless something's up.

"Fine. Fine. Just rushing. Tony will be here in a couple of hours to get me."

"Can we talk? It shouldn't take too long." Her mother swept past her and headed toward the kitchen without first receiving an answer.

"Sure." Alex chased after her. "I made coffee. Want some?"

"Yes. Coffee would be good."

While Alex poured two cups of coffee, Betsy sat at the breakfast room table, smoothing the cloth placemat with her fingers. "How is Tony and Johnny doing?"

"Okay. They're fine, I guess. I haven't seen Tony in a week. Oh, I've seen him a few times in the hallway at school but never long enough to have a conversation. After classes, he rushes to get Johnny from daycare and then heads home to fix his supper."

"When is his sister coming home? He's had Johnny for a while."

"I don't know. He seems a little tight-lipped about the whole situation. He'd originally said he thought she was out West to find a job, so Johnny could be close to both parents. Tony got a card, and Johnny got some things from her at Christmas. But he hasn't mentioned when she's coming home. I know little Johnny misses his Mama.

"I know. Saturday when I babysat for him, he talked about his 'Mommy' a great deal. He asked me if I knew her. When I told him I didn't, he seemed sad. He told me she was pretty, and sometimes at night, he has bad dreams and wakes up crying for her. But he told me the cutest thing. He said, 'But Unky Tony comes in and hugs me and makes me not sad.'"

"Oh. He is so sweet!" Alex agreed. Lack of time gave her courage. "So what did you want to talk about?"

"Sit down, please Alex."

She obeyed and sat opposite her mother.

"Please talk to me about what is wrong between your father and you. I've sensed this horrible strife for several months, actually since summer, and this is entirely too long. I've been sitting back and hoping and praying things would work themselves out. But when Thanksgiving came along, I could have cut the tension between you two. And then Christmas came and…" Her voice trailed off as tears filled her eyes. "We've never been apart for Christmas dinner. Oh, don't get me wrong. I understand you're grown and want to be with your friends, but it really hurt both your father and me. It seemed like sudden plans, like you didn't want to be with us."

"Mama! Please don't do this, not now," Alex groaned. "I don't have time for this! I'm going to be late."

Betsy grabbed a tissue from a nearby box on the counter and dabbed at her green eyes. "I'm sorry. It seems like you never have time anymore. You don't come over; you don't call. When we call you, you don't have time to talk. Is it this book that's taking all your time? Is it work? Is everything okay with your job? Is there something going on with your friends? Help me to understand, Alex. We've always been close, and we've shared so much with each other. Please talk to me."

"Mama, please can we do this later?" She hoped Betsy would agree to buy her more time.

Betsy stared at her manicured fingers. Her bottom lip trembled, and the tears began again. "If I've done something to hurt you, I'm sorry," she whispered barely loud enough for Alex to hear.

Alex arose, coming over to her mother. Tenderly, she hugged her, soothing her shaking shoulders with her hands. "Mama, I love you. You haven't done anything. I promise."

"Then is it something your father did?" she asked. "What could he have done to make you act this way?"

Alex abruptly pulled back. "It's between us." She stood and went to the coffee maker and poured more liquid into her cup.

"Then there is something wrong. Have you given him a chance to make things right?"

"He can't make this right." Her back was to her mother. When she turned around, her mother appeared shocked. The way Betsy rocked her back against the chair was as if someone had slapped her across the face.

"Probably not, because I haven't cared to talk with him. And I don't plan to talk with him about this."

"Alex! You're being so unfair. I've never known you to act like this. You've always been so loving and kind – you've always fought for the underdog, those who are hurt. You and your father have always been crazy about each other. How can you treat him so cruelly?"

She paused but received no reaction from her daughter.

"This is making him sick. I don't know if you noticed at Christmas or not, but your father has lost thirty pounds or more. I'm worried about him."

"I'm sure he is fine. You shouldn't worry about him."

"I love you both, Alex. I can't help but worry. You two are my life."

"And you're mine, but I honestly don't have time to talk about this now."

"Well, I'm sorry. Tony and this book will just have to wait. I believe this is as important as the book or your classes or your friends. I'm talking about family, Alex. Family is important. No matter what he's done, it is possible to forgive and move on."

"I disagree," Alex moaned. "This is so unfair. Why haven't you asked him what's wrong?"

"I have. He won't tell me either. He seems reluctant to discuss anything to do with you. But I can't continue like this anymore. I want my family back. I want my daughter to come and visit her parents. I want us to be welcomed into your home. We haven't been invited to your home since you moved back in after the water damage. I want us to laugh and be a part of each other's lives like we used to be."

"I think you need to talk with him."

Betsy looked dumbfounded. "Why can't you tell me?"

"I think you need to talk with him," Alex repeated.

"Okay. I will," Betsy replied quietly, apparently resigned.

It hurt to see her mother so brokenhearted. Alex's anger began to bubble up to the surface again.

"May I tell you a story, Alex? It shouldn't take too long; you'll still have time to get ready before Tony arrives."

"Sure, if you will promise to hurry."

"I will. Then please give me the courtesy of having a seat." She motioned for her daughter to sit closer to her. Rather than sitting across the table, Alex placed herself in the chair at the end of the table, closer to her mother.

Her mother cleared her voice and paused. She sipped the coffee as if to garner strength, and began. "Once there was this happy family, which consisted of a father, a mother, three daughters, and two brothers."

Alex guessed Betsy was talking about her own family.

"The father had a demanding job working as a project manager in a nationally-owned construction company. The mother was a schoolteacher, who had taught junior high school for sixteen years. Over a series of months, she had begun to lose weight. She wasn't dieting or cutting back on what she was eating. Then one night while taking a bath, she found a lump in her right breast. She waited several more months until she said something to her husband, who insisted she see a doctor as soon as possible. He even took off work to accompany her. Tests were run, and the tests were conclusive. She had cancer. The quick-growing cancer had started in her breast, but by the time she'd gone to the doctors, it had spread throughout her body."

"With heavy hearts, they called the children together and shared her terminal diagnosis with them. The children were devastated. They cried and bellowed and expressed their fears of the unknown to their dying mother. Bravely, she asked each of her children to promise to always turn to God through prayer in times like these. She asked them to attend church regularly and to help their father and each other in the days and years ahead. She explained that even though there'd be rough times, they should always love each other and remember they were family. She warned they'd make mistakes along the way, but as long as they learned from them, then their mistakes could be forgiven and forgotten. Jesus's death on the cross had already provided forgiveness, a release from their sins. Finally, she reminded her children when Jesus came into this world, he accepted the role of servitude – to serve and not to be served. She hoped they would realize these teachings in their own lives and be helpful to others."

"For the few days they had left, she asked them to take turns reading her favorite Bible verses to her. Between the excruciating pain and the debilitating effects of the pain relievers, she led them in prayers and listened to their heartfelt prayers with pleas for their mother's health to be returned through some miracle. But that wasn't God's plan, so they watched as her loveliness disappeared before their eyes."

"When she died within the month, she was only thirty-eight years old. Her husband was distraught by grief, having lost the love of his life. He'd known and loved her since they were childhood sweethearts in the eighth grade. He couldn't accept the emptiness she left behind, so he began working longer hours than normal. He took on additional projects each weekend. He hid his sorrow by filling his days with work. The children were left to fend for themselves."

"The eldest daughter, who was sixteen at the time, became a substitute responsible parent. Her father would cash his paycheck each week and leave household monies in a white envelope. With the money he provided, she saw groceries were bought, meals were cooked, and utility bills were paid. The other children assisted in keeping the house clean and the clothes washed. Her two sisters were thirteen and twelve; her brothers were even younger – ten and eight. Each night, she helped them with their homework and tucked them into bed before completing her own homework assignments. While she was thankful for their collective contributions of performing assigned chores like taking out the trash, mopping the floors, dusting, or vacuuming, she became worn out and depressed. She prayed for her mother's presence, but she needed her father's help. The responsibilities were too much for a sixteen year old to carry alone, but he didn't seem to care. He was wrapped up in his own sorrow. He had forgotten his children were grieving too."

"One night, three of his co-workers invited him to celebrate one of their birthdays by going after work for a few beers. Normally, he had said no to these repeated invitations. He'd never been much of a drinker, and even as a teenager, he hadn't developed a taste for beer. But on this particular night, the first anniversary of his wife's death, he was feeling even lower than usual. So when he agreed, they clapped him on the back and promised he'd have a good time."

"They decided to drive one car, so the four men piled into a car and headed for a nearby bar where they each drank a couple of beers. Next, they decided to frequent an exclusive men's club where they had more drinks and watched a girlie show. The night ended at a third bar where they enjoyed their last drinks. After being returned to his car, the father was drunk. He couldn't even remember driving home that night."

"When he arrived at the house, the eldest daughter was awake in her bed and doing her homework. By the time she'd taken a bath and dressed for bed, the other kids had fallen asleep. A loud bang interrupted her studies. She hurried to the front door and found her dad sprawled out on the porch. He apparently had stumbled while climbing up the front steps and had banged his head on the door casing. There was a dribble of blood oozing out of an egg-sized knot on his forehead. Alarmed, she helped him to his feet, so he could steady his footing. With his arm slung over her tiny shoulders, she slowly led him to the kitchen, where he plopped down in the nearest chair."

"While she ran to the nearby bathroom's medicine cabinet to grab some clean gauze, a bottle of peroxide, and some bandages, he hummed a song to himself and laughed aloud several times. When she returned, she stood in front of him and bent forward to wipe the wound clean, oblivious to the fact her gaping gown provided him with a view of her bare chest."

"Without warning, he shoved her backward with such force, her buttocks hit the floor hard. He was screaming. 'What is wrong with you, girl? You're acting like a whore! I didn't raise you to be a slut. Why are you showing your breasts to me? I'm your father!'"

"'Daddy!' is all she could sob aloud before he began berating her again."

"'Is that what you do on all your dates? Giving those boys a real show, huh?'"

"'No! No! I don't do that.' The girl sobbed from his belittling. This was the lowest moment of her life. She'd never experienced so much hurt, or shame, or so much pain heaved onto her innocence. Her heart was shattered by his cruel words."

"'You're lying. You're lying! No daughter of mine is going to act like all those harlots I saw tonight prancing around without any clothes on."'

"He lunged toward her with an open palm and the intentions of slapping her across the face, but she dodged his hand by half a second when she quickly moved backward. Suddenly, his fingers became entangled in the front of her gown, ripping the cotton cloth away and exposing the pink flesh underneath. She gasped and quickly covered her nakedness with her hands. She began bawling, unaware her sister was watching in horror from the doorway."

"'Stop it!' She screamed at her father as she fell to the floor to embrace her older sister and to block him from hitting her again."

"Startled, he began crying, then repeating, 'I'm sorry. I'm sorry. I didn't mean it. I didn't mean to....'"

"'What's wrong with you, Daddy?' her sister yelled back. 'Come on, Sis. Come on.' Together, the girls disappeared into the hallway, leaving the stunned and embarrassed father sobbing in his open palms."

Alex was captivated by her mother's storytelling. Astounded, she asked, "Oh Mama, how awful! What did you do?"

"The next morning was difficult. Unbeknownst to us, he'd called in sick at work, so he could be there when I awoke. I'd slept restlessly, but Brenda had curled up beside me and fallen asleep. At daybreak, Shirley had awakened to find Brenda's bed empty, so she joined us, unaware of the previous night's events. We stayed in my bedroom until we thought Daddy had left for work. As we crept down the hall to fix cereal, we found him sitting at the kitchen table in the same clothes, unshaven, and looking forlorn. When he heard us, he immediately sought my face with his red-rimmed eyes, now swimming in tears. He mumbled, 'Betsy, I am so sorry. Please forgive me. Can I talk to you?'"

"Honestly, Alex, I was startled to find him at the table, and I definitely didn't feel like talking. I was embarrassed and self-conscious about what he'd seen. After all, he was my father. No one but my sisters and mother had ever seen my bare chest. And I was so hurt by all the mean and terrible things he'd said and called me. I guess I was shocked my father knew those words. I'd never thought of him as a regular man. He was my father; I'd always put him on a pedestal. He wasn't like other men. I didn't think he knew what a whore or a slut was. I thought he was above all this. Maybe his words had shattered the pedestal, as well as the image I had of him. Maybe this is what hurt the most. He'd fallen off the artificial pedestal I'd placed him on. I think this is something we all do to our parents. We place them on a pedestal they can't possibly stand on because they are human – we all are human."

Alex listened intently. Her eyes were brimming with tears. "So, what happened?"

"I asked Brenda and Shirley to leave the room. This was one of the hardest things I'd ever done. Secretly, their being there had made me feel better, more confident, stronger, even though Shirley had no idea what had happened. And later Brenda and I made a pact she never had to know."

"I sat down at the table across from where he sat. He reached for my shaking hands, but I withdrew them and hid them in my lap. I felt so empty, so desolate, and never before had I wanted my mother more than I did at that moment. It felt like I was talking to a stranger. So I said a quick prayer and asked God not to leave me and to give me strength and a compassionate heart for my father's pain. And you know what, Alex. God did. All of a sudden, I felt this warm tingle running through me from head to toe. My hands stopped shaking, and I began crying not for me, but for him."

"I can't remember all my father said to me that day. It's been so long ago, but I knew he meant every word he said from the bottom of his heart. I knew he was sorry and begged for my forgiveness. It would have been easy to pout or not to accept his apology, but I knew he'd never acted that way before to mother or any of us. He admitted to drinking all those beers and where he'd gone the night before, not to make excuses for his actions, but as a confession and promise he'd never drink anything again. Maybe he was trying to assure me the man whom I'd encountered the night before was not the father I knew and definitely not the father I could count on having in the future. I realized by his confession and openness with me, he was holding himself accountable for his actions – not placing the blame or the responsibility on his three co-workers, which is what a lot of people would have done. This made him grow in my esteem for him. And as far as I know, he never drank anything else, not even a glass of wine."

Alex nodded. Loving tears streamed over her cheeks for the brave woman who sat beside her. She'd been terribly hurt by her father, and Alex knew another secret, which would hurt her again. She wished with all her heart her mother's pain could be spared. Reaching over, she grasped her mother's hand in hers.

"So did ya'll live happily ever after?" She wasn't trying to be insensitive.

"As happy as we could be. All of us hurt for a long time after mother died, but we were family, and she'd asked us to remember it always. She'd also asked us to be mindful we were human and would make mistakes but the love we had for each other should be enough to warrant forgiveness. I never forgot what my dad did, but I realized he was only human and had made some mistakes. Jesus died on the cross so all my sins and mistakes could be forgiven; he didn't hold back, so how could I withhold forgiveness from a man I dearly loved – my father?"

"Alex, remember we all make mistakes and fall short of the glory of God. But God loves us so much he gave his only son to die for us so our sins could be forgiven. So as Christians, how can we withhold forgiveness from others – especially those whom we love the most?"

She came over and sat in her mother's lap even though they were about the same size. It felt good to be held by her and to hold her again. It had been too long since they'd opened their hearts to each other. She was grateful for her mother's visit that morning. She'd shared something so intimate, so profound it had left Alex speechless.

After her mother left, Alex returned to the kitchen and dropped to her knees beside the doggie beds where her puppies were napping. She grabbed them into her arms and smothered heartfelt cries into their Yorkies' pedigreed hair and allowed them to lick away her salty tears with unconditional love.

Chapter Thirty One

The Gift of Wisdom

"Turn your wounds into wisdom."
Oprah Winfrey

ALEX WELLS / TONY ADAMS

On the same morning, Tony had gathered together a few of Johnny's toys and packed two snacks and a tasty lunch in his *Star Wars* lunch box. Tony's married neighbors, Tanna and Shauna, who lived in the next condo, had volunteered to keep Johnny for the day. The couple had even insisted Tony allow the little boy to sleep over, which would give Tony the opportunity to invite Alex to dinner after their Saturday trip to Rutherfordton. So Tony was feeling upbeat with the promise of actually having a proper date with her. Working on the book certainly wasn't what he considered dating. Johnny was sitting on the floor, building houses with his new Legos Tony had surprised him with the previous night. That's when the phone rang.

"Is this Mr. Tony Adams?" the woman asked.

"Yes."

"Mr. Adams. This is Wanda Avery. I'm with TriangleCity Memorial Hospital in California. Is Terri Adams Tunney your sister?"

"Yes she is," he said, with a sudden instinct something bad was wrong.

"I'm sorry. I have some bad news."

Tony's legs felt like spaghetti noodles, as he slipped to the floor. This was de ja vu. He'd heard those same words when his parents had been killed instantly in an automobile accident. He started to hang up the phone. He didn't want to hear any more.

"Mr. Adams, are you still there? Mr. Adams?" she repeated.

"Yes, I'm here," he stammered.

"Your sister was admitted here last night. It appears she may have attempted suicide, but she is alive. Our doctors and nurses were able to save her."

"Suicide? What? Are you sure you're talking about my sister?"

"You did say your sister is Terri Tunney, correct?"

"Yes."

"Then your sister is a patient at our hospital. Currently, she is in stable condition. Her roommate found your name and phone number among her personal items. Are you able to come?"

"Roommate?" he stammered. Before she answered, he said, "Of course I'll come. I have .... Let me see. I have to find a babysitter.... Then I need ...."

"Mr. Adams," she interrupted. "I'll tell the doctors you're on your way. Do you know how long it will take for you to arrive?"

"I have no idea. I live in North Carolina. I'll have to catch a plane as soon as I can arrange some things and buy a ticket." His mind was whirling in fifty different directions.

"Okay. I understand. We wanted you to know."

"Thank you for calling, and ma'am, please tell the doctors thank you for helping my sister. Please continue to help her. I'll be there as soon as possible."

"I will pass this along. Goodbye."

"Bye."

Tony wanted to scream. While the ceiling was crashing down, the walls were caving in, too. The room had gotten darker, and it needed to stop spinning. He reached for the phone and dialed the first person he could think of – he dialed Alex's number.

Alex wiped her tear-stained face and running mascara with a damp dishtowel as she answered the phone. "Hello?"

"Alex, this is Tony. I have to ask you a big favor."

"Oh Tony, I'm glad you called. I was getting ready to call you and tell you...."

"Alex. I don't have time to talk. I need you to keep Johnny for a few days."

"Tony! I'm not feeling well today. Did you say for a few days?"

"Yes. I don't have time to explain now. I need to hurry. Can you do it or not?"

"Well, I've never kept him more than a few hours. I don't know...."

He interrupted her. "Alex. I need you. Johnny loves you, and you're the only one I'd leave him with more than a night. Please help me out."

He sounded desperate, so she conceded. "Sure. Of course, I will. What do you want me to do? Do you want me to come and get him there, or will you bring him here?"

"You're out of the way of the airport. Can you come here?"

"Sure. I'll be there in an hour."

"That should be fine. I need to make the next flight to California. If I have to leave before you get here, I'll leave Johnny with Tanna and Shauna, my next door neighbors."

"I remember. Where are you…?"

"I'll explain later. I love you…." He caught himself. "I mean, I love you for doing this," he stammered.

"Sure. But you better call me as soon as possible, and let me know what's going on."

"I will. I promise. And thank you."

The call was disconnected before she could respond.

When Alex arrived at Tony's condo, he didn't answer the door, so she knocked on his neighbors' door. Tanna quickly opened it and welcomed her in. She found Johnny and Shauna blissfully playing on the carpeted floor. They had built a house of Legos.

"Do you know what happened?" she whispered to Tanna. "Why did Tony have to leave so quickly?"

"It had something to do with his sister. He said he'd be gone for a few days, asked us to get his mail, and said you'd be coming soon to get Johnny."

"Oh okay. I figured it might be about her. Well thank you for taking care of Johnny until I could get here. This is going to be a new experience for me. I've never kept a child overnight."

"He's a good kid – really smart. Play it by ear. Let your nurturing instincts kick in."

She laughed. "I'm not sure I have any of those."

Alex took Johnny by the hand and lifted his car seat with the other. Shauna carried a large mesh bag of toys to the car. Tanna followed behind with two small suitcases and helped Alex install the car seat by adjusting the seat belts.

"Thanks, guys. I appreciate your help."

"You're welcome," Shauna said. "And we're here if there's anything we can do to help. I wrote down our home number and our two work numbers in case you need anything. I stuffed those in one of the suitcases. Can't remember which one, but you'll find it."

"Thanks so much. I'll guard it with my life. I may be calling on you," Alex warned. "Johnny, say goodbye to Tanna and Shauna."

"Bye. Bye." He flipped his tiny hand up and waved goodbye like he'd seen his uncle do. "See you next time."

They were laughing when Alex circled through and exited the parking lot.

She adjusted her mirror, so she could see the tiny boy in the backseat.

"Are you excited to be staying with me, Johnny?"

"Yep. Excited."

"We'll have fun together, won't we?" she probed.

"Yep."

"And you'll help me take care of you, right?" she asked.

"Yep."

"Are you excited to see the puppies again?"

"Yep."

"Will you quit being so talkative?"

"Yep."

Before they drove into her driveway, Johnny was asleep. Carefully, she unbuckled the little boy and lifted his body in her arms.

So trusting, she thought. *Poor little fellow. Your mother is who knows where, your father has been who knows where, and now your uncle is going to who knows where.*

He was so sleepy, even the welcoming barks of the Yorkies didn't wake him. Alex pulled back the covers of her bed and laid him on the sheets before removing his shoes and covering him. The Yorkies were jumping on the sides of the high bed and sniffing in the air.

"Come on girls," she whispered. "Let him sleep."

As she gently closed the door and began tiptoeing into the other room, the phone rang.

Charles? I bet it's him calling. We were supposed to meet him at the library.

She hurried to cease the ringing before it woke Johnny. "Hello?"

"Yes ma'am," the feminine voice said. "Are you interested in entering the Publisher's Clearing House Sweepstakes?"

"Lady, only if you can guarantee I'll win and be able to take a rocket to the moon."

"Excuse me?"

"I'm sorry. I'm busy. I don't have time to talk today. Call back another time. Goodbye."

She felt like crying again for the second time that day. Or was it the third time? She'd lost count. She looked at the calendar hanging on the wall. It couldn't be hormonal. She was in the middle of her cycle. Her frayed emotions had to be because of all the crazy things going on in her life, starting with her father. How could she forgive him for what she'd seen? Once her mother found out, her heart would be broken, then she'd be furious at her father again. How could she forgive him for this? Then there was Mama, who was blaming her for everything when she didn't know the truth. And there was Tony who'd left her in a lurch, caring for his nephew when she did well to care for her two Yorkies and herself. Caring for a child would be difficult. Not only was she expected to bathe him, feed him, and put him to bed, she'd have to play with him, read to him, and take him to daycare until Tony returned. Who knew when it would be? She was overwhelmed.

On top of all this, there was their silly idea of writing a book and becoming best-selling authors after selecting a topic like Hutchins and his murders to write about. As the execution date approached, she couldn't get May 31, 1979, off her mind. He'd caused a boatload of misery in other people's lives. As a writer, she understood how Tony was remaining objective and trying to make him a three dimensional human with emotions. But in Alex's opinion, Tony was trying to give him a soul and a conscience, and she wasn't sure it was possible even from a fictional standpoint. Alex shook her head. Her stomach felt knotted. Her hands shook. Her nerves were shot. This had been an emotional day that wasn't ending the way she'd planned. She needed a glass of wine to calm herself, but now with a baby in the house, she decided against it.

The Yorkies barked. "I know. I know. You're hungry," she growled. "This short-order cook, failed daughter, demanding English instructor, want-to-be author, and volunteered babysitter needs a glass of wine, but I can't have one. I need a break."

That's when the phone rang. It was wonderful when she heard Charles's concerned voice on the other end. She felt relieved and as if a prayer had been answered. Suddenly, the little Dutch boy who kept his finger plugged in her emotional dyke had left unexpectedly, leaving her alone for the dam to burst and the floods to come. And the rushing waters swept through the telephone lines, travelling the long distance to the end and splashing an unexpected friend in the face with the cold truth.

Chapter Thirty Two

The Gift of Freedom

"You, my brothers and sisters, were called to be free. But do not use your freedom to indulge the flesh; rather, serve one another humbly in love."

Galatians 5: 13-14 (NIV)

ALEX WELLS / TONY ADAMS

When Alex regained her composure, she assumed Charles was still on the phone, waiting patiently.

"I'm sorry, Charles. I've had such a bad day," she hiccupped. "I'm sorry I didn't call the library and leave a message so you'd know we couldn't meet with you."

"That's okay, Alex. I figured something unexpected had happened. Are you and Tony all right?"

"Yes. We're physically fine. I can't say the same for our mental or emotional states. And to be honest, I don't know all Tony is going through."

"I'm sorry. Tell me what I can do to help you? I'm your friend, and I'm here for you both." His voice was gentle, so inviting, so comforting, so needed.

Without hesitation, Alex began blubbering into the phone's mouthpiece. First she relayed Tony's phone call when he asked her to care for Johnny. This was stressing her out because she'd never cared for a little boy before. Then she rattled off the highlights of her mother's visit that morning and how her mother seemed to be blaming her for the situation between her father and her, even though she had no idea what had caused the problem and how her mother's story about her grandfather had made her sad. Finally, she shared the horrid details of finding her father in the arms of another woman and how it had disappointed her and how it would destroy her mother, upsetting Alex to the point of never wanting to see her father again. She hardly took a breath as she blurted out the litany of problems she faced.

As Alex rambled on for twenty five minutes or more, Charles listened intently and never interrupted, not even to ask a question. His audible breathing was her only way of knowing the call was still connected. When Alex's diatribe ended, she caught her own breath. Immediately, she noticed her body felt lighter, like a heavy backpack full of books had been lifted from her aching shoulders.

"Uh huh. Hmmm," Charles said. "Well, I'm extremely sorry for all you've experienced, Alex. It's easy to understand how hurt you've been and how you've had your mother's best interests at heart. And you're being a good friend to Tony by caring for the little boy in the midst of all the confusion and turmoil you've been feeling. So Alex, allow me to ask you one question."

"Sure," she agreed.

"Alex, how many times have you taken these burdens to God in prayer?"

With that question, he figuratively smacked her between the eyes with a two by four. "I...I...well ...I guess

I haven't. I've been so wrapped up in my feelings I haven't really taken the time to pray. Besides, God has more important things to worry about than my problems."

"You do believe in God, right Alex? You believe Jesus Christ is your Lord and Savior who died on the cross to save you from your sins and who defeated death so you might have a life everlasting, correct?"

"Of course! My parents took me to church for my entire childhood. I do believe in God. I went through Confirmation when I was fourteen. I've learned all the Catechisms, and I believe in the tenets of the 'Apostle's Creed.'"

"Okay. Good. The reason I asked you about prayer is because it's easy for us to believe we are in control of all situations, and we can handle all the turmoil and tribulations, which come our way. It's easy to think of God as some far-away being who is there when we remember or when we go to church. It's easy to forget prayer is a way of conversing with the One who loves us more than anyone on this earth, the One who knows us better than we know ourselves, the One who knows every secret of our hearts or every burden weighing us down. Prayer is an opportunity to communicate with your best friend. It's a time to express thanksgiving and give praise for all the blessings you've been given. It's a time to ask for help, Alex. We are so inadequate to handle the turmoil and the tribulations that come our way each day. Besides, God already knows what we're going through and is in control of all things. God can take the chaos we create or others create in our lives and turn it into something good. You haven't been alone, Alex, and

Tony is not alone, now. Your Father is walking beside you every step of the way. Am I making sense?"

"Yes, Charles. It's easy to want to cram all the bad down deep inside and not express it to anyone – not even God."

"Which is futile because God already knows. And let me correct one thing you said earlier, Alex. God loves you more than anything. Your problems are important. There are no problems you have that can't be fixed if you call upon the name of the Lord. Okay?"

"Yes, okay."

"Now Alex, there is something else I want to talk to you about. Do we have time?"

"Yes. The baby is still asleep. Talk away, Charles."

"Your feelings today aren't about your mother's visit and your grandfather's transgressions against her. Your feelings aren't about caring for Johnny for an unknown period of time. Your feelings today are a culmination of all these things, but to me, it seems like you're difficulty in forgiving your father is compounding your emotions and interfering with other relationships and your overall outlook on life. Am I correct?"

"Yes. Probably. But in all honesty, Charles, I want to forgive him, but I don't know if I can."

"If you want to, then this is most of the battle. And maybe you're hesitation is because you're having a hard time forgiving yourself?"

"Me? What have I done?" she asked.

"For committing your un-Alex-like actions. You're not acting like the Alex I know. For not forgiving your father. For withholding your love from him -- someone who loves you deeply. For hurting your mother with your absences and neglect. Does any of this make sense?"

"I guess," her voice was low. She felt ashamed, embarrassed. "I guess you're right."

"In John 8:32, we're told 'And you shall know the truth, and the truth shall make you free.' Alex, sometimes forgiving others seems like an impossible thing to do. Because of the excruciating pain you've experienced, the initial reaction may be to become confused. I'm sure you were shocked at what you saw. You couldn't believe it was happening. And then the natural reaction is to avoid feeling the pain again. We look for ways to avoid pain. You've quit referring to your father as 'Dad' or 'Daddy.' I've noticed. Instead you refer to him as 'he.' You've avoided visiting your parents' home and participating in family activities the three of you always enjoyed. And sometimes forgiveness is hard, especially when we don't see others as human beings and when we view them as being exalted. It is like when we put someone on a pedestal and the person falls off. That means we were wrong, and we don't like to make mistakes. Our feelings become bruised and sensitive. We've discovered the person is nothing more than a human being, capable of making mistakes and committing sins like us. Forgiveness doesn't come easy when we focus more on our hurt instead of focusing on the person and realizing he/she is fallible as we are. When Christ was dying on the cross, He was able to focus on the love he had for the people, not on their horrible acts to him, not on the physical pain they caused him, not on the ultimate betrayal they had chided him with, or not on the mockery they had shown him by not recognizing He was the true Son of God. That's how He was able to ask God to forgive those who crucified him."

"Alex, when we forgive someone, we demonstrate a loving heart, God's heart; when we forgive someone, this is the closest we ever get to God. When we forgive someone, we demonstrate our awareness of all God has given us."

"Charles, talking about it sounds easy. Doing it is really difficult. I can't forget."

"But I'm not asking you to forget. I believe once the forgiveness is given, the painful memory fades and a peacefulness replaces it, so the memory no longer hurts – even though it is still there in the past where it belongs. How can we accept God's forgiveness for our sins when we can't give the same forgiveness to others? Why do we expect God's mercy when we don't give the same mercy to others? Alex, when we don't forgive the debts or trespasses of others, then we block ourselves from loving others and accepting love from others."

"You don't know how many times I've cried over this. Charles, you don't expect to walk into your home and find your father with another woman."

"No, you don't, Alex, but your father is a man. He has problems and doubts and desires and dreams and fears of his own. He's growing older. He's questioning his time left on this earth. He's questioning his virility as a man. He's questioning his effectiveness at work. These are not excuses for what he did; but there can be healing and understanding for what he's done – for him and for you. You may not ever forget what you saw. But it is possible to begin the healing process for those wounds as long as you're willing to accept his apology and try to forgive him. When you are able to do that, you'll set him free from his pain, and in the process, you'll set yourself free from your pain, too. Alex, don't you agree you've been withholding your respect, your time, your kindness, and most of all your love as a punishment to your father?"

"Yes, I suppose so."

"That's what's eating you inside. Withholding your love is contrary to whom you are as a person. You're a very loving, giving, and accepting person. You've had a strong family unit until these last few months. And if you'll think about it, your resentment toward him has affected your other relationships, like with your mother. She hasn't done anything to you, but you are punishing her by your actions and resentment toward your father. And perhaps, your resentment gets in the way and prevents you from realizing or nurturing other relationships."

"What do you mean?" she asked.

"Take James, for example. His childhood was hard because of poverty, hard work in the share-cropping fields, his lack of education, and his abusive, wife-beating father who rejected him. The male role model in a boy's life is his father. He was the authoritarian figure in his life, as well. I'm sure James has always had unresolved resentment toward his father, which spilled over into his other relationships, causing him to continue the cycle of abuse with his own family. And sadly, he never received an apology from his father so there could be healing and perhaps a closure for the wrong he'd experienced. In addition, his dislike for authority was probably born from this resentment. He never developed a healthy acceptance for the law, rules, or law enforcers."

"But Alex, we don't have to sit around and wait for someone to apologize; it can be futile if the person is unwilling or unable to say 'I'm sorry' or if the person dies before it's possible. As a result, if we don't deal with the hurt ourselves, days and months and years can pass, and before we know it, the seeds of an unforgiven spirit have taken us hostage, separating us from God."

"God loves you, Alex, and God wants to share your burdens. Take them to God in prayer and ask for help. Your prayers will be answered. I'm sure."

"Thank you, Charles. I need to digest all you've told me."

"I hope you will, young Alex. And above all, pray about it."

"I will," she promised. "I will. Already the world seems a little brighter."

Chapter Thirty Three

The Gift of Love

"Love is patient, love is kind. It does not envy, it does not boast, it is not proud. It does not dishonor others, it is not self-seeking, it is not easily angered, it keeps no record of wrongs."

1 Corinthians 13: 4-5 (NIV)

ALEX WELLS / TONY ADAMS

Tony sat at his sister's bedside, watching as she slept. He felt an overwhelming amount of gratitude to God that his prayers had been answered and Terri's prognosis was good. After extensive questioning of Terri and her former college friend, Carol, with whom she'd been staying the past few months, it was determined what had initially been considered an attempted suicide was now deemed irresponsible and precarious behavior. When her friend, Carol, had been unable to awaken Terri when she'd returned from work, she didn't hesitate to call for an ambulance. Of course, the two empty bottles of wine and the half-empty bottle of sleeping pills presented fear and suspicion to those first responders.

Carol informed the doctors Terri was depressed, but Carol was adamant Terri had never exhibited any behaviors or indicated she wanted to "end it all." Yes, Terri had been going through a tough time in her life, but she had been gradually getting better, especially after a recent meeting she'd had, which had cleared up a lot of things for her. Carol had remained vague about Terri's turning point, but the doctors believed her.

Thankfully, when Terri was conscious again and alert, she was able to convince everyone – doctors, nurses, psychiatrists – she had no intentions of taking her own life. She admitted to being depressed since her husband had left her – and even before then, when her parents had died accidentally in a car accident. And she did admit to taking several sleeping pills while she was in a wine-induced haze. She couldn't remember if she'd taken a pill before retiring or not, so she had taken another one; possibly, she had even repeated the same sequence of events a third time. She couldn't be certain. She did agree she'd taken more than one and had had drank two bottles of wine in a short while that afternoon before Carol had returned home.

The doctors had agreed she would be discharged the following day as long as Terri promised to enter an outpatient rehabilitation program and receive counseling for her depression when she returned to North Carolina. They repeated the same recommendation to Tony and emphasized her need for therapy. He heartily accepted responsibility for seeing it was done. Tony and Terri thanked them, thanked Carol for saving her, and expressed their eagerness to return home to North Carolina – especially to Johnny!

After signing the discharge papers at the hospital the following morning, Tony met Terri in her room. The nurse already had her sitting in a wheelchair and was preparing to wheel her downstairs when he appeared in the doorway. She had glanced in his direction and managed a half-smile before turning her face away. Tony had spent the night on Carol's couch the night before and had packed his sister's things. He had a taxi waiting to drive them to the airport.

After finding their seats and buckling their seat belts on the plane, Terri was unusually quiet. Once the plane had successfully lifted into the air and everyone could relax, Tony listened to the free music channels through the provided ear phones. Even though he was trying to read a new spy novel, he was distracted by his sister's stillness. He realized he'd already read the same page three times and still didn't comprehend what he'd read.

"Sis, are you okay? Do you need anything?" he asked.

"No. I'm fine. I'm not hungry," she said quietly.

"How about something to drink? Want a tea or coffee or water? I'll ask the stewardess to get you something."

"No, Tony. Really, I'm fine." She emphasized the word "fine."

"Okay." He wasn't able to mask the dejection and exasperation he felt. "Don't you want an update on your son, Terri? You have yet to ask me about Johnny." Tony shut the novel and jerked off the earphones, relenting to his sudden anger. "You've yet to ask me how I've been."

"Of course, I do. How's Johnny?" Her tone was meek. "Did he get my Christmas presents? I hope he liked them."

Tony stared out the window before answering, as if his reply was the only thing he could withhold as punishment or ransom.

"He's fine. Just fine. Yes, he got the presents. He loved them." Tony's displeasure mounted.

As twins, Tony and Terri had always shared an inherent understanding of each other's emotional state. Even if they were not twins and ordinary siblings, she easily could have grasped his concealed anger and annoyance with her.

"Tony, I know you're angry with me, and you have every right to...."

"Yes I am angry," Tony felt stormy, but as he looked into his sister's penetrating eyes, the gratitude he'd felt yesterday morning when he'd found her okay was slowly filling his soul, edging out his irritation with her. "Yes, I was angry," he clarified. "I was mad at you, Terri. I couldn't understand how you could up and leave me like that with Johnny. I've never cared for a child before. I have a job to go to everyday. I have papers to grade at night. I'm interviewing people and researching articles and newspapers and everything I can get my hands on, so Alex and I can write a book. I have a life, too, you forgot about when you left. You transferred your responsibilities onto my shoulders."

"I know, I know," she stammered. "I'm sorry."

"But I was left to figure out how to become his mother, as well as his uncle -- his main caretaker. I had to figure out how to find the time to prepare my lesson plans, how to find time to grade my papers, and how to schedule time to get him from the daycare every afternoon, how to fix him dinner, how to give him a bath, how to play with him, and how to read him a bedtime story within a twenty-four hour timeframe, all while trying to decipher notes from interviews and papers and schedule interviews for our book. This is something that is important to me, but with no forewarning, I became a parent. I had to put Johnny first and rightfully so." His anger was swelling again.

"I'm sorry. I'm sorry. What else can I say, but I'm sorry. I mean it," she whispered loudly. Neither of them had realized the approaching snack cart.

"Excuse me, but would you like a soda and some peanuts?" the stewardess asked.

"No thank you," Terri replied.

"No thanks," Tony responded with a slight smile.

Terri grabbed his hand. He didn't jerk it away, so she surmised his anger was dissipating.

"Believe me when I say how grateful I am to you for all you've done for Johnny – and me. You're the ONLY person in the world I can trust my son with. You're the only one I can depend on. You and Johnny are all I have, Tony. Will you please forgive me? I didn't mean to hurt you and place my burdens on your shoulders."

He hung his head, wanting to allow the stinging tears to flow. But since it wasn't a manly thing to do, he rubbed his eyelids with the back of his free hand. He heard the sincerity in her voice. "Terri, there isn't anything to forgive. Besides, we're family. Who else can you place all your burdens on?" He asked with a forced smile.

"You're crazy," she joked. "I love you."

"Love you, too."

They sat quietly until their raw emotions caught up with their calmer thoughts.

"He was so excited to get the new movies you sent; we've about played out the others. And instead of sleeping with Big Bird, he's now sleeping with *E.T.* Big Bird has been replaced and sits in the rocking chair beside his bed."

She giggled softly. "That's so sweet, but I feel sorry for Big Bird. He's been number one for so long. Now, he's been replaced. Did ya'll have a good Christmas?"

"Yeah. It was fine. We actually had a better Thanksgiving. We went to Wilmington and visited with Eddie and Pat."

"That's good! How are they?"

"Fine. Johnny enjoyed playing with their kids. They were kind enough to insist we stay the entire weekend. We had fun. We took the kids to the Aquarium at Fort Fisher, to see the Battleship North Carolina, and to the movies. We ate out a couple of times at the restaurants we used to enjoy as kids."

"How did Johnny like everything?"

"All he could say was 'wow' everywhere we went. 'Wow' this and 'Wow' that."

She wore a happy smile.

"As far as Christmas was concerned, we had a quiet one. Other than asking me every other minute 'Is Mommy coming home today?' I made sure Santa brought most of the things on his list, even though his list changed every day, especially whenever he'd watch television and see another toy advertised."

She giggled. "So you didn't spend the day with anyone?"

"No. It was just the two of us, which was fine. When he napped, I was able to sort through some of my notes and read some more articles."

"Thank you, Big Brother. And, I'm sorry I didn't send you a present. Money was really tight. I've been using the money I'd saved from Mark's checks to live on. That's how I was able to buy Johnny a few things and give Carol money for groceries and toiletries. But I will make it up to you. I promise."

"You don't owe me anything. I want you to take care of yourself – and Johnny. Having you home again is what I've been wanting. You are my present."

She changed the subject. "How is the book coming along?"

"Well, we're hoping it will be a book someday. We're still interviewing and researching and trying to figure out where we're headed with this. He is scheduled to be executed March 16."

"That's so depressing. And how is Alex?" she asked with a sly smile.

"Why are you smiling?" He felt embarrassed.

"I think you know," she answered.

"Well, I don't." He tried to sound convincing. "Alex is fine. She's going through some issues of her own, but we've been able to meet on Saturdays with a retired photographer who seems to know a lot about the case. And he's actually friends with the murderer."

"Interesting. And I like Alex, by the way. She's neat and very pretty."

"Yeah. She is." He reversed the conversation to focus on her. "Terri, we've missed you. The first week or so, Johnny cried every night for you. He still does every now and then, but he usually is able to fall off to sleep. The first week, neither of us got any sleep."

"I'm sorry. My poor baby. I feel so bad for leaving him, but I really needed to get away by myself to think. I couldn't handle being depressed, drinking wine, taking pills, and then not being able to function and care for him. You were right. He was in danger with me. I couldn't handle what I'd allowed to happen that night with the stitches. I couldn't handle my guilt and what it was doing to you. By the way, does he have a scar?"

"No, you can hardly see where the gash was. It healed fast."

"Good. I was hoping he wouldn't."

"So, California was the place you decided to go?" he asked.

"Yes. It was the only place I could go. Carol and I have stayed in touch since college. After Mark left, we've talked sometimes two or three times each week. I'm sure you've noticed your phone bill has increased."

"I did, but I assumed the calls to California had to do with Mark or his parents."

"Nope. When Carol invited me to come, I decided I would. Plus, I wanted to see Mark in person. I needed him to tell me in person he didn't love me anymore. And if he didn't love me, then I needed him to explain how he could live his life without his son. I knew he could be selfish, but I never thought he could give up his own son."

"What happened?" Tony exclaimed.

A single tear strolled down her face. She brushed it away with her index finger.

"Probably what you expect happened. I went to his parents' home in Anaheim. They were really kind, welcoming, and even apologetic about Mark. They are as distressed and even flabbergasted about his lack of interest in Johnny as I am."

"Remember what Mom always said, 'Blood is thicker than water,'" Tony said.

"I know. And while we didn't sit around and bash Mark or his choices or who he is with or any of that, we focused on Johnny and his welfare. They want to be a part of his life, and they need to be. They are the only grandparents he has."

"Yep, you're right."

"They want me to bring him out twice a year for a visit, and they hope to come here to visit once Johnny and I have our own place. In the meantime, they've promised to write to him, telephone him, and send him gifts – all the things grandparents do. Remember ours?"

"Yes, and I miss them a lot. Anyway, it's really good news. I'm glad Mr. and Mrs. Tunney are smart enough to be involved in their grandson's life. He's a super kid. It's Mark's loss. One day, he'll regret his decision."

"And Johnny's loss, too," she said softly. "Johnny deserves a father, and even if his father doesn't want me, he should want his son in his life."

"So what happened with Mark?"

She shrugged. "Nothing good. I telephoned and asked him to meet me at a restaurant down the street from where Carol lives. Of course, he was surprised I was on the West Coast. But he met me with his charming smile and flashy grin. I wish he wasn't so darn handsome," she injected. "Anyway, we sat there for a while and talked like old friends about Johnny. He asked a lot of questions and seemed pleased and excited over his progress. He even asked about you, Brother."

"Isn't that nice? I'm sorry, but I have lost all respect for him, Terri. I can't forget how he treated you and how he's treating his son."

"I know. So I came right out and asked him why he stopped loving me. What had I done?"

"And?"

"He said it was because I had changed. When my parents' died. Mark said I became depressed, no longer interested in things, which made him happy. He thought having a baby would help pull me out of my depression. But it didn't. Mark said he'd always love me, but he wasn't in love with me any longer and hadn't been for several years. He even admitted to having an affair with his secretary while we were still married, after he'd fallen out of love with me. You remember the one I always wondered about? I was right. It was her."

"You're kidding?" Toni was amazed.

"No, I'm not. When he told me he'd had an affair, it was like I was seeing him for the first time --- probably the only time I'd taken a good look. And while I was looking at him in amazement, bewilderment, and shock at his confession, he was ogling the waitress who brought our coffees. Honestly, I did see him for the first time that day and couldn't believe how blatantly disrespectful he was acting toward me. And even though I still care about him, Tony, and I always will, I know I'm not in love with the Mark who sat across the table from me that day. This man was not the man I had married."

"What did he say about Johnny?"

"Not much. He promised to continue sending the monthly checks and to fulfill his obligations regarding his college education – what we had written into the divorce and custody papers. He'll also keep Johnny on his medical and dental insurance plans, but other than that, he thought it best he not complicate his life anymore."

"Whose life?"

"Uh, I assumed he meant Johnny's life. But now that you ask, I'm not sure."

"Well, be sure of this, Terri. You and Johnny and I are going to be fine. I can see you've already made a lot of progress, but we're going to get you completely well. Afterward, I think we're taking a vacation to visit the Tunneys. Isn't Disneyland in Anaheim?"

She giggled loudly; they bumped shoulders affectionately. Then Tony reached for the passenger light above his seat. Suddenly, he felt like reading again.

Chapter Thirty Four

The Gift of Forgiveness

"For if you forgive others their trespasses, your heavenly Father will also forgive you, but if you do not forgive others their trespasses, neither will your Father forgive your trespasses."

Matthew 6: 14-15 (NIV)

ALEX WELLS / TONY ADAMS

It was March 10, 1979. According to the news channels and newspapers, James Hutchins's execution was scheduled for the following Friday at 2:00 a.m. Tony and Alex were planning to attend because of the extended essay or writing project they hoped to one day write about.

Even so, Alex's heart was lighter than it had been in a while, especially since Tony had returned home two weeks before. The first person he'd telephoned had been her, and it was from the airport after they landed to inform her he and Terri were on the way to get Johnny. Over the three days and two nights she had kept him, she and the Yorkies had fallen in love with the tot and his squeaky voice. She loved the way he pronounced her name as "Allie." He played well with the puppies, never trying to squeeze them or hurt them.

The only thing she had to caution him about several times was carrying them around. She'd worried he might drop them and break one of their bones.

After her mother's visit, Alex naturally had been upset to learn about her grandfather, the man she'd loved as a small child. He'd died when Alex was five, but she felt like her fond memories of the kind and gentle man she'd known as "PawPaw" were now tainted. But she and her mother had shared phone calls over the past two weeks, which allowed her to ask more questions about her grandfather's erratic and hurtful actions. Repeatedly, her mother had assured her nothing like this had ever happened again and she'd forgiven her father. He had been a wonderful parent.

Alex remembered their last conversation. *"Alex, I had so much love and respect for my father all my life, and I still do. He was a good man; he was going through a difficult time in his life. He was weak. We all make mistakes. We all hurt the people we love the most, those who are the least deserving of the pain we inflict. But it is love that allows us to forgive, and I forgave him as soon as he asked me, even before, if you can believe it"* her mother had said. *"Sure it hurt at the time, but there were so many good things he'd done for me all my life, it was easy to cover up the bad things he said that night."*

"You're a good woman, Mama. I love you. And I've probably never said this enough, but I admire you so much. Do you think I still have a chance of growing up and being like you?"

"Hmmmm. I think so. There's still hope." They'd giggled. It had been so long since they'd laughed together like girlfriends. It was euphoric.

The phone interrupted her thoughts. Alex answered the phone. Her mother's voice was on the other end.

"Alex, what are your plans for tonight? Want to go and see a movie with me? Your daddy doesn't want to see this one, but I want to see *Norma Rae.* I like Sally Field. Interested?"

"Oh, I'm sorry, Mama. But -- I have a date," she said slyly.

"What? You do? With whom?" From her mother's voice, it was easy to tell she was delighted.

"Guess!" she teased.

"Tony? I hope Tony," she almost screamed his name in her excitement.

"Yes. He finally asked me out on a date! A real date! We're going to dinner and then maybe to a movie."

"Wonderful! I'm so happy he's finally asked you out on an official date!"

"Me, too. But I do wonder why it's taken so long."

"Just be glad, Alexandra, it didn't take longer."

They both giggled.

"Yeah. You're right, Mama, as usual."

"Well then. If you can't go to see a movie with me, will you come to church tomorrow?"

"Isn't Daddy going?"

"Probably. He normally does. But I'd really like you to come tomorrow."

"Mama!" she groaned. "Why are you doing this?"

"Because Alexandra. You haven't been in a while, and I'd really like to have you sitting by me tomorrow. And in all fairness and honesty, you and Tony are getting ready to witness something very difficult to watch next week. I think visiting the Lord's house might be a good place to spend some time and prepare your heart."

Alex's mood changed. She had pushed all thoughts of Friday away, instead trying to concentrate on the excitement of a first date with Tony. But now, her mother had mentioned the execution, and now it was moved to the front of her thoughts. She hadn't been able to sleep throughout the past two nights without waking and feeling the dread. It was as if someone were tightening a lasso around her heart, threatening to stop its beating. Maybe attending church wasn't a bad idea, after all; she didn't *have* to sit beside her father.

"Okay, Mama. You've beaten me down. I'll come."

"You will?" Her mother's voice betrayed shock and surprise. "That's wonderful! I'm so pleased."

"Eleven?" Alex asked.

"That's right. Nothing's changed. Same time, same place. Well, you two have a wonderful time tonight. Say hello to Tony for me. I'll find a girlfriend to go with, so don't worry about me, which I know you won't."

"That's not fair!" Alex laughed.

"I love you," her mama said.

"I love you, too."

The three parishioners, Alex and her parents, sat quietly on a wooden pew amidst the congregation, waiting for the worship services to commence. Betsy sat uncomfortably between her silent daughter and husband. Alex noticed how subdued her mother seemed and knew this separation was weighing her down.

"Did you have a good time last night," she whispered to her daughter.

"Yes. We had a great time. We went to a neat out of the way Italian restaurant Tony's family used to frequent in uptown Charlotte. The food was delicious! I'll take you there sometime. Instead of a movie, we came back and had a glass of wine and watched a television show together."

"I'm pleased," she stated. But she didn't ask any more questions like Alex anticipated she would.

Alex noticed her father had leaned in, probably trying to overhear the conversation. No doubt, her mother had informed him of last night's date with Tony. In the depths of her heart, she wished she could forget what she'd seen that day and could somehow move on. She missed her father and his contagious laughter. He always was the life of the party, but even with other folks, he was noticeably withdrawn and unobtrusive. And she had noticed when she politely hugged him a few minutes ago that he'd lost weight. His cheeks were sunken, and his eyes lacked their normal sparkle. Alex's uneasiness was increasing as the minister and choir members took their places. After announcements, the call to worship, the prayer of confession, the pardon of sins, and the children's message, Alex's experienced an overwhelming desire to excuse herself and leave, but the minister's voice held her back as the sermon began.

She listened closely after his first sentence.

"One of the most beautiful aspects of our Christian faith and life is forgiveness. The prolific and most astute of American authors, Mark Twain, wrote, 'Forgiveness is the fragrance that the violet sheds on the heel that has crushed it.' His words alone are enough to say all I could say, and if my sermon were to end here, it would be as wonderfully simple and wholly pure as I could ever say. But at the risk of imperfection, we will continue."

"Perhaps one of the hallmarks of our faith, forgiveness, is also one of the most challenging things each of us are required to do every day we live. We must forgive others who wrong us, as instructed by Christ when he taught us to pray the Lord's Prayer – and as we pray it each time, we recite his prayer. We must ask for God's forgiveness for our sins. We must seek forgiveness from others for the wrongs we have done against them. And as you know, often we have to forgive our very own selves; maybe this last one is the most difficult. Forgiveness isn't a condition of who we are – it isn't a natural action that comes simply through proper education or upbringing. It is a challenge. It is difficult. But it is one thing we *must* do."

As Rob listened intently to the minister's words, he felt belittled by the truth within the words. He thought, *I believe God has already forgiven me, but how can I expect Betsy to forgive my betrayal of her and our marriage? She's been a good wife and mother all these years – never asking for anything. Always thinking of Alex and my welfare before her own. I feel so ashamed. She never deserved this. What was I thinking? And Alex. How can Alex ever forgive me for stooping so low? I'm her father. I'm supposed to be an example. I feel lower than a snake crawling through the grass.*

"In Ephesians 4:32-5:1, Paul tells us to 'be kind to one another, tenderhearted, forgiving one another, as God in Christ has forgiven you. Therefore be imitators of God, as beloved children, and live in love, as Christ loved us and gave himself up for us, a fragrant offering and sacrifice to God.' I love the verses from Psalm 130.3-4 (NIV), 'If you, O Lord, should mark iniquities, Lord, who could stand? But there is forgiveness with you, so you may be revered.' Both Testaments declare the stories of forgiveness time and again. They tell of the Lord's perfect grace, and they instruct us to have as much grace amongst ourselves in order to follow the Lord's precepts."

"This week's lectionary text from the Gospel tells one of these stories very well. It reminds us of the holes into which each of us often finds himself/herself because of the actions we have done or the words we have spoken. Each one of us ought to be able to recognize ourselves as the woman who bathed Christ's feet with her tears. Each of us should be able to imagine pouring out our love upon him in a sign of hospitality and appreciation. We may not have long, flowing locks of hair (and even this is not an accurate depiction, if we consider her hair may have been oily, tangled, and not 'Pantene' perfect), but we can imagine ourselves leaning over his traveled and dusty feet. And if we cannot, Jesus provides us with the image of the debtor – one with whom (and without any other known characteristics) we can perfectly identify."

"The image of her affection marks us. It humbles us. For which one of us would not wish to be in her position, at the feet of our Lord, in submission and praise? Who of us would not willingly give the opportunity to touch his human feet, knowing about the divinity they walked to spread? Who of us would not be moved to tears and would offer our kisses? Who of us is not in need of the forgiveness this woman sought?"

"Of course, we can pretend we would emulate her and be like her. But let's not fool ourselves. Let's not try to deceive God or this community with false piety. For if we are not willing to express this same kind of devotion and affection with one another as we seek forgiveness from each other or as others seek our forgiveness then we are just the Pharisee who scorned this woman for her love."

"Forgiveness is a beautiful thing. It is humbling to receive. It is honorable to give. It is our command and instruction. And here's another aspect that makes forgiveness such a radical notion in matters of life and faith – it is free. Not one of us needs to feel we are out anything when we give it away. In fact, rather than being depleted of our resources to offer forgiveness, it is one of those rare treasures that increases joy, happiness, and community the more we give it freely and unconditionally."

"And who merits forgiveness? Who merits God's forgiveness or your own forgiveness? The answer is everyone. You. Me. The similar. The different. The neighbor. The stranger."

Betsy's ears devoured the minister's message. Her heart was bleeding from the tatters and tears of her husband's confession the night before about his "almost infidelity." Alex's visit that day had been a blessing; she was grateful Alex's arrival had interrupted the lustful act he'd already committed in his heart.

It's not about what he did as much as it is about whether or not I can ever trust him again, Betsy thought to herself. Then she silently prayed. "Dear Father, heal my wounds. Help me to truly forgive him because I can't do it by myself. Help me to learn to trust my husband again for the sake of saving our marriage. Please help us."

She listened to the Minister's sermon.

"Forgiveness knows no bounds because it exemplifies God's mercy and love. It is the manifestation of all that brings us back into relationship with God and with each other. Along with the lectionary text from the Gospel according to Luke, this morning, comes a less familiar story from the Hebrew Testament. Those who recall the story of King Ahab, Queen Jezebel, and the prophet Elijah may recall the story of Naboth and his vineyard. It is a story of culture, politics, and faith. It is a story that requires more time than we have to read through its whole, and the lectionary cuts short the essence of the story."

"Naboth owns a vineyard that has been in his family for generations. King Ahab wants to take possession of it so he can grow a vegetable garden. Naboth refuses any transaction, and the King is sad but respects the decision. The queen schemes to ensnare Naboth, accuses him of false unfaithfulness, and has him killed by religious leaders. And in the end, Ahab takes control of the vineyard for his own purposes. An innocent man is killed through the hijacking of the name of God. As the story continues, God reveals this information to Elijah, who confronts the King and declares doom upon the King. This is where the lectionary ends."

"If we continue onward just a few verses more, we see that Ahab – certainly not one of God's favorite children – is scared of the prophecy that Elijah declares for him. Immediately, the King repents of his actions, and God forgives him (in that moment)."

"But by the end of one more chapter, Ahab is back to his deceit and sin, and he is killed."

"The point here is not Ahab's death, but that God had forgiven him. Even a man who acted through the villainy of his wife to have a faithful man killed. This is not permission for us to go into the world to commit whatever sins and atrocities we would like. As Christians, we are instructed not to do this. Yet the point remains that an unchanging God, is willing to forgive even the greatest debt a person can have. God is willing to forgive us of whatever separates us from each other or has put a stone in the shoe of our relationship with Him. As Paul also writes, 'nothing will ever separate us from the love of God in Christ.' This is forgiveness."

I wish James Hutchins could hear this sermon, Alex thought. *He killed innocent men, yet God has forgiven him. I hope he knows God's forgiveness is real. He only has to accept it. He only has to forgive himself. Just like me. I need to forgive my father. He's only a man. Only a man who is fallible, who is able to make mistakes like the rest of us. My father is sorry. I know he's sorry. He's tried to tell me, but I've not given him a chance. I kept saying I was thinking about mama, but I wasn't only thinking of her, although I hope she never finds out. I was being stubborn and withholding my love from him. I was thinking of myself, too. I was trying to punish him like you punish a child. But more than anything, I need to ask for forgiveness for being such a brat. My parents love me; regardless of what they've done, they love me, and I love them. We can survive anything.*

Their minister seemed to be wrapping up his message for the day. "Me, I love the smells of the South in the summer. I love the smells of honeysuckle, gardenia, and magnolia. I love these fragrances, and I cannot help but think maybe these wonderful aromas are creation's reminders of forgiveness. Perhaps these are the fragrances creation sheds for the sins that have wronged it. At least, for me, they can become smells of reminder. I think Mr. Twain was correct."

"Each of us is forgiven. Christ did that long ago. God did that before even then. In the unity of Christ's Spirit, we are now reminded of a task – a difficult task – that calls us to do what we may sometimes think impossible and improbable. We are called to forgive as we are forgiven. When we do this, we are blessed in love. And when we find it in ourselves to become humble before one another and God in the way of a woman's humility – to wipe each other's feet with love and tears – then we are stronger and better for it."

Once the organ music of "Amazing Grace," John Newton's masterpiece, began, Alex didn't hesitate to slide behind her mother and reposition herself between her parents. Her father wrapped both arms around her, hugging her closely, as if she were a precious life preserver, and he was a drowning man in a river of rushing waters. Unabashed tears flooded both of their faces as they clutched each other tightly. Alex never wanted this moment to end.

"I'm sorry," he whispered into her ear, repeating the words again and again.

"Me, too," Alex cried. "Me, too."

Rob peered over his daughter's head to find his wife had stopped singing and had happy tears streaming from her swollen eyes. Hesitantly and shamefully, he ventured a timid smile. Regardless of the pain and heartbreak he'd caused her with his honest confession the night before, the corners of her lips turned up in response to her husband's smile. She was thankful to watch her husband and daughter reconciling before her eyes. Prayers had been answered. Her eyes, weary from crying, now sparkled with renewed hope and love. As she bowed her head to praise God, she felt her daughter's arm slip around her waist, hugging her tightly. She joined them in singing the remaining verses of the beautiful hymn, which was so timely and appropriate for today.

Chapter Thirty Five

The Gift of Closure

"In God's wisdom, He frequently chooses to meet our needs by showing His love toward us through the hands and hearts of others."

Jack Hayford

JAMES WILLIAM HUTCHINS

At 5:00 a.m., James was awakened to live his last day as the execution was scheduled for 2:00 a.m. the following day. He wasn't hungry; he hadn't really had an appetite for several days. After declining breakfast, he drank several cups of coffee and opened his mail, which had been averaging seven pieces each day. Outwardly, he remained calm, while inside, he had died a thousand deaths. As he read the mail, he simultaneously relived his fifty four years. Seven days earlier, he'd been moved from death row for the last time and brought back to these four holding cells. On the way, he got to see his last glimpse of the outdoors.

At 6:00 a.m., there was a mandatory head count. He was the only one occupying one of the four holding cells. Later in the morning, he was given a physical exam. *I can't believe they are examining me to see if I'm well enough to be executed.* The doctor found he'd gained two pounds since the previous day. Odd since he hadn't been eating. He was deemed to be in good health.

During the morning, his attorneys appeared and regrettably informed him the governor had made his decision despite meeting with the N.C. Council of Churches, the Baptist State Convention, and representatives of Presbyterians, Episcopalians, and Lutheran churches. Hunt had received over 404 calls with all but 18 being against the death penalty, 157 letters with only 2 for the death penalty, and 10 telegrams against the proposed execution. Governor Hunt would not overturn the state and federal courts' decisions and grant a request for clemency. Hutchins was not crushed even though all hope was now gone. This would *not* be a repeat of January 13, when the N.C. Supreme Court had blocked his execution with forty-nine minutes to go. He shook hands with the attorneys who had tried to save him and thanked them for all they had done.

He was glad he'd told his attorneys on Wednesday not to beg Hunt. "I want to die with dignity and not continue with this legal process. My pleas for life have been turned down too many times." And after approximately twenty hearings and six execution dates, his hopes were depleted. His attorneys had agreed that further appeals would be pointless.

Dismayed, Geneva began crying. Any hope or optimism she'd had evaporated into the thin air. She was especially disappointed because she and her sister, Emily, and her husband, Jim Roper, and a family friend and member of North Carolinians Against the Death Penalty, Kristin Paulig, had met with the governor in

January in hopes of swaying his decision then and now. The meeting had lasted for fifteen minutes. She had left the meeting hopeful, but guarded. And even though the execution had been halted in January, she'd hoped he'd remember their meeting before making a final decision this time.

At noon, Hutchins refused to eat his lunch. Instead he busied himself by watching television. At 1:00 p.m., he was reading the local newspaper and fourteen letters Geneva had brought from home, among them a letter from his son, Jamie. Being the thoughtful wife, Geneva also had included a folder of past letters, school pictures of the kids, and a few drawings they'd made throughout their school years. These pictures and drawings lifted his spirits, as well as the letters, which he read several times.

The governor held a press conference to announce his decision regarding the execution. He stated Hutchins had received a fair trial, which had been presided over by one of the state's best judges and had been found guilty. Governor Hunt stated, "...the murder of a law enforcement officer is not only the cold-blooded killing of a human being. It is an assault on the fundamental rule of law in our society."

Dejectedly, Geneva and James had listened to the "breaking news" press conference on the small radio in the Waiting Chamber outside the four cells – hoping beyond hope the governor might have changed his mind before the press conference began. Even though the governor stated this was one of the most difficult decisions he'd ever had to make during his two-terms in office, he stated he was comfortable with his decision.

Hutchins showed no outward emotion; he remained calm.

"Who were we kidding, Geneva? We should have expected nothing more. I guess it was supposed to be some kind of consolation for me that I had a fair trial. During my life, things have always seemed to take a negative turn, especially where I was concerned. Bad luck, bad things, and bad people have seemed to follow me everywhere I went. I brought it on you and the kids, too."

"What did you decide to have for supper?" Geneva asked trying to change the subject. She couldn't bring herself to say "your final supper."

"Nothing. They asked me twice, but I didn't think I'd want anything. What's the use of eating?"

"You should try to eat something," Geneva suggested. After saying it, she felt silly. The only reason he should eat would be for enjoyment now, nothing more.

"Maybe I'll order a steak and cheese sandwich and a piece of chocolate cake for a late lunch, along with a *Dr. Pepper* and cup of coffee. That's what I ate yesterday. They'll get it from the canteen, so it won't take long. Maybe I can keep it down."

A prison official came by and explained the procedure again so Geneva could understand. There would be three trained personnel whose identities would be obscured by a curtain. Neither of these people would know which one of them gave the lethal drug to him. In addition to the two intravenous lines of saline, which would be shut off when Warden Rice gave the signal to begin, Hutchins would be given sodium thiopental, which would put him into a deep sleep. Procuronium bromide (Pavulon) would then be given; this was the muscle relaxer that would cause his breathing to stop and his death shortly afterward. Watching from an adjacent room, a physician would monitor his heart sounds via cardiac monitor leads. At the appropriate time, this physician would come into the room, check his pupils, and pronounce him dead.

He took small bites of the steak sandwich and drank the soft drink that was delivered to him.

Warden Rice had visited him. The warden was a small, dark-haired man, who had been a corrections worker for twenty-three years. He was business-like and had always spoken kindly and respectfully to him, even when initially denying the contact visit request.

At the end of their short conversation, he'd asked, "James, do you have any last words you'd like to say at the appropriate time?"

James shook his head. Words seemed useless, somewhat trivial, at this point.

His next visitor was the Reverend Guy Johnson of Spindale to whom Hutchins repeated what he'd said on the previous afternoon. He told him he felt "just awful" about the deaths. Later, after the minister left, he agreed to meet with a representative from the North Carolinians Against the Death Penalty. He wasn't sure what good the visit was going to do, but, hey, he only had time – at least for a little while.

"Why don't you go take a break and get something to eat, Geneva? I know you're hungry," he suggested. It was easy to see she was visibly shaken. But she was trying hard to be strong for him. "I'm allowed visitors until 10:00. You have time to go and get something. Go on; take a break."

"Are you sure?" she asked. "I don't want to leave you. We have such little time left."

"I'm not going anywhere, at least for a few more hours. Go ahead."

She relented, promising to return as soon as possible.

He spent the remainder of the afternoon reading his Bible and resting until Geneva returned. He was allowed to speak with his five children over the telephone. That's how they were going to say goodbye. He had declined to see them in person; he didn't think he could survive their tears or his, and he didn't want his children to experience this process.

Shirley Jane and James Jr. were grown now and on their own and doing well except for this thing, which had been hanging over their heads for five years. He was sorry for their sadness. Charlotte, now 23, was strong-willed like her father, so he didn't doubt she'd be okay. Jamie had the makings of a fine man. He was sensitive yet strong, like his mother. He hoped his son would have a successful life, unlike him. Baby Lisa seemed to take this the hardest. She'd always been a daddy's girl and was the one child he worried about the most.

But he'd gotten choked up when he talked to Jamie. He asked for permission to call him once more, and it was granted. There was something he wanted to say to his son. He wanted to say five words to him he meant from the heart. "I'm proud of you, son." These were words he'd never heard from his own father. Their last call had lasted less than two minutes.

He and Geneva talked softly, reminiscing about the good times in their past. They even laughed as they recalled some of the mischievousness the kids had gotten into. Immediately, the loss of not experiencing milestones in his children's lives overwhelmed him.

Dear Jesus, he prayed silently, *please make right the things I've wronged in their lives. Please bless them and help them to move on and somehow forgive me for all the hurt I've caused. I did my best to care for my family. I worked hard in whatever job I could get to feed them. I'm no saint, but I did try to provide for them. I hope they can remember that and some of the good times.*

But all too soon, it was time to say goodbye to Geneva for the last time; he held back the stinging tears. The warden had granted him a contact visit, so he could hug his wife one last time. The initial request had been denied, but somehow, he guessed the prison-higher-ups had reconsidered and granted him the request. He felt her shaking and sobbing in his arms even though she'd promised to be brave. She seemed so tiny, so skinny when he embraced her. It had been a year since she had last visited, so he had readily noticed she had dropped several pounds. But by holding her, it was even more obvious. Her wet eyelashes brushed his cheek when she whispered into his ear, "I love you." He had nodded in return because he was unable to speak. *I hope she can see it in my eyes,* he thought. *I've always loved her.*

Part Three:

Coming Full Circle

The End and the Beginning

March 16, 1984

As sinful humans, our actions are enough to convict us to death, but the mercy and grace of God permeates that sentence. Because of Jesus's atonement, our stories don't end with a death sentence; rather we are pardoned, and our prison doors are thrown open. We are freed by the only key that could unshackle death's claim, and that key is Christ's love.

The Reverend Chas. Jeremy Cannada

Chapter Thirty Six

The Act of Reliving Three Day Nights

"Regret, which is guilt without the neurosis, enables us...to move forward instead of back."
Jane Adams

ALEX WELLS / TONY ADAMS

Alex and Tony had searched the daily newspapers and watched the different news stations on television throughout the past two months and final days preceding the execution to glean all articles and possible. There had been strong speculation there might be another stay, but Charles felt it was unlikely. They read reactions from many people who were for and against the death penalty, which hadn't been exercised in twenty three years. And in the state of North Carolina, lethal injection was new. As Charles had predicted, Hutchins had chosen it as his preferred method of execution. He also had the option of wearing a mask, but he declined it. It was hard to believe March 15 had come and gone and midnight was finally here. In two hours, the execution was scheduled to happen. Alex and Tony had arrived in Raleigh earlier around 10:00 p.m., dreading the event they were about to witness. The letter had told them to report to the Visitors Center at 1:00 a.m., so they went to an all-night restaurant and drank coffee while they read the newspapers they'd gathered.

"Listen to this," Alex said. "One of the officers, who is going to be a witness to the execution, was reported to say, 'You're reading a book. The book was opened in 1979. I'm at the last chapter and I'm fixing to close the book. When it's all over with, I believe I will be able to live with the knowledge they did not die in vain. You sit down and you talk about people's rights. Why sit back and forget about their victims? They have no rights. They have no appeals. Hutchins had a choice between the gas chamber and lethal injection. To me, I can live with myself better after it's over with.'"

"Okay. Let me read you this one. 'I want to see him go. I'd love to see him go some other way, but I reckon this is the best,' another officer was quoted as saying. 'He killed the boys I worked with for a long time,' said a jailer, according to a newspaper article. He was 'delighted to be chosen as a witness.' And he said he'd asked to see Hutchins die when he was sentenced, 'Because I think he deserves it. The ones he killed were friends of mine. I worked with them.'"

Tony continued. "This same newspaper reported another officer, a strong supporter of capital punishment, as saying, 'It could have been me. I was with Roy and Messersmith at the gas pumps. We were changing shifts. If it had been 15 to 10 minutes earlier, it would have been me. I believe that day he [Hutchins] wouldn't have liked anybody coming down there. The only reason I'm going to watch the execution is because of my friends that were killed.' 'It [Capital punishment] will be a deterrent to people just shooting police officers because they're in the way or breaking into old ladies' houses and robbing and killing them. If they start executing people, it might slow them down a little.'"

"Let me read you what the newspaper writes about Alice Messersmith. 'Alice Messersmith, wife of one of Hutchins's victims, said she would be very, very relieved if they do go ahead with the execution. If it doesn't happen, she said, then there is no point in having law officers.'"

"Here's what Sheriff Damon Huskey says," Tony added. "'I'm not too enthused about killing anybody, but I don't know how [Hutchins] felt about killing these officers either. God have mercy on his soul. That's all I can say.' Isn't that something? And it was his brother who was killed."

"Yes, but he also is quoted as calling Hutchins a 'coward' when he chose lethal injection. He said, 'I think on murders that however a person was killed, the person convicted should be killed the same way. Hutchins should have been killed by a firing squad.'"

"I guess you can understand how he feels," Tony said.

"JoAnn Huskey Keyser said, 'I'll go to bed as usual and assume that it went as planned.' She stated she was satisfied that the death sentence is justified. 'However, I don't feel any personal satisfaction. I'd rather for the whole thing not to have happened.' As a death penalty advocate, she has pity on the man that killed her husband. 'I feel pity on him and his family as human beings. I do feel a great deal of sympathy for them. But I don't think that relieves him of having to accept the consequences of his actions.'"

"I think we need to go, Alex. We're supposed to be at the prison at 1:00. It's quarter till now."

"Okay," she groaned. "If we must."

At 1:40 a.m., a guard entered the Central Prison's visitor center where Tony and Alex sat waiting among the other fourteen selected eye-witnesses to the execution, which included eight law enforcement officers, two officials from the Department of Correction, and four media representatives. The guard was all business – very professional – as he cleared his throat and ordered them to line up to be escorted to the Witness Room. The captain of the prison guards stepped forward as the witnesses gathered behind him. In a single file, they shuffled forward in silence as he led the way up a steep hill to the prison doors. The anticipation of this dreaded event was ending; James's execution was imminent. After passing through security, the captain stood to the side of a doorway and motioned for them to enter an elevator, which was a one story ride. When the elevator doors opened, they immediately crossed a hallway and entered a claustrophobic room where sixteen empty plastic blue chairs waited. As they filed into the Witness Room and took the next empty seat, Tony and Alex found themselves in the back of the room in the last two seats. Charles was nowhere in sight. They faced a large glass window with metal mesh and a drawn blue curtain on the other side of the window to obstruct their views.

Tony glanced at his watch and breathed audibly. "It is 1:55," he said in a whisper.

"I've never seen anyone die before," Alex whispered. Curiously, she scanned the faces of the other observers to read their non-verbal reactions. Their faces were stoic, nothing to read. Her teeth began chattering uncontrollably. "I honestly don't think I can do this, Tony."

"Shhhh," Tony cautioned. "Sure you can. We're here for our book and because of Charles."

When she didn't respond, he gently took her chin and turned her face toward him. He stared into her frightened eyes. "Alex, look at me. We knew what we were getting into when we agreed to be witnesses. Focus on our purpose. As writers, it's important to experience this for our project. Take mental notes. Besides, I'm here with you." Timidly, he reached over and grasped her cold and shaking hand firmly in his. The warmth he transmitted surged throughout her body, providing courage.

It will be over soon, she told herself.

Tony examined his father's Rolex and compared it to the digital clock hanging on the white wall. "It's 1:57. They'll open the curtains in three minutes."

Alex dreaded the opening of the curtains.

Then to ease her fragile nerves, Tony elbowed her arm and silently motioned to the grey-haired man sitting on the second row. "Isn't he the famous columnist from the *Charlotte Observer*? The one who's been following all of this for the newspaper?"

"Yeah, I think so. His badge says, 'Press.' And the guy beside him is with the *Associated Press.* Those two men are with the press, too, to get eye-witness accounts for their newspapers. I heard them talking in the Visitors Center."

"This is an oddly-shaped room. It has six sides but the front three are smaller than the back wall and two sides. It's probably eight feet across at the window; each of the two front sides are about 3.5 feet wide and then the back wall is about 15 feet across."

She nodded, uncrossing her legs. The plastic blue chair groaned under its weight. Two of the Rutherford County deputies peered around. She and Tony had interviewed them several months ago. They exchanged blank stares, then nodded in acknowledgement before returning their attention to the window. They had waited a long time for justice and this moment of retribution.

Alex noticed the reporters scribbling on yellow legal pads. "I forgot my pad. I'll have to rely on my memory," she whispered to Tony. "It seems so cold to take notes when someone's lying there dying. Do you think he'll look at us, the witnesses? Gosh, I hope not. I hope I don't cry."

"Put your professional hat on, Alex." Tony squeezed her hand. "Detach yourself if you can. Breathe in and out slowly."

She tried to obey, but her breathing was shallow. Her temples throbbed.

"I know how you're feeling; it's weird for me, too."

"It's sad another person has to die – and to die with lethal injection." She involuntarily shuddered.

Her thoughts raced back to the painful Sunday three years ago when she had to put down her beloved Yorkshire terrier. Neely had been fifteen. Her death was one of the only ones Alex had experienced in her twenty six years of life, except for her grandfather's.

Neely's initial diagnoses seemed like a death sentence hanging over their heads. She had rejected the inevitable, replacing it with desperate hopes and prayers she'd get better. Somehow the veterinarians at the specialty hospital worked miracles over eighteen months with a regime of daily medications and monthly EKGs and other blood tests to ensure her quality of life was maintained for the duration.

Then, like overnight, the congestive heart condition worsened, her trachea began collapsing under the expansion of her heart, and edema set in. Neely's difficulty breathing had escalated to suffering and pain. It was inhumane to watch her suffer; Alex loved her too much. Her foe was fate, and fate had dealt a bad hand, leaving Alex forced to make the inevitable decision: euthanasia. Beyond being miserable and sobbing uncontrollably, Alex and Neely were accompanied by Rob and Betsy to the twenty-four hour emergency animal hospital. Neely was wrapped in her favorite afghan, the one Alex had made her when she was a puppy after Alex learned how to knit.

The compassionate nurse had ushered them silently into an examination room. Alex smothered Neely to her chest and massaged each of her tiny four paws. "I'm giving you your favorite – a foot massage." Then she scratched her furry head behind her ears – the way she loved it. Alex closed her eyes, compelling her fingers to memorize each crease of the dog's body, her wet nose, and her little paws.

Her heart had dropped when a doctor entered the room to administer the drug.

She gently inserted the catheter and patted Neely's head and scratched under her chin. Sympathetically and empathetically, she asked, "Are you ready, Alex?"

If Alex could have taken her index finger and reached to the back of her throat, she could have touched her displaced heart. It was literally high in her throat. She swallowed hard to return it to her chest where it belonged, so she wouldn't choke. Then the young woman took a deep breath and nodded. She couldn't speak.

Alex hugged the Yorkie close to her as the doctor silently squeezed the lethal drug into the catheter. As Alex watched the last of the drug disappear, a rush of emotions seized her, and she began speaking from her heart, calling the dog's name as a last gesture of love and comfort as much for her friend as for her. In the future, the name "Neely" would connote a memory of what once was instead of a denotation of what is now – for a few more fleeting moments.

"Neely, you've given me so much love and joy. We've shared some beautiful memories. Neely, you taught me what love is all about. Now I have to love you more than I ever have. That's why I have to let you go, Neely. I can't let you suffer any longer. You're my best friend, Neely. I'll never stop loving you. I'll think of you every day. You'll live here always," she said pointing to her heart.

Alex licked a stray tear at the corner of her mouth. "It's okay for you to go, Neely. I'll be all right." She swallowed back the melon-sized lump in her throat and forced a smile. She fought the strong urge to cry and wash away the sting from her eyes. A smile would be her last gift to Neely. But the dog upstaged her. Alex would never forget how Neely's black eyes had searched for hers. And when they found them, they reached deep into her soul. Her final look conveyed a mixture of emotions: unconditional love, ultimate surrender, and welcome relief before closing her eyes the last time. Alex remembered how it felt the exact moment when life left Neely's small body. On one side of the nanosecond, there had been a beating heart and struggle, with life pulsating through the muscles and sinew of her body. On the other side, there was tranquility, an abrupt void that couldn't be described in words.

Now they were going to watch a man go through the same process of being lethally injected and dying. The euthanasia of thousands of unwanted dogs and cats took place daily in countless animal shelters across the United States, and people shuddered with sadness at these acts. Even the euthanasia of a rabid dog would have been heart-felt and sorrowful. Because the dog, at one time, had had purpose and meaning and an instinct to survive before the demon disease had claimed and possessed its body. Is this what James Hutchins had become? A rabid dog who had been diseased by poverty, ignorance, perceived persecution and bias, abuse, and alcoholism in a society who believed him to be more dangerous than to have purpose?

She remembered the verse she had recited in the Vacation Bible School program:

To everything there is a season, and a time to every purpose under the heaven.

A time to be born, and a time to die; a time to plant, and a time to pluck up that which is planted.

To everything there is a season, and a time to every purpose under the heaven:

A time to kill, and a time to heal; a time to break down, and a time to build up;

A time to weep, and a time to laugh; a time to mourn, and a time to dance;

A time to cast away stones, and a time to gather stones together;

A time to embrace, and a time to refrain from embracing.

A time to get, and a time to lose; a time to keep, and a time to cast away;

A time to rend, and a time to sew; a time to keep silence, and a time to speak;

A time to love, and a time to hate; a time of war, and a time of peace. (Ecclesiastes 3:1-8, NIV)

As she wiped a memory-induced tear from her eyes, Central Prison Warden Nathan Rice solemnly walked into the Witness Room and announced the procedure was beginning. After he repeated the state-required litany of sentencing, a uniformed guard in the Execution Chamber parted the blue curtains to reveal James Hutchins lying on his back on a hospital gurney. His body was completely covered by a green sheet over which two brown leather straps were fastened. They assumed his ankles and wrists, which were covered by the sheet, were also held by straps. It was 2:00 a.m.

The wooden chair with heavy leather straps sat empty and forlorn in the background.

"This is it," Tony warned. "Prepare yourself." He squeezed Alex's hand so tightly, it ached.

Before a quick prayer could be offered, Tony shifted his body away from Alex to improve his line of vision. Without consciously realizing it, their own breathing stopped. James was closer than could have been imagined. If the officers on the front row could have extended their arms and reached through the window, they could have touched him. That's how close they were. All eyes were transfixed on him – no one moved or spoke or even cleared a throat. This reality was too eerie – too real.

Chapter Thirty Seven

The Gift of Writing

"You gain strength, courage, and confidence by every experience by which you really stop to look fear in the face. You are able to say to yourself, 'I lived through this horror. I can take the next thing that comes along.'"

Eleanor Roosevelt

ALEX WELLS / TONY ADAMS

Tony thought James Hutchins looked younger than his pictures, maybe because of his clean-shaven face, instead of the brownish red and gray stubble, which had been in the customary pictures shown in the newspaper articles. His hair was neatly parted and combed to the side. He lay so motionless, Tony had to peer closely at his chest to see if it was rising and falling. His upper body was elevated thirty degrees, so the witnesses could see his face, now turned slightly away to the right toward a white drawn curtain that would hide the identities of the three people, an anonymous doctor and two staff technicians, who would be responsible for opening the valves for the chemicals to be released. These three people would not know which of their syringes held the lethal chemical.

Tony watched intently as Hutchins's only movement was his Adam's apple jumping up and down twice when he swallowed. Alex drug her eyes away from the convicted man to focus on the faces of the two officers she could see from her angle. The jailer and captain sat upright with stern, unexpressive looks – no outward emotion. Tony caught Alex's eyes before turning back to watch Hutchins. The convicted man had fixed his eyes above his head and never looked toward the glass. Obviously, he felt the presence of the witnesses. He knew they were watching his every move.

Tony dragged his eyes from the condemned man's face for a quick second to check the clock's face: 2:02 a.m. That's when Hutchins's lips began trembling. Or were they moving? Was he trying to say something? Was he praying? Then his eyes flew open, and his eyebrows moved up and down several times.

"He's fighting this," Tony whispered. "He's trying to stay awake."

When his eyes closed again – for the final time -- his body jerked and experienced recurring spasms. Then it was as if he'd drifted off to sleep. His lips parted and his mouth dropped open. Tony checked the clock on the wall: 2:04 a.m. Alex leaned toward Tony so their arms could touch.

Was he dead? *What was happening*?" she wondered. But no one in the room dared to move.

With curiosity and with what they'd like to call "respect," they watched in silence as the coloring in his face paled, slowly spreading to his ears and lips. There was no movement, so at 2:15, a man in a black suit, presumably the doctor or a staff technician, appeared from behind the white curtain, carefully keeping his back to the witnesses to protect his identity. The man pulled the green sheet below Hutchins' shoulders and placed a stethoscope on his chest in three different places, listening intently each time. Tony checked his father's watch, while Alex checked the wall clock: 2:17 a.m. The anonymous man repeated the process again. Finally, he pulled the sheet over Hutchins's face and disappeared behind the heavy white curtain beyond the gurney, successful because no one ever saw his face.

It was so silent. So final. So sad. Alex let out a long breath and fought back hot tears while reaching blindly for Tony's limp hand. He squeezed it tightly. She noticed his eyes were glistening, too. He cleared his throat. It was 2:20 a.m. when the warden appeared again, announcing Hutchins's official time of death was 2:18 a.m.

Immediately, armed guards appeared. Because of their "Press" credentials, they, along with the other "Press" people followed a guard who escorted them to the elevator. No emotions registered on any of their faces. Another guard escorted the remaining witnesses to a different elevator. No one said a word. No one sighed. No one emoted.

They were ushered in separate groups to the Visitors' Center where the lonely podium was surrounded by reporters and camera men and brightly lit camera flashes and television spotlights. Tony gazed at the hundreds of death penalty protestors singing hymns and lifting makeshift signs that read, "Thou Shalt Not Kill" and "Jim Hunt is not God," and rhythmically waving lit candles and flashlights back and forth.

One of the protestors that night, a member of the Citizens Opposed to Capital Punishment, which was based in Greenville, N.C. said, "Nobody in this entire crowd wants to see James Hutchins back on the street, but there is a way other than capital punishment."

A supporter of the death penalty said, "I feel we should have a prayer vigil for the victims" and he should not be spared because of the "holocaust he put the victims through."

"Look!" Tony gasped. He pointed behind them toward the prison building's windows. The glow of match lights flared and flickered briefly. Then they were randomly extinguished. When Alex smiled in acknowledgement, Tony motioned with a nod of his head for her to look at the prison doors where they had entered earlier. Parked close to the entrance was a white van – the hearse that would take Hutchins's body to a nearby hospital where a medical examiner would certify his death. Earlier, they'd been informed the body's transport would occur around thirty minutes after the execution, and everything was moving along as scheduled. The crowds became still as the media conference began.

The monotone voice of the prison spokesperson announced that James W. Hutchins had received a lethal injection according to state law and the order of the court. He was pronounced dead at 2:18 a.m. The spokesperson also stated the execution had gone smoothly and without incident. He informed the room full of people the Hutchins family would claim the body. After the other "Press" witnesses shared statements about their observations, a fifteen-minute question and answer session followed.

According to Hutchins attorney, "He had felt awful for months and years about his inability to provide for his family, and he had just that day reached the lowest point that he had ever remembered in his life. At that moment, Roy Huskey drove up the driveway. He expressed the wonderful wish that all of us have thought from time to time that if he could turn the clock back and undo it all, his choice would be to let them kill him rather than taking their lives."

Tony and Alex blended into the crowds of reporters and interviewers to observe and listen to the recitations, questions, and answers. They were silent and lost in their individual thoughts in the chilly night air. Alex looked toward heaven and noticed the dark, vast sky was sprinkled with thousands of blinking stars, stars James Hutchins hadn't seen in five years and would never see again on this side of eternity. She hugged her woolen jacket closer to her body; her teeth were chattering audibly while a single tear traced a new path down her cheek.

The four Rutherford County officers were surrounded by questioning reporters, who were shoving microphones and cameras in their faces. One officer compared being shot with a .30-06 and a lethal injection as being very different. Another officer expressed his relief it was over. The third officer said he hoped the victims and their survivors could rest easier now. The fourth officer summarized his thoughts in one statement: "Justice has been served." One of the officers added, "It was too easy...it was just like going to sleep."

As the last officer said the word "Justice," Tony nudged her arm and nodded with his forehead. The white, windowless van was moving slowly down the paved drive toward the prison's only exit. Once through the gate, it turned to the left onto Western Boulevard and disappeared. As they turned right toward the Visitors' Center parking lot to leave, they heard chants from proponents of the death penalty. The opponents were slowly dispersing and extinguishing their flash lights and candles.

Tony's face was stern as they solemnly drove through the prison's gate. One of the demonstrators held up his sign, which read "Pray for the Victims." Tony gave him a thumbs up before pressing the accelerator and turning right onto Western Boulevard. With grateful relief, they were headed back home.

"Why did you give a thumbs up, Tony? Do you believe he deserved to die?"

"I gave a thumbs up because we're all victims, Alex. We all become victims anytime there is a senseless murder and especially when there is disregard for the law. When you commit a crime, you should be held accountable for your actions. That's how our system of justice works."

"I know," she said. "Hutchins was a convicted murderer. He did a bad thing by killing those officers in cold blood. But even so, he was a human being. Is it right for society to take his life? It took fifteen minutes for the chemicals to kill him. Is it right for us to kill like this or gas chamber or hanging or electrocution in the name of justice?"

"Well, until someone changes the sentencing laws, Alex, then we all have to abide by those statutes."

"Well, it was extremely difficult for me to witness a human being's execution," she replied. "Tony, if you think about it, Hutchins became a victim, too. He was a victim of capital punishment – more specifically, lethal injection."

Tony shook his head in disgusted resignation. "It's so senseless, Alex. He murdered innocent, hard-working officers who were just doing their jobs. He robbed their families of a future with them. He shattered their hopes and dreams. He took away fathers and husbands and friends. And yet, I believe the execution of a 54 year old man seems senseless, too. But he made choices that day – three times he made choices – bad choices to end innocent lives. Who gave him the right to take their lives? He was mad? He was drunk? Life was not fair?"

"But what have we gained for him to die this way, Tony? Sadly, those men can't come back from the dead," she argued.

"But then you have to think of the families, Alex. The survivors on both sides – those of the victims and those of the convicted. The families of the officers deserve justice. They have a right to have closure, so they can move forward with their lives. Their lives may never be normal again, but they have to try and have some semblance of normalcy."

"I know. I know. I'm so confused. You know, I've been a proponent of capital punishment. You know how hard I was in the beginning. I couldn't wait for him to be executed. But now, even after these past few months of researching this case and interviewing the people who were impacted and are still hurting, I'm not sure what I believe."

"Then you're showing a level of maturity, Alex. You're growing into your own and not just following the paths of others or adopting other's beliefs and opinions. We all have to form our own convictions. Let your heart be your guide, Alex, in all things rather than allowing your head to lead. Confusion is when your heart says one thing and your head says another. We can be educated, but I believe somewhere in our hearts, we have an innate goodness – a desire to do what's right. We have to listen with our hearts instead of reacting with our minds."

Her head ached; her brain felt sore inside her skull; her emotions were raw. She quit talking. She quit staring at the oncoming headlights, averting her eyes to the car's floorboard. She quit reliving the sights and sounds of this night, which had seemed to last three days – a three day night. She quit questioning the futility of life. Instead, she leaned her head against the cold window and softly wept for the waste of lives, the waste of time, the waste of unshared love, and the waste of not forgiving.

Concerned with her silence and freshly fallen tears, Tony smiled tenderly. He turned his hand over, palm up on the seat between them. She accepted the invitation and softly laid her hand in his, allowing their fingers to entwine. This time she didn't pull away; she didn't want to – ever again.

Alex had been a bystander, an innocent victim in the path of a stray bullet, this time perpetrated by someone she had loved and wrongfully idolized. Bitterness and resentment had pierced her heart and inflicted an indescribable pain and infection that had oozed and seethed through every pore of her body. She had been angry, stubborn, self-righteous, and unforgiving. Most of the responsibility for her long suffering, disappointment, and pain rested on her shoulders when she had placed her father's feet on a pedestal on which he could not stand. No human could. Lefrere had helped her to realize too many people's expectations of each other are based on a fallacy that men and women can be sinless, mistake free. He'd read a verse to her from Romans 3:23 (NIV): "...for all have sinned and fall short of the glory of God."

Unlike the victims of May 31, 1979, Alex was alive. Her journey had not ended; rather, it was continuing and a new path was being established with Tony. Her scarred heart was beating; there was hope for healing and a full recovery. All she had to do was to reject the prognosis of a marred spirit caused by the residual poisons of judgement, hurt, and disappointment. Instead, she had chosen soothing antidotes based on the teachings of our Lord and Savior concerning love and forgiveness. By spreading healing salves and Christ's blood over her gaping wounds, they could be cleansed and closed forever.

She couldn't wait to at her parents' home. There she could fall into their loving embraces and forget a "sometimes ugly" world of death and dying and sickness and pain and hatred and anger that waited outside the locked door. She closed her eyes and welcomed the darkness.

Epilogue

ALEX WELLS / TONY ADAMS

Eager to introduce Rob and Betsy to Charles Lefrere, Tony and Alex drove them to the library in Rutherfordton where they hoped they'd find their inspirational friend. Alex and her mother sat in the back seat, while her father sat in the navigator's seat and dutifully suggested driving techniques to Tony. The women giggled softly in the back seat because they were watching Tony's back stiffen each time he did. Occasionally, Alex looked lovingly at her hand where the antique engagement ring was mounted in a platinum setting. It had been Terri's and Tony's grandmother's ring.

"But what about Johnny?" She had asked Tony when he proposed. "Don't you want him to have it for his wife one day?"

"No," Tony had whispered. "Terri and I want you to have our grandmother's engagement ring. Our grandparents were married for fifty two years. Besides, Terri is saving our mother's engagement ring for Johnny."

"Oh! It is absolutely beautiful, Tony." She'd stared at the lovely blue sapphire with the two diamonds on both sides. "Was a sapphire her birthstone?"

"No. It was the month they were married – September."

"That sounds like a perfect month for our wedding, too."

That's when he'd kissed her gently on the lips.

Betsy had been watching her daughter admiring her engagement ring.

"It's lovely, honey," Betsy whispered. "I'm so happy for you."

"Thanks, Mama. I'm really happy, too. I can't wait to show Charles. He'll be happy for us, I know."

"Tony, how's Terri doing in her rehab?" Betsy asked.

"She's great!" Tony glanced at her in the rearview mirror. He was beaming. "She'll finish the program in a few weeks. She's joined AA, and her doctor has prescribed something for depression. My sister seems like her old self again. She's been interviewing for jobs; hopefully, she'll get one soon. There's one she really wants, so she has her fingers crossed."

"What is it? I don't even know what your sister does."

"She's a social worker. She's hoping to get a job at the *Salvation* Army. They have an opening for someone to work with the homeless by coordinating housing for women and families. If she gets it, she'd supervise the evening staff, which means she'd be working late afternoon and evening hours. That would give her more time with Johnny during the day. We've decided to send him part-time to daycare, so we can get caught up on some bills. At night, I'll be home to help with him. So, like I said, keep your fingers crossed."

"How about we pray about it? If it is God's will, then it will happen," Betsy suggested.

"Even better," Tony conceded. "Thank you."

"How's our little man?" Rob asked.

"Let me answer," Alex began. "Begging to come and spend a weekend with ya'll. After all, you're like grandparents to him."

"Aw, he is so sweet," Betsy cooed. "We'd love to keep Johnny anytime, wouldn't we honey?"

"As long as I have a day off afterward to re-cooperate. He wants to ride the donkey all the time, and my poor back is noticing its age. Plus, he likes to pretend he's wearing spurs and kick the donkey to giddy-up. My ribs are still sore from the last time."

"But why are you a donkey and not a horsey?" Tony asked.

"I think we all can answer that."

Everyone laughed good-naturedly, including Betsy.

"Tony, what happens if Charles isn't at the library this morning? After all, we didn't schedule a meeting to occur after the ...uh...you know," Alex stammered.

"Well, I'm hoping. He usually came on the days when we asked him to meet us; but he's always there on Saturdays. If not, I figured we could ask the librarian where he lives, and maybe surprise him with a visit."

"He wouldn't mind if we just dropped in?" Betsy asked.

"Charles is one of the most polite people you'll ever meet. He's so laid back; I'm sure he wouldn't mind if that's what we end up doing."

After they pulled into the parking lot, and Tony parked the car, Alex flung open her door and hurried to the library's door. "Come on," she rushed them.

As they hurried into the library and looked around at its emptiness, Charles wasn't visible. Tony walked up and down the book aisles to ensure he wasn't there. "It looks like he's not here."

Alex's shoulders dropped with disappointment.

"Maybe he's already come and gone. Let's ask the librarian if he's been in this morning," Tony suggested.

"Sounds like a good idea to me," Betsy agreed.

As they approached the familiar librarian, Tony cleared his throat.

"Hello," she said politely. "Welcome back. How can I help you?"

"We were hoping to see Charles Lefrere this morning. We wanted to introduce him to my fiancé's parents."

Alex smiled; she liked the way he enunciated her new title.

"I'm sorry." The librarian frowned; her eyebrows knitted together. "I don't understand. With whom did you wish to speak?"

Alex decided to step in. "Charles Lefrere. You've seen us meeting with him here many times."

"No miss, I'm sorry. I've seen you and this young man here many times, but there was no one with you," she stated. "Especially not Charles Lefrere."

Alex wanted to laugh at this absurdity. *Was this woman a victim of dementia? If so, how could she be working in the library?*

"Sure there was," she argued. "We've met Charles Lefrere, the white-haired gentleman here almost every Saturday since the first of the year. You've seen us together," Alex insisted. "He's the retired photographer. Do you remember now?"

"Yes ma'am. I remember you and your friend being here most every Saturday, but there was no one meeting you. Especially not the gentleman you're speaking of."

Tony asked, "Why do you say 'especially not Charles Lefrere?'"

"Wait just a minute. I'll be right back." The librarian disappeared into a back room.

"Uh oh. We've upset her," Alex whispered.

"Maybe she's gone to call Charles," Tony suggested.

"Maybe she's gone to take a memory pill," Alex said sarcastically.

"Is there another librarian who works here who might remember him?" Rob asked.

"She's the one who has been here every Saturday, Rob. She was here some of the weekdays – not all -- when we came during the summer. She should remember us meeting with him with no problem," Tony stated.

"Yeah, because she's the one who always stared at us whenever we got loud," Alex offered. "I remember apologizing to her several times when Charles made me laugh."

They stopped talking when they heard her approaching footsteps. "Here you are." She spread open a newspaper on the table beside them. They all gathered around to read what the headline read.

In disbelief, Alex read the words aloud: "Popular Photographer Accidentally Killed. Oh no!" She turned to Tony, reading disbelief in his eyes. There on the front page of the local newspaper was a large picture of smiling Charles Lefrere. His favorite camera hung from his neck. Gilkey Lumber Company was in the background.

Loudly, her mother gasped, "Oh how awful!" Betsy covered her mouth. "I'm sorry."

"When did this happen? Did it just happen?" Tony cried to the librarian.

She pointed to the date of the newspaper: October 17, 1976.

"That's not possible!" Alex sunk into a nearby chair and buried her face in her hands. "Tony," she muffled her cry. "I don't understand."

"Nor do I, Alex. Nor do I."

Rob began reading the smaller print. "Charles Lefrere, a popular friend of many people in the county, died on October 16, 1976. His death was ruled accidental by the Medical Examiner. After careful investigation by law enforcement, they determined he was accidentally struck in the chest by a ricocheting bullet while taking pictures in the woods across from Gilkey Lumber Company."

"Lefrere was an international freelance photographer who had resided in the area since his retirement in 1973. The accomplished photographer had worked for many well-known magazines, such as... they named them all here. It's quite a list." Rob continued. "When asked what he enjoyed most, his response was always the same: 'I enjoy traveling and seeing this beautiful world and all of its interesting people God has created.'

Lefrere was unmarried and left no known family survivors. It is interesting to note the name 'Lefrere' means 'the brother,' and this brother will certainly be missed by all those who had the pleasure of meeting him."

"Lefrere – the brother. How appropriate," Alex sighed.

Bewildered, all Tony could do was shake his head.

"I'm sorry," the librarian said kindly. "I don't know what else to say."

"There isn't anything to say, ma'am," Alex responded. "We've witnessed something so magnificent we'll never comprehend it fully. Thank you."

In shock and disbelief, the four adults wandered toward the door as if in a dream.

"Oh, I'm sorry. I never knew your names," the librarian called. "Are you by any chance Alex and Tony?"

"Yes," Tony replied.

"Here's an envelope with your names. It must have been left yesterday on my day off."

Tony returned to the desk and retrieved the envelope. After thanking her, he began opening it. Alex watched as he withdrew a folded piece of white paper.

"Whose it from?" she asked.

After reading the note, Tony found it difficult to break his stare from the cursive handwriting. Each letter was perfectly formed.

"Tony?" Alex called. "What is it? What does it say?"

Tony beamed as cold chills ran up and down his spine. He reread the note's contents and the familiar words from Philippians 4:7 (NIV): *And the peace of God, which transcends all understanding, will guard your hearts and your minds in Christ Jesus.* It was signed CL-TB.

"Something real," he replied. "Something beautiful. Something great."

"The Mindless Menace of Violence"

Robert F. Kennedy, April 5, 1968

This is a time of shame and sorrow. It is not a day for politics. I have saved this one opportunity, my only event of today, to speak briefly to you about the mindless menace of violence in America which again stains our land and every one of our lives.

It is not the concern of any one race. The victims of the violence are black and white, rich and poor, young and old, famous and unknown. They are, most important of all, human beings whom other human beings loved and needed. No one - no matter where he lives or what he does - can be certain who will suffer from some senseless act of bloodshed. And yet it goes on and on and on in this country of ours.

Why? What has violence ever accomplished? What has it ever created? No martyr's cause has ever been stilled by an assassin's bullet.

No wrongs have ever been righted by riots and civil disorders. A sniper is only a coward, not a hero; and an uncontrolled, uncontrollable mob is only the voice of madness, not the voice of reason.

Whenever any American's life is taken by another American unnecessarily - whether it is done in the name of the law or in the defiance of the law, by one man or a gang, in cold blood or in passion, in an attack of violence or in response to violence - whenever we tear at the fabric of the life which another man has painfully and clumsily woven for himself and his children, the whole nation is degraded.

"Among free men," said Abraham Lincoln, "there can be no successful appeal from the ballot to the bullet; and those who take such appeal are sure to lose their cause and pay the costs."

Yet we seemingly tolerate a rising level of violence that ignores our common humanity and our claims to civilization alike. We calmly accept newspaper reports of civilian slaughter in far-off lands. We glorify killing on movie and television screens and call it entertainment. We make it easy for men of all shades of sanity to acquire whatever weapons and ammunition they desire.

Too often we honor swagger and bluster and the wielders of force; too often we excuse those who are willing to build their own lives on the shattered dreams of others. Some Americans who preach non-violence abroad fail to practice it here at home. Some who accuse others of inciting riots have by their own conduct invited them.

Some look for scapegoats, others look for conspiracies, but this much is clear: violence breeds violence, repression brings retaliation, and only a cleansing of our whole society can remove this sickness from our soul.

For there is another kind of violence, slower but just as deadly destructive as the shot or the bomb in the night. This is the violence of institutions; indifference, inaction, and slow decay. This is the violence that afflicts the poor, that poisons relations between men because their skin has different colors. This is the slow destruction of a child by hunger, and schools without books and homes without heat in the winter.

This is the breaking of a man's spirit by denying him the chance to stand as a father and as a man among other men. And this too afflicts us all.

I have not come here to propose a set of specific remedies nor is there a single set. For a broad and adequate outline we know what must be done. When you teach a man to hate and fear his brother, when you teach that he is a lesser man because of his color or his beliefs or the policies he pursues, when you teach that those who differ from you threaten your freedom or your job or your family, then you also learn to confront others not as fellow citizens but as enemies, to be met not with cooperation but with conquest; to be subjugated and mastered.

We learn, at the last, to look at our brothers as aliens, men with whom we share a city, but not a community; men bound to us in common dwelling, but not in common effort. We learn to share only a common fear, only a common desire to retreat from each other, only a common impulse to meet disagreement with force. For all this, there are no final answers.

Yet we know what we must do. It is to achieve true justice among our fellow citizens. The question is not what programs we should seek to enact. The question is whether we can find in our own midst and in our own hearts that leadership of humane purpose that will recognize the terrible truths of our existence.

We must admit the vanity of our false distinctions among men and learn to find our own advancement in the search for the advancement of others. We must admit in ourselves that our own children's future cannot be built on the misfortunes of others. We must recognize that this short life can neither be ennobled or enriched by hatred or revenge.

Our lives on this planet are too short and the work to be done too great to let this spirit flourish any longer in our land. Of course we cannot vanquish it with a program, nor with a resolution.

But we can perhaps remember, if only for a time, that those who live with us are our brothers, that they share with us the same short moment of life; that they seek, as do we, nothing but the chance to live out their lives in purpose and in happiness, winning what satisfaction and fulfillment they can.

Surely, this bond of common faith, this bond of common goal, can begin to teach us something. Surely, we can learn, at least, to look at those around us as fellow men, and surely we can begin to work a little harder to bind up the wounds among us and to become in our own hearts brothers and countrymen once again.

The Aftermath

"But the world moves on, even when you don't want it to, even when change feels like the end of everything. It never stops."

Ann Aguirre, Author

In a profession where death is always present, the police officer rarely considers the final and ultimate danger until one of our brothers falls in the line of duty. Trying to make a better place for the American citizen to live in this country sometimes takes all a man can give; such was the case in Rutherford County where three officers died in the line of duty. Three men, each with families and dreams of his own, went to work on May 31, 1979, and never returned home again. These men left behind hurt families, robbed of their loved ones, unanswered questions, and dreams left forever unfulfilled. It's difficult to understand why some things happen, when they do, and how could anything as tragic as three beloved police officers being killed have a meaning. Perhaps it's not our providence to know. All we can do is remember and cherish a memory of what that individual stood for. It is no different than dying in war while defending our country.

These individuals gave the ultimate sacrifice so that each of us may live, hopefully free of a person who would deprive another of his most cherished possession, his life. (*The Magnum,* Fraternal Order of Police*)*

"It didn't bother me either way, just as long as they put him to death. If they ever turned him loose, he would have killed again. He was really too mean to live."

-Hazel Peterson, mother of Pete Peterson

"He was a good father to his children. He loved them all, and they loved him. But when he drank, he always upset me and the children...."

--Geneva Hutchins

"He supposedly was good-hearted except when he'd get to drinking. There was nothing to lead you to think something like this would happen."

"I pity his family. I believe the Hutchins family were victims just like my husband was a victim. He [James] disrupted my life and tore my children's lives apart. He owed society for what he'd done."

"When they re-worked the county roads, they re-named all the roads, and ours was named Roy Huskey Road. It took me a long time before going out that way [Hutchins's house] from my home because we lived within eyesight. I thought about what happened every time I did."

"On Execution Day, I was at work at the WAGE radio station and was greatly concerned that Governor Hunt might commute the sentence. When I heard his speech earlier that day, I felt relieved. We had lived for almost five years in a state of suspension. It would be ended, and we could get on with our lives."

-JoAnn Huskey Keyser, widow of Roy Huskey

"'I was in front of the *City News* in Forest City that day working with Ken Hunsucker and had to break up a fight. We wanted to go (to Gilkey where the shooting occurred, but (Forest City) Chief McDevitt gave us our orders to take care of the town. We worked the second, then the first shift before we got off,' Crisp said" (www.the digital courier.com).

-Retired Officer, Lt. Lamar Crisp

"McDevitt was cited for several incidents of meritorious conduct during his career, including placing murderer James Hutchins under arrest after an overnight manhunt in Rutherford County in 1979. Hutchins who hours before had killed two sheriff's deputies and a highway patrolman, was sentenced to death and later executed on March 16, 1984" (www.burkesheriff.org).

"Now, Therefore, Be It Resolved: That the North Carolina Board of Transportation names the bridge carrying traffic on U.S. 221 over U.S. 74 in Rutherford County the **Trooper Pete Peterson Bridge** for his dedicated service and for his ultimate sacrifice that made the highways in Rutherford County and the state safer for all motorists (January 5, 2001) (www.ncdot.org).

God's way is to take the chaos and bad we humans create in our lives and in the lives of others. God uses the bad to create order and something good from it. The deaths of these three heroes were not in vain. Their senseless slayings and untimely deaths left behind shattered hope and unfulfilled dreams, but because of the love and admiration of a community of people who took the pieces and glued them back together, there were positive changes in statewide law enforcement protocols.

1. Interagency reporting of officer murders began.
2. Radio-cross-communication between local agencies and the N.C. State Highway Patrol, which dispatches for most N.C. state law enforcement agencies was created.
3. The N.C. Criminal Justice Training and Standards Commission changed their domestic disturbance protocols and standards for response, tactics, and training of basic and in-service N.C. peace officers based on this incident and to emphasize and enhance officer safety. Law enforcement personnel to this day continue to chronicle the Rutherford County tragedy to emphasize the dangers involved in domestic disputes when law enforcement officers are responding.

These slayings were not high profile, being as this was a small town in the North Carolina foothills, but there were a number of lessons learned and a number of procedures changed for the better. You see, God has a way of taking the chaos we create and using it to make something good.

But an unfortunate number of records were set and recorded in history. Here are a few of the sad facts.

- Hutchins, an enigma, had turned fifty on March 26, 1979.

- Roy Huskey and Owen Messersmith were the first Rutherford County deputies to be killed in the line of duty since 1895.
- Pete Peterson was the forty first North Carolina trooper to be killed in action and died during the fiftieth anniversary year of the North Carolina State Highway Patrol.
- During 1979, seven officers died in the line of duty – only four others than Huskey, Messersmith, and Peterson.
- Never had three officers lost their lives on the same day in the same county in North Carolina by a single killer.
- In 1984, Hutchins became the first person executed in North Carolina after a 23 year long moratorium of the death penalty.
- Hutchins's choice of lethal injection was the inaugural use of the method in North Carolina.

In Honoria

The North Carolina State Highway Patrol

In Memoriam

Patrolman R. L. Peterson – Rutherford County – Died May 31, 1979, of a gunshot wound received while pursuing a man for speeding who earlier had murdered two county deputies (www.ncshp.org).

Officer Down Memorial Page

In 2016, the North Carolina State Highway Patrol named the physical training field and running track at the agency's training center in Raleigh as "Peterson Field" in honor of Trooper Peterson's legacy as the agency's most famous physical training instructor and in honor of his service (www.odmp.org).

North Carolina General Assembly 1979 Session
Resolution 81 House Joint Resolution 1532
A Joint Resolution Honoring Robert L. Peterson, Roy Huskey, and Owen Messersmith

Whereas, on May 31, 1979, Robert Lee (Pete) Peterson, Roy Huskey, and Owen Messersmith were killed near Rutherfordton after a domestic disturbance; and Whereas, the 37-year old Robert Peterson was a 10-year veteran of the Highway Patrol; and Whereas, the 48-year old Roy Huskey was a captain in the Rutherford County Sheriff's office, where he had served for 11 years, and was the brother of Rutherford County Sheriff, Damon Huskey; and Whereas, Owen Messersmith, 58 years old, was a Sergeant and 4 1/2-year veteran in the Rutherford County Sheriff's office; and Whereas, all three men were killed while answering a call;

Now, therefore, be it resolved by the House of Representatives, the Senate concurring:

Section 1. The General Assembly honors the service and lives of Robert Lee (Pete) Peterson, Roy Huskey, and Owen Messersmith, and expresses its sympathy to their families. Sec. 2. The General Assembly thanks Sheriff Damon Huskey and his staff, the Highway Patrol, and all other law enforcement officers who were involved in the search for and arrest of the man suspected of killing the officers. Sec. 3. The Secretary of State is directed to send copies of this resolution to the Rutherford County Sheriff's office, the Highway Patrol office in Rutherford County, and the families of Robert Peterson, Roy Huskey, and Owen Messersmith. Sec. 4. This resolution is effective upon ratification. In the General Assembly read three times and ratified, this the 8th day of June, 1979.

North Carolina General Assembly 1979 Session Resolution 81 House Joint Resolution 1532

Captain Roy Huskey Bridge, Seargeant Owen Messersmith Bridge Dedication Ceremony
Monday, June 9 at 2: p.m.
Cool Springs Administrative Offices Building
382 West Main Street
Forest City, N.C. 28043

The N.C. Department of Transportation Chief Deputy Secretary Nick Tennyson will join law enforcement and other local officials at a dedication ceremony to honor fallen Rutherford County Sherriff's deputies Capt. Roy Huskey and Sgt. Owen Messersmith. The bridge along U.S. 74 over Oakland Road will be dedicated as the Captain Roy Huskey Bridge, and the bridge along U.S. 74 at Bethany Church Road will be dedicated as the Sergeant Owen Messersmith Bridge.

Both officers were killed in the line of duty on May 31, 1979. The bridge dedications were requested by the Rutherford County Board of Commissioners, and approved by the N.C. Board of Transportation on January 9, 2014.

In Memory of My Fallen Comrade – Pete Peterson

YOU WERE MY FRIEND

You were my friend when I didn't need you
But most of all you were my friend when I needed you.
I could count on you as
You could count on me.
I trusted you and
You trusted me.
We shared the same views and
We fought the same fights.
We laughed together yet sometimes
We cried together.
I respected your philosophy of life, and, yes,
You respected mine.
At times we were slow
But we were also diligent.
We were persistent and
We were faithful.
Certainly, we both realized that our job was not easy
But we were dedicated.
It could have been me and not you,
But it was you and now I am alone, my friend.
Your body is gone
But not your memory.
My friend, I shall never forget you because
YOU WERE MY FRIEND.

Trooper Dan J. Good

End Notes / Chapter Notes

Introduction

Page 8 Quoted in article

Shepard, Charles. E. "A Life Marked By A Sudden Temper, Violence And Troubles With The Law." *The Charlotte Observer.* N.d. Print.

When the jury sentenced Hutchins to die, the trial judge editorialized him as "the most dangerous man I have ever seen."

Page 8 Hunt, Governor James quoted in article:

Parris, Lou. "N.C. Executes Hutchins: Convicted Police Killer Injected With Lethal Drug." *Spartanburg Herald-Journal.* 16 Mar. 1984. Print.

"...the murder of a law enforcement officer is not only the cold-blooded killing of a human being, it is an assault on the fundamental rule of law in our society."

Page 8 *Damon's Law / Rutherford County Line.* Dir. Thom McIntyre. Perf. Earl Owensby. Owensby Studios. 1985. Film.

Page 9 Keyser, JoAnn Huskey. Personal interview. 8 Nov. 2003.

"He supposedly was good-hearted except when he'd get to drinking. There was nothing to lead you to think something like this would happen."

Page 9 Owens, Steve quoted in article:

Shepard, Charles. E. "A Life Marked By A Sudden Temper, Violence And Troubles With The Law." *The Charlotte Observer.* N.d. Print.

"They had to work for everything they had. It didn't come easy. They weren't like an *Eight is Enough* type family, but they loved one another."

Page 8 Summers, Lt. Mike. Personal interview. 4 Nov. 2003.

"The whole thing took four or five minutes, but it felt like fifteen or twenty. His face went cherry red, then ash gray."

Page 8 Peterson, Hazel quoted in

Aycock, Anthony. What Thing in Honor (non-published essay). 2004. Print. 2016.

"It really didn't bother me either way [electric chair or lethal injection] just as long as they put him to death."

Prologue

Pages 14 -22 Acree, Keith. Personal interview. 31 Aug. 2016.

Pages 14-22 Drawn from articles in

Allen, Ken. "A Day of Promise That Ended In Gunshots And Death." *The Charlotte Observer.* 13 Jan.1984. Print.

Blanco, Juan Ignacio. "James W. Hutchins." *Murderpedia: The encyclopedia of murderers. www.murderpedia.org.* n.d. Web. 20 Apr. 2016.

Parris, Lou. "N.C. Executes Hutchins: Convicted Killer Injected With Lethal Drug." *Spartanburg Herald-Journal.* 16 Mar. 1984. Print.

Chapter 2: The Gift of Grace

Pages 28-32 Drawn from article:

Allen, Ken. "A Day of Promise That Ended in Gunshots And Death." *The Charlotte Observer.* 13 Jan. 1984. Print.

Chapter 3: The Gift of Today

Pages 33-39 Keyser, JoAnn Huskey. Personal interview. 8 Nov. 2003.

Keyser, JoAnn Huskey. Email to Sandi Edwards. 9 Nov. 2003. Email.

Brooks, Faye Huskey. "The Thomas Clifford Huskey Family." Sources: Census records. Bible records. Family records. Cemetery records.

Drawn from article:

Allen, Ken. "A Day of Promise That Ended in Gunshots And Death." *The Charlotte Observer.* 13 Jan. 1984. Print.

Pages 37-38 Epley, R.H. (Fripo). Personal interview. 4 Nov. 2003.

Chapter 4: The Gift of Victory

Pages 40-45 Keyser, JoAnn Huskey. Personal interview. 8 Nov. 2003.

Pages 40-45 Drawn from and quotes in article

Allen, Ken. "A Day of Promise That Ended in Gunshots And Death." *The Charlotte Observer.* 13 Jan. 1984. Print.

Keyser, JoAnn Huskey. Personal interview. 8 Nov. 2003.

Philbeck, Det. David. Personal interview. 4 Nov. 2003.

Chapter 5: The Act of Duty

Pages 46-50 Drawn from

Allen, Ken. "A Day of Promise That Ended in Gunshots And Death." *The Charlotte Observer.* 13 Jan. 1984. Print.

Good, Sheriff Dan. Personal interview. 4 Nov. 2003.

Philbeck, Det. David. Personal interview. 4 Nov. 2003.

Summers, Officer Mike. Personal interview. 4 Nov. 2003.

Page 50 Lake Lure's Medical Examiner, Dr. William Burch, as quoted in article:

Hendrick, Marny. "County Endures Long Night Of Tragedy And Tension."
*The Enterprise.*6 Jun. 1979. Print.

"He never knew what hit him. The bullet tore off the top of his head."

Chapter 7: The Gift of Safety

Pages 55-57 Drawn from article:

Hendrick, Marny. "County Endures Long Night Of Tragedy And Tension." *The Enterprise.*

6 Jun. 1979. Print.

Chapter 11: The Act of Resistance

Page 74 Drawn from article:

Hendrick, Marny. "County Endures Long Night Of Tragedy And Tension." *The Enterprise.* 6 Jun. 1979. Print.

Chapter 12: The Gift of Surrender

Pages 83-87 Drawn from

Good, Dan Sheriff. Personal interview. 4 Nov. 2003.

Hendrick, Marny. "County Endures Long Night Of Tragedy And Tension." *The Enterprise.* 6 Jun. 1979. Print.

McDevitt, Tom. Officer quoted in "County Endures Long Night Of Tragedy And Tension."

"Bring him out one way or another. I don't want any more officers hurt. Do not make any concessions – don't listen to anything he says. Put him in custody one way or another."

Chapter 13: The Gift of Comfort for the Grieving

Pages 88-89 Drawn from

Hendrick, Marny. "Rutherford mourns its dead." *The Enterprise.* 4 Jun. 1979. Print.

Chapter 14: The Act of Justice

Pages 90-92 Allen, Ken. "A Day of Promise That Ended in Gunshots And Death." *The Charlotte Observer.* 13 Jan. 1984. Print.

"Hutchins Being Held Without Bond; Hearing On Murders Set June 12." *The Enterprise.* 8:22. 6 Jun. 1979. Print.

"Probable cause hearing set for June 12." *The Enterprise.* 8:22. 6 Jun. 1979. Print.

Chapter 15: The Gift of Innocent Anticipation

Page 94 Permission to use "Café 100" in Huntersville, N.C., by Jay Hill, Manager, on April 6, 2017.

Chapter 19: The Gift of History

Pages 116-122 Hutchins, Glenn. Personal interview. 4 Nov. 2003.

"I believe if someone else had shown up, it wouldn't have happened."

Page 119 Freeman, James. Personal interview. 24 Oct. 2003.

"I believe in my heart if someone else had shown up, it wouldn't have happened."

Chapter 20: The Gift of Compassion

Page 125 — Permission to use "Café 100" in Huntersville, N.C., by Jay Hill, Manager, on April 6, 2017.

Chapter 21: The Gift of Memories

Pages 128-129 — "Interlaken, Switzerland. *Trip Advisor. Tripadvisor.com.* N.d. Web. 6 Jun. 2017.

"Rutherford County Official Site." *Rutherfordcountync.gov. N.d.* Web. 6 Jun. 2017

"Voidomatis River." *The Greek Island Specialists. Greeka.com.* N.d. Web. 6 Jun. 2017.

Pages 129-136 — Drawn from

Allen, Ken. "A Day of Promise That Ended in Gunshots And Death." *The Charlotte Observer.* 13 Jan. 1984. Print.

Hutchins, Geneva quoted in article:

Shepard, Charles. E. "A Life Marked By A Sudden Temper, Violence And Troubles With The Law." *The Charlotte Observer.* N.d. Print.

"My husband was the kind of man who thought that what was his, was his – and he could do anything he wanted with it. If he wanted to beat his wife, that was his business. Nobody had the right to interfere with that. When those lawmen came up there, to him they were trespassing. It was his house and his business."

Hutchins, Glenn. Personal interview. 4 Nov. 2003.

Parris, Lou. "N.C. Executes Hutchins: Convicted Killer Injected With Lethal Drug." *Spartanburg Herald-Journal*. 16 Mar. 1984. Print.

Chapter 24: The Act of Humility

Pages 145-151 Drawn from

The Charlotte Council on Alcoholism and Drug Dependence. *Drugs of Abuse & Their Effects*. Charlotte: The Charlotte Council on Drug Dependence. Nd. Print.

Pages 145-151 Good, Sheriff Dan. Personal interview. 4 Nov. 2003.

Philbeck, Det. David. Personal interview. 4 Nov. 2003.

Summers, Officer Mike. Personal interview. 4 Nov. 2003.

Chapter 25: The Act of Searching

Pages 152-154 Epley, R.H. (Fripo). Personal interview. 4 Nov. 2003.

Chapter 27: The Gift of Friendship

Page 162 North Carolina Department of Correction: Division of Prisons. Letter to Capt. Ray Dixon. 7 Jan. 1984. TS.

Chapter 29: The Gift of Mercy

Page 171 Drawn from and quoted in

Allen, Ken, Marilyn Mather, Lolo Pendergrast. "Late Appeals Sought A Stay Of Execution." *The Charlotte Observer.* 12 Jan.1984. Print.

"Hutchins has no fear of dying and he believes he was 'going to be in a better place' and 'the sooner the better.'" She had also testified that Hutchins "is mentally ill," but "he knew the difference between right and wrong." She concluded by saying Hutchins was in a "severely paranoid state and believes every event is fixed against him" and "because Hutchins feels he shot the two deputies in self-defense, he was in the right and will go to heaven."

Chapter 34: The Gift of Forgiveness

Pages 203-211 Cannada, Chas. Jeremy, Rev. "Forgiveness." Amelia Presbyterian Church. Amelia Courthouse, Virginia. 12 June 2016. Sermon.

Chapter 35: The Gift of Closure

Pages 212-216 Drawn from

"North Carolina Man Executed in Deaths of 3

Police Officers." *NYtimes.com.* The New York Times. 16 Mar. 1984. Web. 20 Apr. 2016.

Parris, Lou. "N.C. Executes Hutchins: Convicted Killer Injected With Lethal Drug." *Spartanburg Herald-Journal.* 16 Mar. 1984. Print.

Parris, Lou. "Hutchins' Last Day Spent With Visitors." *Spartanburg Herald-Journal.* 16 Mar. 1984. Print

White, Katherine. "Death Penalty Protest Draws 100 to Capitol." N.d.

Page 213 Hutchins, James quoted in article.

Parris, Lou. "N.C. Executes Hutchins: Convicted Killer Injected With Lethal Drug." *Spartanburg Herald-Journal.* 16 Mar. 1984. Print.

"I want to die with dignity and not continue with this legal process. My pleas for life have been turned down too many times."

Page 213 Governor James Hunt quoted in article:

Parris, Lou. N.C. Executes Hutchins: Convicted Police Killer Injected With Lethal Drug." *Spartanburg Herald-Journal.* 16 Mar. 1984. Print

"...the murder of a law enforcement officer is not only the cold-blooded killing of a human being. It is an assault on the fundamental rule of law in our society."

Chapter 36: The Act of Reliving a Three Day Night

Pages 218 – 225

Chief Jailer Luke Roberson quoted in article:

Parris, Lou. "N.C. Executes Hutchins: Convicted Police Killer Injected with Lethal Drug." *Spartanburg Herald-Journal.* 16 Mar. 1984. Print.

"I want to see him go. I'd love to see him go some other way, but I reckon this is the best. He killed the boys I worked with for a long time. Because I think he deserves it. The ones he killed were friends of mine. I worked with them."

Alice Messersmith quoted in article:

"Hutchins' wife appeals to Gov. Hunt for stay." *The Daily Courier.* 12 Jan. 1984. Print.

"Alice Messersmith, wife of one of Hutchins' victims, said she would be 'very, very relieved if they do go ahead with the execution.' If it doesn't happen, she said, 'then there is no point in having law officers.'"

Sheriff Damon Huskey quoted in article:

"Hutchins' wife appeals to Gov. Hunt for stay." *The Daily Courier.* 12 Jan. 1984. Print.

"I'm not too enthused about killing anybody, but I don't know how [Hutchins] felt about killing those officers either. God have mercy on his soul. That's all I can say."

Det. Mike Summers quoted in article:

Van Dyke, Jeff. "Deputies selected to witness execution." *The Daily Courier.* N.d.
Print.

"You're reading a book. The book was opened in 1979. I'm at the last chapter and I'm fixing to close the book. When it's all over with, I believe I will be able to live with the knowledge they did not die in vain."

"You sit down and you talk about people's rights. Why sit back and forget about their victims? They have no rights. They have no appeals. Hutchins had a choice between the gas chamber and lethal injection. To me, I can live with myself better after it's over with."
Dixon, Ray. Quoted in article:

Van Dyke, Jeff. "Deputies selected to witness execution." *The Daily Courier.* N.d. Print.

"It could have been me. I was with Roy and Messersmith at the gas pumps. We were changing shifts. If it had been 15 to 20 minutes earlier, it would have been me. I believe that day he [Hutchins] wouldn't have liked anybody coming down there. The only reason I'm going for is to watch the execution because of my friends that were killed. So that it will be a deterrent to people just shooting police officers because they're in the way or breaking into old ladies' houses and robbing and killing them. If they start executing people, it might slow them down a little."

Parris, Lou. "Prison Workers Just Did Their Jobs." *Spartanburg Herald-Journal.*
16. Mar. 1984. A3. Print.

"JoAnn Huskey Keyser said, 'I'll go to bed as usual and assume that it went as planned.' She stated she was satisfied that the death sentence is justified. 'However, I don't feel any personal satisfaction. I'd rather for the whole thing not to have happened.' As a death penalty advocate, she has pity on the man that killed her husband. 'I feel pity on him and his family as human beings. I do feel a great deal of sympathy for them. But I don't think that relieves him of having to accept the consequences of his actions.'"

Pages 218 - 225 Acree, Keith. Personal interview. 31 Aug. 2016.

Flesher, John. "James Hutchins executed: His last requests were to wear wedding band, avoid autopsy." *The Daily Courier.* 16 Mar. 1984. Print.

Page 223 Drawn from

Gary, Kays. "Execution eyewitness says 'eyes never moved.'" *The Charlotte Observer.* 16 Mar. 1984. Print.

Chapter 37: The Gift of Writing

Pages 226--231 Drawn from

Gary, Kays. "Execution eyewitness says 'eyes never moved.'" *The Charlotte Observer.* 16 Mar. 1984. Print.

Quoted by member of Citizens Opposed to Capital Punishment in article

Parris, Lou. "N.C. Executes Hutchins: Convicted Police Killer Injected With Lethal Drug." *Spartanburg Herald-Journal.* 16 Mar. 1984. Print.

"Nobody in this entire crowd wants to see James Hutchins back on the street, but there is a way other than capital punishment."

Pages 226-231 As quoted by Lee Churchill of Raleigh, supporter of the death penalty,

White, Katherine. "Death Penalty Protest Draws 100 to Capitol." N.d. Print.

"I feel we should have a prayer vigil for the victims" and he should not be spared because of the "holocaust he put the victims through."

As quoted by Atty. Roger Smith in article:

"Condemned murderer felt regret, attorney Smith says." N.d. 19 Mar. 1984. Print.
"Hutchins felt remorse." N.d. 19 Mar. 1984. Print.

"He had felt awful for months and years about his inability to provide for his family, and he had just that day reached the lowest point he had ever remembered in his life. At that moment, Roy Huskey drove up the driveway. He expressed the wonderful wish that all of us have thought from time to time that if he could turn the clock back and undo it all, his choice would be to let them kill him rather than taking their lives."

Pages 226-231 Drawn from and quoted in

Paris, Ron. "It was different this time: Atmosphere at prison was less hectic…." *The Daily*

Courier. 16 Mar. 1984. Print.

The fourth officer summarized his thoughts in one statement: "Justice has been served." One of the officers added, "It was too easy…it was just like going to sleep."

Pages 237-239 Kennedy, Robert F. "The Mindless Menace of Violence." Cleveland City Club. Cleveland, Ohio. 5 Apr. 1968.

-

In Honoria

Page 240 "Domestic Disturbance." *The Magnum: Official Publication of the Charlotte-Mecklenburg Fraternal Order of Police* 1.4. Jul 1979. Print.

Page 241 Gordon, Jean. "Sheriff's Officer Retires After 31 Years." *The Digital Courier.* 30 Jan. 2003. Web. 16 Sep. 2003. (www.thedigitalcourier.com)

Page 241 Burke County Sheriff's Office. "Press Releases: Sheriff Receives National Award." 20 Mar. 2002. Web. 16 Sep. 2003. (www.burkesheriff.org)

Page 241 "Resolution for Trooper Pete Peterson." *NCDOT January 2001 Board of Transportation Minutes.* 5 Jan. 2001. Web. 16 Sep. 2003. (www.ncdot.org)

Page 245 "Patrolman R. L. Peterson." *The North Carolina State Highway Patrol In Memoriam.* N.d. Web. 16 Sep. 2003. (www.ncshp.org/memoriam 1.html.

Page 246 Good, Dan Sheriff. "In Memory of My Fallen Comrade – Pete Peterson: You Were My Friend." (Published with Good's permission).

Miscellaneous Documents Accessed / Read / Researched

Allen, Ken. "A Day of Promise That Ended In Gunshots And Death."
The Charlotte Observer. 13 Jan.1984. Print.

Allen, Ken, Marilyn Mather, Lolo Pendergrast. "Late Appeals Sought A Stay Of Execution."
The Charlotte Observer. 12 Jan.1984. Print.

Aycock, Anthony. What Thing in Honor (non-published essay). 2004. Print. 2016.

Blanco, Juan Ignacio. "James W. Hutchins." *Murderpedia: The encyclopedia of murderers.*
www.murderpedia.org. n.d. Web. 20 Apr. 2016.
"James William Hutchins – North Carolina – March 16, 1984." *Crime & Capital Punishment.*
www.cncpunishment.com.
12 Nov.2010. Web. 20 Apr. 2016.

"James W. Hutchins." *Wikipedia.org.*
(en.wikipedia.org/wiki/James_W._Hutchins. n.d. Web.
20 Apr 2016.

N.C. State Cases: James Hutchins. "State of North Carolina v. James W. Hutchins."
LexisNexis@prod.lexinexis.com.

8 Jul. 1981. Web. 7 Oct. 2003.

N.C. Federal and State Cases: James Hutchins. "Woodard, Secretary of Corrections of North Carolina, et al. v. Hutchins." *LexisNexis@prod.lexinexis.com.* 3 Jan. 1984. Web. 7 Oct. 2003.

"Offender Data Screen: Hutchins, James W." *North Carolina Department of Correction Public Access Information System. www.webapps.doc.state.nc.us.* N.d. Web. 16 Sep. 2003.

Meet the Author

Sandi Huddleston-Edwards is a proud North Carolinian native where she has lived all of her life. She earned an A.A. degree from Central Piedmont Community College and B.A. and M.A. degrees in English from the University of North Carolina at Charlotte.

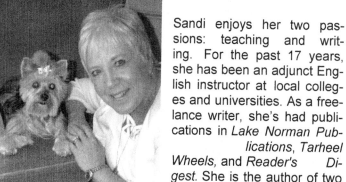

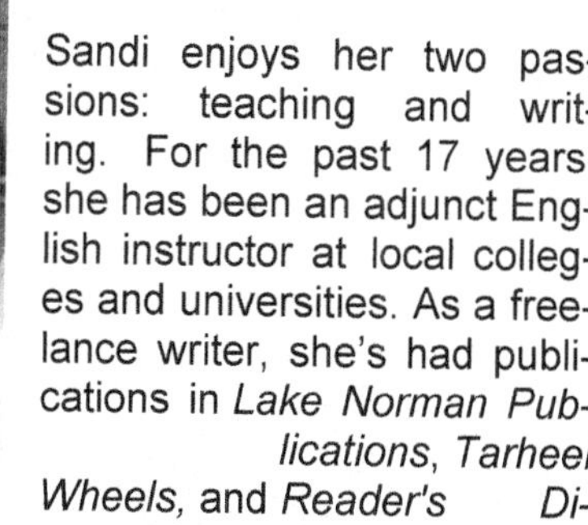

Sandi enjoys her two passions: teaching and writing. For the past 17 years, she has been an adjunct English instructor at local colleges and universities. As a freelance writer, she's had publications in *Lake Norman Publications*, *Tarheel Wheels,* and *Reader's Digest.* She is the author of two novels, *Richard's Key* and *Roy's Sandman, a memoir, A Stranger to Myself* and a children's book, *The Guardian Angel.* She is in the process of writing more projects. "All glory goes to God."

In addition to teaching and writing, Ms. Huddleston-Edwards, a proud mother of three sons and four grandchildren, enjoys bike riding, reading, traveling, watching old movies, and spending time at Myrtle Beach with her husband, Barry, and their two Yorkshire Terriers, Maddie and Abbie. She and Barry reside in Huntersville.

(Sandi is shown above with her beloved Neely Noel, who patiently waits at the Rainbow Bridge.)

CPSIA information can be obtained
at www.ICGtesting.com
Printed in the USA
BVOW10s2356101217
502439BV00001B/41/P

9 781945 620324